LACIE'S
SECRETS

Teresa Sorkin and **Tullan Holmqvist**

BEAUFORT
BOOKS

All quotations from Hansel and Gretel come from *The Brothers Grimm Fairy Tales*. Grimm,
Brothers. "The Brothers Grimm Fairy Tales." Project Gutenberg, April 2001/June 28, 2021,
https://www.gutenberg.org/cache/epub/2591/pg2591-images.html

The Alfred Lord Tennyson quote is from his work titled *Maud*.

Library of Congress Cataloging-in-Publication Data

Hardcover 9780825309793
eBook 9780825308581

For inquiries about volume orders, please contact:
Beaufort Books
27 West 20th Street, Suite 1103
New York, NY 10011
sales@beaufortbooks.com

Published in the United States by Beaufort Books
www.beaufortbooks.com

Distributed by Midpoint Trade Books,
a division of Independent Publishers Group
www.ipgbook.com

Printed in the United States of America
Cover design by Laura Klynstra
Interior design by Mark Karis

TERESA

*Thank you to my Husband Ian and children Jaden and Isabella
who give me purpose and lasting memories each day.*

TULLAN

*For my wonderful sisters—Malin and Linda—
Thank you for the gift of true sisterhood in this life,
Sharing joy, compassion, home and love.*

KATE'S FAMILY TREE

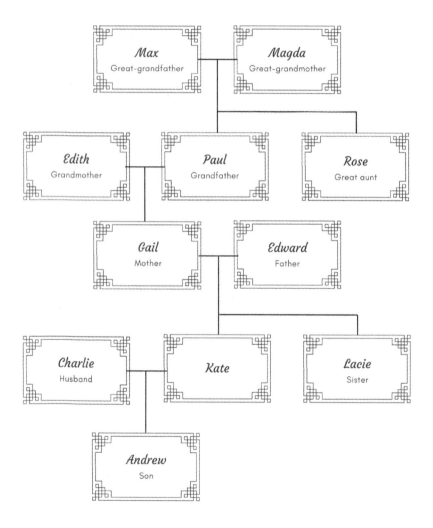

"So now I have sworn to bury
all this dead body of hate,
I feel so free and so clear
by the loss of that dead weight."
—ALFRED LORD TENNYSON

It was never supposed to have happened. Not like this. A serene summer week with friends was all it was supposed to be. Yet, there it was. A body, floating aimlessly in the murky pool, like a mystical, otherworldly creature, devoid of the life that once pumped through its veins. The stark image was like a still painting; quite beautiful and distant.

The harshness of the moonlight accentuated and outlined the body perfectly, its arms spread out like wings, its hair a halo, the blood draining from it, slowly creating a swirl of pink hues in the oval pool. They had all been swimming and laughing in the pool earlier that evening. Well, most of them had. Some had been preoccupied with the events of the week. None of them ever imagined that one of them would later be back in the pool, lifeless. The body had been alive just a few hours earlier, full of energy and promise. And now, it was just a shell, and soon it would decay, its eyes nothing more than cave dwellings for maggots, its withering skin falling off, leaving only bones to be reclaimed by the earth. Yet this very moment was special because everything looked peaceful.

The first rays of sun would bring the horror into full light. Soon enough, all would be exposed to outsiders. The house had been filled with friends, enjoying a week away from their normal lives. That was certainly how the week had started. But tensions had been running high the last few days and had threatened to boil over. By the look of the body in the pool, someone had reached their boiling point.

On the terrace above the pool, a dark figure appeared. It stood still and silent, observing the floating body, not wanting to wake the others just yet, wondering how they would react once they saw it. There would be lots of questions, that was certain, disbelief and shock. But some of them would not be surprised at all. Some would have been expecting it as if something terrible had been bound to happen all along. The house would stir as it always did when tragedy came to visit. It was a house that had seen things, both awful and wonderful, and now, awakening like a lion, it called on someone else. They were now part of the house, of its past and its future, part of its story. It would haunt all of them forever.

As dawn slowly broke through the darkness, a scream tore through the house, and life as they knew it would never be the same.

PART ONE

*"Near a great forest there lived a poor woodcutter
and his wife and his two children:
the boy's name was Hansel and the girl's Gretel."*
—HANSEL AND GRETEL, GRIMM BROTHERS

When the call came, Kate was not expecting it. It was eight o'clock on a Tuesday, at the end of May. It came out of the blue, on an early summer breeze, while everything seemed to be humming along. It came as she enjoyed a sip of her morning coffee and was looking at the first blooms outside. Her peonies had just sprung pink buds, and she could hear a bird crying in the distance.

Kate Williams had just said goodbye to her husband Charlie and their son Andrew after a quick breakfast. She loved that moment of the day, alone in the kitchen, enjoying the quiet of the empty house. The sun shone in through the window and she opened it wider to let in some air. Warmth spilled in, announcing the arrival of a new season. The first days of summer excited her and also made her a bit nervous.

The phone rang, the unexpected sound startling her. She looked down at her cell phone, but it was dark. It must be the home phone; everyone she knew called her on her cell phone. She looked around for the landline, barely remembering where they kept it. It was half-hidden on a shelf in the kitchen, behind a blue ceramic bowl filled with trinkets collected from summer travels. She hesitated before picking it up.

"Katie?" said the voice on the line. No one called her Katie anymore, not in years. She knew who it was right away, the voice ragged and gruff from years of abusing it with too many cigarettes and strong coffee. It was Susan Dresden, who, along with her husband, Doug, lived on her mother's property in Maine as the estate's caretakers. Kate closed her eyes and braced herself for what was coming. If Susan was calling her, the news could not be good.

"Oh, Katie…" said Susan again.

"She's gone, isn't she?" Kate whispered, the words getting stuck in her throat. There was silence at the other end, a deafening silence. She wondered for a moment if the line had been dropped. "How did she…?" Kate wanted to know, even though it didn't matter.

"In her sleep. She was fine last night, save for a cough she had. I gave her her favorite tea, like always." The words now came rushing out.

Kate knew all too well that "tea" meant gin or bourbon. Her mother, Gail, drank every day and called it tea. *Had they enabled her for all these years?* Kate wondered as she slumped down on the kitchen chair.

Susan continued through the phone, "She seemed happy. Well, happier than usual. Doug and I were surprised, to tell you the truth. We hadn't seen her like that, well since…"

"Lacie." Kate swallowed. It felt strange saying her sister's name after all these years.

"Doug found her this morning. She looked peaceful." It was hard to imagine her mother ever being peaceful. She had been sick for some time, suffering from many ailments, a broken heart being one of them. It must have all caught up with her. Kate's gaze wandered out through the window to a red-tailed bird fluttering around her big oak tree.

Kate felt her chest tighten, and her eyes filled with tears. Her sadness surprised and overwhelmed her. She shook the tears away and stood up. She didn't want to be on the phone any longer, remembering the past. She thought she had moved beyond it, but it came crashing back in an instant.

"Your mother didn't want a funeral, or a memorial even. But of course, you knew that, didn't you? She certainly mentioned it enough times to make it stick. She wanted to just pass quietly," Susan continued as if somehow talking would make all the hurt better. "She was so private these last few years. Never had many visitors; just us and some town folk from time to time."

A funeral. Kate hadn't even thought about a funeral and wondered what else she would have to arrange. She was relieved she would not have to say anything about her mother at a funeral. It would have felt unnatural and she was afraid of what might come out if she had to speak. The truth was better left unsaid, she thought, as she took a deep breath. She looked out at the garden as Susan's voice droned on. The bird on the tree flapped its wings rapidly and flew off. She realized she had no choice—she would have to go back.

"I'll come up soon then." Kate tried to keep her voice level.

"Are you sure? All the way from Connecticut?" The surprise in Susan's voice was evident.

"We'll have to clean it out to get it ready for sale. It certainly won't be easy to do, a house of that size. And after four generations."

"For sale? Are you sure?" Susan asked.

"Yes." Kate had already made up her mind.

"Doug and I, well… We thought that you may want to keep it in your family. It's such a beautiful summer house, and it's been in your family for so many years." Her voice trembled and then she paused. Kate could tell she was upset. Susan was a proud woman, though, and her voice regained some strength. "But it's your home to do with as you wish. We've loved every moment in this house."

Kate's heart softened, and she felt a twinge of guilt. Maybe she could try to convince the new owners to keep Doug and Susan on. They knew the house's ins and outs better than anyone else and had been loyal caretakers for so long. They were like family.

"It'll be okay. I'm sure whoever buys the house will need help, and who better than the both of you to do that," Kate reassured Susan.

"Now are you sure you need to come up, Katie? Doug and I are happy to take care of things around the house. We can put Gail's belongings in storage."

"Thank you, Susan, but I'm sure. Maybe it's time for me to come back."

"I understand. We'll be happy to have you," Susan said, as if the house were hers. "Would you like us to take care of your mother, her body?"

"Please." Kate's heart was heavy in her chest as she thought about her mother, now gone forever. "I'm so sorry you have to deal with all of this."

"It's our honor, Katie. We loved your mother like our own family. Doug and I will be there for the burial."

"Thank you. Andrew has his high school graduation in a couple of weeks, so we can come up to deal with the house after that." Kate sighed, looking at the calendar she had pinned to the fridge.

As Susan explained how they would deal with the death as quietly as possible, Kate thought about how it would feel to be back at Villa Magda for the first time in almost twenty years. She hadn't seen her mother in years and had never been back to the house since that fateful summer. Now, she just needed to go back, clean everything up, and finally get rid of the house along with all of its terrible memories.

"Is she… was she still in her bed?" The words slipped out of Kate before she could stop herself.

There was a pause on the other end of the line. When Susan finally answered, her voice shook a bit. "Well, Doug found her in Lacie's room. She was holding onto that bunny." Susan's words spilled out and then stopped abruptly. She had said too much. Of course, Kate knew what bunny Susan was talking about: Lacie's favorite stuffed animal, the one she had received on her fifth birthday. She wouldn't let go of it when she was a kid.

Kate remained silent for a few moments. *Lacie's room?*

"I thought she didn't go in there?"

"She'd kept it locked for years," Susan confirmed. "The last time she was in there was the end of that summer." She sighed. "She said she would only ever open that room if Lacie came back."

"Came back?" Kate repeated, a shiver running through her.

She hadn't thought about Lacie and all that happened that summer for years. Long ago, she had locked the events of the summer away in her mind, and she knew there might be things that she would never be able to recall. Over the years, Kate had come to terms with it, imagining the part of her brain where her memories were jumbled like a messy room hidden behind a closed door. Truthfully, a part of her preferred not knowing. It made it easier to sleep at night. But Susan talking about it brought feelings of dread, and Kate desperately wanted to hang up.

"Well, thank you for all you did. My mother appreciated you so much. So do I."

"Gail had a difficult life. She was…damaged. And small towns hold onto things. We understood."

Kate knew that all too well. It was another reason she had never gone back.

"Yes, they do."

As she hung up, Kate felt a strange mix of emptiness and confusion, guilt and sadness, but she felt it all from a distance, as if it were happening to someone else. Even though she had been abandoned many years ago, Gail was still her mother. To compensate for her own childhood, Kate had tried to be the best mother she could be, giving up everything for her son. But now, she grieved for the mother she never had, and tears streamed down her cheeks for what never was and never would be.

* * *

When the front door slammed shut, Kate jumped. She hadn't realized how long she had been sitting there. Her coffee had grown cold. She looked at the clock and realized who it must be. Molly Evans was one of Kate's closest friends, and their children,

Andrew and Ben, had gone to school together since kindergarten. Molly walked in, her dark hair, normally down and curly, was pulled back in a bun and her body toned as ever—she practically lived at the gym. "Morning! Ready for our workout?" Molly had grown up in a suburb outside of Philly, but her accent was mid-Atlantic, having acquired it while at boarding school during her formative years. She smiled at Kate, but her face fell when she saw Kate's expression.

"What's wrong, honey? You look like someone died."

Kate looked at her, stricken.

"Oh my God, did I just put my giant foot in my mouth?" Molly asked.

Kate let out a big sigh. "My mother died this morning."

"Oh, Kate, I'm so sorry. I'm such an idiot!" Molly enveloped Kate in her strong arms. Kate let Molly hold her for a few minutes, the two women standing in silence. Then Kate eased out of Molly's embrace.

"She was sick for a long time," Kate said, as she sank down on the kitchen bench.

"You never talked about her," Molly said gently.

"We have… we *had* a complicated relationship."

"I get it, my mom is difficult at times," Molly responded. "I'm here to help however I can."

Kate pulled back, an idea popping into her head. "Actually, can I ask you a favor? Later this summer I have to go up to my mother's house in Maine and get it ready to sell. I would love to have your opinion on the house. I have no idea what shape it's going to be in," Kate admitted. Molly was one of the top architects at her firm, and she was always looking for inspiration. Kate knew she would love seeing Villa Magda's opulent architecture, and she could use Molly's expertise when preparing to sell the house. "And Sam and Ben can join us for the week if you would like. I don't want to be alone, and I know Andrew would love the company."

"Of course," Molly said without hesitation. "Like I said, anything I can do to help."

Kate sighed in relief. "Thank you."

* * *

Thank goodness for Molly, Kate thought, as she watched Molly walk to her car. With all the hours of Pilates and SoulCycle, Molly's spark was finally coming back. The past winter, Kate had gotten a call on a Saturday at 2 a.m., the buzz waking her from her slumber. Charlie had been fast asleep beside her. The number was listed as private. Worried, Kate had picked up. Her first thought had been Andrew, but instead it had been Molly, hysterical and crying on the line. She was still drunk, Kate could hear it in her voice. Only this time, she was drunk and in jail.

"Kate, I need you!" Molly had cried to her over the phone.

"I'll be right there. Don't worry. We've got this," Kate had promised. Kate would never let her friends down if they needed her. A therapist had said that she was still desperately trying to save her sister, and any friend needing her triggered that. So when Molly called for help, Kate ran to her rescue.

Not many people knew what had happened that night, not even Sam. Only she and Charlie knew, and Molly wanted to make sure they kept it that way. The arrest had been wiped from her record because no one was hurt while she was driving. Molly assured Kate that she wouldn't have a drop of alcohol after that night, and Kate was proud that she had kept her promise. Kate's mind jumped back to Maine. For years, her mother had tried to get her to go back for summers and bring Andrew along with her. "Mom, Andrew has a lacrosse sports camp all summer. Maybe we can try and come up next year?" Kate lied time and time again, until one day her mother just stopped asking.

* * *

Throughout her day, Kate kept returning to the question of why her mother had decided to go into Lacie's room right before she died. Maybe she knew her time was almost up and she was desperate to be close to her favorite child, even if that meant going into a stuffy room that hadn't been opened in nearly two decades. Gail had always kept that room locked, adamant that no one be allowed in. It was Lacie's room. Period. Forever locked in time.

The summer that Lacie disappeared had, of course, changed their lives forever. The search was exhausting, continuing day and night for weeks, until they all started to lose hope. The disappearance had been national news for a while, with news crews swarming the gates of the estate, trapping Kate and her family inside. The relentless headlines were all variations on a theme: *"Disappearance of sixteen-year-old devastates small-town Maine."* And then, seemingly just as fast, it had become a cold case. After weeks of searching for Lacie, the police and townspeople had given up on the idea of ever finding her. Kate's family had, too, except for her mother.

Kate had never wanted to go back to Villa Magda, at least not alone. But the thought of her dearest friends and family going with her gave her courage. It was just a house after all, and maybe this was the last chance to make happy memories there before saying goodbye for the final time.

2

"We will take the children early in the morning into the forest.
They will never find the way home again."
—*HANSEL AND GRETEL*, GRIMM BROTHERS

That evening, when Charlie and Andrew came home, Kate broke the news about her mother and the house. They hugged Kate, and for the first time that day she was able to take a deep breath, exhaling into their embrace.

As a teenager, Kate had been so madly in love with Charlie, and still, after all these years, she sometimes felt butterflies when they were together. His boyish good looks were marred only by slight grayish streaks at the sides of his sandy brown hair. He took immense care of his body and worked hard to keep fit. She wondered sometimes what he saw in her. Kate had never been conventionally pretty, not like Lacie. Her dark auburn hair, once straight and smooth, was hard to tame most days. Kate had always thought that her eyes, now framed by slight crow's feet, were the color of a dark, mysterious lake, and her part-Irish heritage marked her with freckles that everyone found cute when she was a kid, but not as much now that she was in her mid-thirties.

Charlie was her rock and had changed so much from the young teenager she had met. Sooner or later, time changes everything, but Kate could not imagine her life with anyone other than Charlie. As young parents, Kate and Charlie had grown up together while raising their son. She was grateful for how sensible he was and the way he took care of her and Andrew. Sometimes, though, he treated her as if she would break, and those times she wanted to scream. She wanted to shake him and tell him that she was so much stronger than he thought. But in the end, she didn't say anything. She knew that he wanted to take care of her, and she let him think that was what she wanted, too. Their relationship worked that way—it made him feel needed. "It's going to be okay," Andrew said, bringing her back to the moment. He was such a good, kind kid, Kate thought as she held him. She couldn't believe how quickly the years had gone. In just a few months he would be starting his first year of college. Looking at Andrew, she thought he seemed so much younger than she had felt at his age.

Andrew hugged his mother a little extra, and when he let go, she could see he had tears in his eyes. He always had a cool exterior, but Kate knew he had a sensitive side too. But he wore his heart on his sleeve only briefly, before asking what's for dinner.

Thankfully, Charlie could sense that Kate wanted to avoid the subject over dinner, and he kept the conversation moving by asking Andrew about school. Finally, during dessert, Kate couldn't ignore it any longer, and she shared her idea of going back to the house with their friends. To her surprise, Andrew liked the idea and went upstairs to text Ben.

Charlie got up and cleared the plates. He had been quiet for most of the discussion. "Are you sure you want to go back there?" He asked, his deep voice laced with worry. He knew how complicated her past with the house was. "We haven't been there in so long. Not since we were kids."

"I know, but I have to do this. You understand, don't you?"

Charlie looked at her, eyebrows knit together. She pressed on, continuing to make her case.

"We have to get it over with. Waiting will only make it harder. And I need to get the house ready to sell. There are decisions only I can make." Kate paused, standing to take the rest of the dishes to the sink. "Besides, it's a beautiful house despite everything else. We'll enjoy it, and the ocean is glorious. You loved it there once too, remember? I think maybe we will again."

"I know you're right, but it's just… I'm afraid it could trigger you, all those memories. I don't want you to go back there. You've done so much work to get beyond all that happened." Charlie paused, and spoke softly. "Going there can't bring Lacie back, you do know that, right?"

"Of course I know that." Kate didn't want to worry him, and did her best to steer away from any mention of Lacie.

Charlie took her into his arms, his rough stubble scratching her face. She liked the gruffness of it. She looked into his bright blue eyes and the creases around them. So much time had gone by, and they had built a wonderful life together. She would not let this ruin any of that.

Kate started talking about the details of the trip as she put away the leftovers. Charlie walked over to the sink to pour himself a glass of water.

"I don't know why you would want to go back," he admitted after she was done talking, his body still turned toward the sink. "I don't particularly want to, especially that week in August. Besides, I thought you hated it there."

"Look, I know that you're just trying to protect me. I do. But I don't have a choice; my mother is gone. Decisions need to be made regarding the estate," she said, prompting Charlie to face her. "Besides, if we're going to sell it, I need to see if any major renovations need to be made. Molly is an architect, after all. It won't hurt to have her opinion."

"What kind of decisions need to be made? And what do you mean by 'if we're going to sell?' Maintaining a house like that is very costly, and Andrew is about to start a very expensive college."

"I don't know. But I hate to take Doug and Susan's home away from them. They've been there longer than I've been alive."

"They can't stay there forever, Kate."

"I'm sure my mom set something up in her trust for them. Look, can we not worry about this right now? It's been a long day."

He sighed and admitted, "I should know better than to ever try and change your mind."

"Yes, you should," Kate said playfully. "Now, stop worrying and let me organize this."

Charlie half-smiled. "Okay, I hope I won't have to say I told you so." He took her hand and pulled her close. "I want to protect you, always," he whispered in her ear, sending shivers down her arms.

She kissed his cheek as he held her. Charlie looked down at

Kate as if she were a specimen he was studying.

"Look, I don't mean to keep bringing this up, but don't you think it will be a little strange?"

Kate glanced up at him. "Maybe, but the three of us would be too lonely. There is no way that I could go back there without friends around me; it's just too sad. I need to make new memories, happy ones. Besides, it's my birthday too. I think after all these years it's time to celebrate, don't you?"

"Well, I suppose," Charlie said begrudgingly.

"And it will be good to see Alice again. I am sure she will want to join us."

Charlie's shoulders stiffened, a slight frown forming on his face. "Alice? I thought the two of you had stopped talking."

"I guess it has been awhile. But you know that is normal for us; one of us will get busy and forget to call. But we always show up when the other one is in need."

Charlie murmured something under his breath, but Kate paid no attention to him. She left the rest of the dinner clean-up to Charlie and walked out of the room like a woman on a mission.

* * *

Kate felt surprisingly good about her decision to return to Villa Magda. It would be the first time she would acknowledge her birthday in years. She hadn't celebrated it since her sister disappeared on her eighteenth birthday. Most years, it would just come and go like any other day. Andrew had questioned her about it once, and Kate had replied that she didn't like to celebrate herself. He had shrugged his shoulders and just thought it was one of his mother's quirks. But Kate knew it was time to stop running from what happened. Didn't her therapist tell her she needed to confront those memories? Tackle them to the ground, she had said. Kate had laughed, but she knew what she meant. The memories were all jumbled, causing her stress and anxiety deep down. Freeing herself would be a godsend. Kate suspected that her mother's death would make it easier for her to start the healing process. Now, finally, she could let some of the guilt go. And in the process, Kate hoped that her friends would enjoy themselves, even as she held them close to her like talismans to ward off the house's effects. She was determined to turn the necessity of dealing with her mother's estate into more than just a sad event. She would not let the past mess with her plans.

Memories were like words—they could not break her.

3

*"When it was mid-day, they saw a beautiful
snow-white bird sitting on a bough.
It spread its wings and flew away before them,
and they followed it until they reached a little house."*

—HANSEL AND GRETEL, GRIMM BROTHERS

The next day, Kate went down into the basement and searched for a box she had stored away after her father had died. She found the cardboard box with "Villa Magda" in big letters across the top and brought it to the kitchen, setting it on the marble countertop and ripping off the packing tape. In the box were several big, yellow envelopes that her father had saved with information regarding the house. She quickly shuffled through them. Most of them contained official documents, including bills and permits, plans, and photos. And then she found the envelope she was looking for: "History of Villa Magda." It was filled with loose letters and handwritten notes, most about her great-grandfather,

Max, who had built the house in the early twentieth century.

She pulled out one photo that featured Villa Magda looming large on a cliffside, the shimmering ocean in the foreground. Villa Magda was a beautiful home on the southeast coast of Maine, in a town called Aria. It was a quaint old beach town, its population less than a few thousand people, that was bustling in the summer and dormant in the winter. Aria had only eight miles of beach lined with sharp cliffs, woodlands, and rocky coves—if you blinked you would miss it, the townsfolk said. And they liked it that way. The village itself was simple and populated by a small group of families that had been there for generations. In the summer, Aria overflowed with beautiful flowers, fruit trees, and out-of-towners—usually families who brought their rambunctious children on summer holidays, and writers who came to write the next great American novel. The villa had been built by Max for Kate's great-grandmother, Magda. Her mother had often claimed that her grandpa Max had fallen totally and madly in love with Magda at first sight. Magda was mesmerizing, with long golden hair and deep blue eyes that reminded Max of the open sea. Kate picked up a picture of Magda and marveled how she looked strikingly like Kate's mother, Gail—and Lacie. Kate herself took after her father, with his dark hair and eyes; she had inherited his temperament as well.

The house was built entirely in stone, and the original construction had been maintained and updated over the years, but not so much as to change the original feel of the home. The villa had two main floors with a side tower and an attic. It had rows of windows that were draped with lush curtains that Kate's grandmother handmade herself, which is why they were never replaced despite the heaviness they brought to the rooms. The ornate doors had stained-glass windows that illuminated the rooms inside with pools of color.

Surrounding the house was a magnificent landscape with views stretching toward the sea. Behind the house and down a short flight of marble stairs, there was a large swimming pool, located on the edge of a perfectly manicured lawn. It was all framed by a panorama of incomparable beauty—the lawn stretched out toward the edge of an imposing cliff with jagged edges that led to the ocean. The cliff was steep, and Doug and Susan would often refer to terrible accidents that could occur if one went too close. Because of them, Kate had always steered clear of the cliff as a child. And then there were the woods behind the house that went on for miles. Those, too, had been off limits to Kate and Lacie when they were kids.

Kate looked at Magda's picture again, at her golden-blonde hair surrounding her face like a halo, just like Lacie's. Magda had come from Germany to live with her cousins. Max wooed her with the promise that he would build her the grandest house on the Maine coast. He worked day and night and poured all of his family's money into the home to impress her, importing marble from Italy, furniture from France, and planting trees that would remind her of home. But she remained unimpressed, always seemingly wanting more. It took him several years to add to the house. In year two he added a tower and secret rooms and passageways that he thought would entice her curiosity, but nothing seemed to move her. He then built an extension to the side, and finally the caretaker's cottage that was nestled in a grove of birch trees. He was almost ready to give up when Magda walked the grounds, through the home and the cottage, and then looked out over the cliff and the vast ocean and declared she was ready. The townspeople were dying to finally see what Max had built for love and couldn't stop talking about the fairytale wedding. It was Aria's version of a royal wedding, and the villa was their palace.

Also included in the envelope were newspaper clippings and family photos from the wedding that Kate studied carefully. They all looked beautiful, and it seemed like a joyous and extravagant celebration. It was clear that her great-grandfather had believed that he could build Magda a home that would make her fall as madly and deeply in love with him as he had with her, but he had been wrong. According to family stories, on their fifth anniversary, Magda announced that she had fallen for a gentleman farmer who lived a few towns over. She left Max to tend to their two small children alone in the villa he had built. He fell into a deep depression, and the villa had become dark and full of sadness. Magda never came back to the house, not even to see her children. According to a note written by Paul, Max and Magda's oldest son, Max had died young, leaving the kids to be raised by his sister.

Kate put the folder down and thought of the house and how much her mother loved it. As an only child, the house went to Gail, along with a healthy inheritance. After renovating it and adding her own touches, they soon began spending their summers there as a family. Kate's father, Edward, was a corporate executive, which meant he had to be in New York City most days. He would visit Gail and the girls as often as he could. But Edward hadn't liked coming to the Villa; he preferred staying in the city or traveling, so Gail and the girls spent many weeks alone.

Thinking back, Kate remembered feeling all the sadness in the house as a little girl and, at times, she even thought she could hear sobbing. Once, when she tried to find where the crying was coming from, it led her to the library, where a pair of portraits hung, featuring her great-grandparents. She'd told her mother about it and Gail had brushed it off, claiming that Kate had an overactive imagination, just like her sister. As she grew older, she heard fewer and fewer sounds, until they stopped altogether. Her mother had been right—it had been just her imagination.

It certainly would not be an easy task to pack it all up, Kate thought, but she was ready to immerse herself in this project. She had always suspected that the house had many secrets buried deep in its walls, under the floorboards, in the garden, and in the maze, and she found herself suddenly thrilled at the prospect of investigating every inch of the property to her own satisfaction. Despite its dark history, Kate was looking forward to sharing the house with some of her favorite people—it was where she had spent her childhood summers, where she learned to swim and fish, where she first met and fell in love with Charlie. It had been a magical place until the one day that changed everything as she knew it. But that's what tragedy did. It pulled the rug out from under you, and it made all the good disappear in an instant.

After Lacie disappeared, Kate had gone from loving Villa Magda to despising it. She had felt as if the walls were closing in on her, and she wished that it would burn to the ground. But now, after all these years, her mother no longer casting a shadow over what the house represented, she hoped to see the beauty Villa Magda held once again, standing majestic and proud on its seaside cliff.

As she put the file back, she saw a yellowed envelope with *Lacie* written across it. She picked it up, her hands shaky. It held newspaper clippings from the time of Lacie's disappearance.

STORY OF MISSING TEEN GRIPS POPULAR VACATION SPOT IN MAINE.

The search of the woods in Aria, Maine, began several weeks ago and involved more than a dozen police officers, police dogs, and local residents. Sources have reported that the police have received hundreds of tips from the general public. Witnesses have reported seeing plaster casts of tire tracks near the girl's summer residence, Villa Magda, which were collected by police among other evidence, including strands of hair in the nearby woods. According to the Maine News, *the search has been unsuccessful to date and the active search will be suspended. The chief of police will be holding a press conference with further details by the end of day tomorrow.*

MISSING TEEN'S SISTER WAS THE LAST ONE TO SEE HER. LAPSE IN MEMORY OR SOMETHING ELSE TO BLAME?

The search for Lacie Cambria, a teen who went missing more than three months ago in Aria, has not brought conclusive results, sources report. The person who last saw her was her eighteen-year-old sister, Kate, who has claimed she remembers very little from that day, especially the hours leading up to Lacie's disappearance. Police confirm the teen had gone to the movies with a friend and was not present during the hours that they believe Lacie left the home. Investigators have eliminated Kate and her family as suspects at this time. The small summer enclave of Aria has been suffering since this tragic event and is eager to find out what happened that day. The gardener from the property, Carl Warren, was questioned, but has since been excluded as a person of interest in this case. The question remains all these months later: What happened to Lacie Cambria?

Kate's head was spinning and she couldn't read anymore. She stuffed all the articles and envelopes back into the box and sealed it shut again.

Reporters had been everywhere, Kate remembered, lurking in the shadows. Her mother tried keeping them away, but they were relentless and they were desperate to talk to Kate. Gail forbade Kate to leave the house, in case she did or said something wrong. Kate missed Charlie; he had all but disappeared. But she couldn't blame him.

After days of being holed up in her room, her eyes had been raw from nights she spent crying herself to sleep. Each morning she hoped she would wake up and find that it had all been nothing more than a vicious, cruel dream. Finally, one day, Kate decided to sneak out to the beach to meet Charlie at their special spot. It was after a big storm, and she knew that no one else would be there. But when she got there, Kate saw a different man standing by the shore. She had recognized him from the group of reporters. His hair was blond and tousled from the salt air. He smiled at Kate, warmly. She smiled back. She knew why he was there, but she didn't care. She wanted to tell someone how she felt. So she did. She told him everything. All of it was taken out of context and chronicled on the front page of the local newspaper and then picked up nationwide, culminating in a story on *Inside Edition*. They made Kate out to be the jealous sister, the less attractive one whose mother didn't pay attention to her. She was portrayed as a resentful teen who may have done something to Lacie.

Her mother had been furious with her. The house had been so important to her mother, who had insisted on staying there to wait in case Lacie returned—just like Max had never left the house, always waiting for Magda. For a long time, Kate had resented Lacie for having taken her mother's love away from her, for preoccupying her attention for the rest of her life. Even so, Kate couldn't keep herself from obsessing over what had happened during those few hours when she was out of the house. Where had Lacie gone that day? She couldn't know. There was no way to find out. The question had haunted her for years and years, reasserting itself over and over like a wound healing over only to reopen.

Kate folded the article and shut the box. It had been almost twenty years. She was stronger and wiser, and by now, she hoped that nobody would remember her as the sister of the girl who had vanished into thin air.

PRESENT DAY

POLICE FILE—ARIA, MAINE.

CASE 1583

Q: What can you tell us about last night?

A: It was Kate's birthday. We had steak and great wine. It seemed normal enough, except...

Q: Except what?

A: This place, the mother, the sister—nothing seemed right. It seemed as if it was all coming to a head. I thought maybe we pissed off the house, you know, all here trying to pretend everything was normal. Just bullshit.

PART TWO

MONDAY

4

*"When they approached the little house
they saw that it was built of bread and covered with cakes,
but that the windows were of clear sugar."*
—HANSEL AND GRETEL, GRIMM BROTHERS

The day they finally arrived at Villa Magda, the summer air was extremely dense and humid, and the bumpy car ride was long. Kate was tired—she had hardly slept the night before in anticipation of the trip. As the green fields and rugged coastline flashed by their windows, the farms and summer homes appeared fewer and farther between on the winding roads leading toward the estate. She had forgotten how far Villa Magda was from anything most people would consider civilization.

Kate peered out the window, remembering just how excited she would feel each Memorial Day weekend as they drove to the house when she was a child. She and her sister would always talk about what adventures another summer would bring. Her mother's garden parties, Doug and his boat, the corn and fresh lobster, Susan's apple and blueberry pies, and the local friends. Even if they were "from away," as the locals called them, they felt at home here for a couple of months each year.

When they were little, Lacie pretended she was a princess and Villa Magda was her fairytale castle. Kate would often join in and together they would play make-believe for hours, Lacie insisting that Kate play the role of the witch or the wicked queen. They would have elaborate tea parties where they invited all of their imaginary friends and stuffed animals. They would dress up, do their hair, make cupcakes, and play until their mother or Susan called them in for dinner.

Kate couldn't remember when it had happened exactly, but one day, they stopped playing pretend. Reality began to set in as they got older, and their dolls were packed away into the attic along with the tea sets and their vivid childhood imaginations. The house was no longer a castle, Kate was no longer a captor and Lacie no longer a princess. Even though they were close in age, Lacie started to annoy Kate as they got older, and whenever her little sister asked her to play, Kate would make a million excuses why she could not. Kate had started dating Charlie, and after that she had no time at all for Lacie and her games.

Lacie had been a late bloomer, but when she did, she was a stunner. Kate sometimes felt inadequate when she stood next to her. Lacie didn't realize how beautiful she was. She still saw herself as a little girl. Now, all these years later, Kate wished she had had one more day to play with her. Kate often thought that one more day was all she needed.

As the car hummed along, Kate looked over at Charlie, who

was focused at the steering wheel, far off in his thoughts. Andrew was focused on his phone, ignoring the tension between his parents. Kate scanned the straight road ahead and she felt her eyes growing heavy. As she drifted off, the sounds of the road turned into a chorus of laughter and music. In her dream, she was now walking down the path through Villa Magda's garden. As she drew closer to the house, the music grew louder and she saw the table under the big pear tree set with pink flowers, teacups, and cupcakes decorated with a black script that read "Eat Me." Her mother was hosting one of her magical parties for Lacie—this year's theme was *Alice in Wonderland*—and she was giddy. Kate only saw her mother really happy when she was in the middle of preparing and hosting a party, with Susan always by her side helping with the food, cutting flowers, and checking the guest list.

Susan was busy making Gail happy, an orchestrated dance that Kate had seen over and over again. Gail always said she was made to socialize and that it was a true artform. As the first guests started arriving, they milled around the garden and gulped drinks, in awe of the dreamland they entered into. "No locals," Gail would emphasize whenever they sent out the invitations, causing Susan to roll her eyes behind Gail's back.

The garden was now full of people, with kids running around with candied apples and Susan bringing plates of cookies shaped like grinning cats and mushrooms. Kate felt dizzy as the music became too loud and the kids started spinning in circles. She could see Susan rush out of the house toward her mother, holding something in her hand amid sounds of hushed whispers. She couldn't hear what was being said, but she moved closer as Susan swiped by her and she saw towels in her hand, dripping with blood. She heard one word: "Lacie."

Gail rushed past, muttering to herself, "The house is only content with chaos. When things are too quiet, bad things happen." Kate felt a shiver down her spine. "Lacie. What's wrong with Lacie?"

No one answered. No one even heard her, but the movement around her sped up. Some of the guests noticed Gail's fear and began gathering the children in a chaotic rush, heading toward the gates. Kate looked up at the house, and there was a glow from the windows shining down on her.

Kate jolted awake as the car hit a deep pothole. Her forehead shone with sweat, and it took her a few moments to remember where she was. As her eyes readjusted to the bright sunlight, she tried to make sense of the dream.

As the images faded, Gail's words were the only thing echoing in Kate's head, "The house is only content with chaos. When things are too quiet, bad things happen."

* * *

The car bumped and swayed along the dusty roads leading them through miles of dense woodland and beautiful coast. Kate bounced around like a weary rag doll. Kate's throat clenched immediately as the car approached Villa Magda's massive iron gates. Nothing much had changed, she thought, as she felt her chest tighten and her palms become damp with sweat. Doubt seeped in. Was it a good idea for her to bring all these people to this place? She wasn't so sure anymore. What was she trying to prove? Arriving at the entrance, she worried that she might never get beyond what had happened there. But as she looked back and saw Molly and Sam pulling up behind them, she knew it was too late to turn back.

They pulled up to the house, the sign on the gate reading

Villa Magda in gothic lettering, and sweat formed under her armpits from heat and anxiety. No one needed to know how she truly felt, not even Charlie. She didn't want him to tell her that he told her so.

The car came to a sudden halt. Kate slowly opened her door and took a deep breath. She could taste the salt in the air. She turned to the rest of them, the house looming behind her, and she could only imagine what they were thinking as they looked up at it. The first view of the house was always impressive.

"We're finally here!" Kate called out, and plastered a smile on her face as the others rolled down their windows. "Welcome to Villa Magda, everyone!" She noted the anticipation in their eyes as she imagined they were thinking of days of languishing by the ocean together, eating local foods, and drinking wine. Five adults and two kids. They would be spending the next seven days eating, drinking, and basking underneath the Maine sun. None of that sounded terrible—there would be no mention of that summer or of Lacie. Most of them had no idea about her history, and she would make sure Alice and Charlie kept it a secret. No one had to know.

* * *

The house stood imposingly against the backdrop of the sea with a tennis court, pool, and garden adorning the property. Kate had to smile when she saw it all. Over the years, Kate's mother had sent pictures of the house and the work she did, hoping to entice Kate with the promise of a glorious summer.

"This is absolutely gorgeous!" Molly exclaimed as she stretched her long, dark legs, toned and muscular from all her exercise classes.

"That was quite the long ride," Sam grumbled.

"But it looks like it will be worth it," Molly continued, ignoring Sam as she glanced around the grounds with a wide smile. From where they were standing, the curve of the rocky coast just barely peeked out past the edge of the house, but the faint crash of the waves could be heard slapping against the shore.

"What a view, truly breathtaking. And I can run on the beach. So perfect. You must be thrilled to be back. Even though, under the circumstances..." Molly apologized, realizing her gaffe. "I'm sorry, I didn't mean to bring it up."

"It's okay," Kate said, shrugging off the comment. Molly had been thinking about Kate's mother, but Kate was thinking of Lacie. Her therapist had explained that trauma-based memory loss can easily occur when the trauma creates stress that negatively affects the brain, which kept her from having proper memories. Lacie's disappearance had done some real damage to her.

"Lacie," Kate whispered to herself.

"Hey, Katie," Charlie said, startling her. "You okay?" His kind eyes twinkled. She realized that he never called her that at home, and it surprised her that he did so now. He kissed her cheek softly, making her feel like a teenager again. She loved him so much.

"I'm better than good, believe it or not. Maybe it's the ocean air, but I don't feel as upset as I thought I would." It was a half-lie. She wanted to accept what happened to her sister. If only she could remember some of that day leading up to it. But it was still such a blur. "Detachment from trauma and guilt," her therapist had said, like a jigsaw puzzle that she couldn't quite find all the pieces to. Fragments all jumbled together. It was all there, but locked away—the protective door she had closed years ago in her mind now stood in her way as she tried to piece together what had really happened. She was ready to uncover the truth, to confront what she had repressed, but her own mind seemed to be hiding the solution from her. Memories don't go anywhere, the therapist had explained; they are embedded in us. Kate just had to figure out how to open that door, how to open herself, to retrieve the answers.

The sounds of the circling seagulls interrupted her thoughts. Kate turned to look at the others. Molly had pulled her hair back in a bun and was admiring the view. Charlie was unpacking their car. They all looked exhausted from the long drive as they picked up bags and suitcases and lumbered toward the entrance, Sam jogging ahead of them.

"Alright Kate, I'm a big guy, I need the biggest room. Where is it?" he jokingly called out as he left Molly alone with the bags.

"So typical," Molly sighed. "I'm sorry, he is such a man-child."

Kate couldn't help but chuckle a bit. This is what she wanted: normalcy.

"Idiots," Ben muttered as he passed by his mom. Though Ben was easygoing and quiet, he was outwardly judgmental of his parents. Ben watched them like a hawk, disapproving of their shenanigans.

"Can you just wait for the rest of us?" Kate called after Sam. "I'll show you the guest rooms and you can all choose, like out of a hat or in some other dignified fashion."

Andrew poked Ben. "Race you to the pool." The two boys sprinted off toward the backyard, leaving a trail of shirts and shoes in their path. Andrew and Ben had hit it off in kindergarten and had grown up together, spending most weekends together at one house or the other. With Andrew so busy with lacrosse, Kate had noticed that the two boys had been spending less time together, so she was glad they would have this week to spend hanging out and relaxing.

"Just stay out of the woods!" Kate called out after them. The woods edged the side of the property adjacent to the cliff and went on for miles, part of an untouched reserve that could not be built on. These woods had always scared Kate as a kid, even before Lacie disappeared. Lacie, on the other hand, loved the woods and insisted they were enchanted. But Kate knew better. To her, they were dark and uninviting, easy to get lost in. Kate gazed at the gently swaying pines, wondering if Lacie was still lost somewhere deep inside the labyrinth of trunks and branches. She shivered and hugged herself.

"Mom, we're not five. We get it; no woods. Just pool, okay?" Andrew called out as he raced Ben around the side of the house.

Kate marveled at them being so carefree. The last summer before the end of childhood—it was bittersweet. It had all come so fast. She had started dating Charlie around the same age. Kate had been smitten with him from their first date. They had been so young and clueless when they'd had Andrew, but they stuck with each other and look at them now, she thought. Andrew was their pride and joy. Her mom had warned her when she and Charlie had gotten engaged, "Only fifty percent of teenage sweethearts stay married past ten years," much to Kate's annoyance. But they proved her wrong. Kate was now in charge of the house and was an adult, with her only child all grown up. Time had flown by for Kate and Charlie, but glancing up at the house, Kate wondered what memories were still buried deep within its walls. Time had stood still at Villa Magda.

5

"How can I bear to leave my children alone in the forest?
—the wild animals would soon come and tear them to pieces."

—*HANSEL AND GRETEL*, GRIMM BROTHERS

Alice was already there, standing at the edge of the cliff like a Roman statue gazing out onto the sea, her translucent skin dewy and her golden hair free and flowing in the wind. As Kate walked across the lawn toward Alice, she remembered how windy this place could be, but despite the wind, as always, Alice looked perfect. Kate had always wished she could be more like Alice—confident in her beauty and grace. While Alice was lithe and tall, Kate was shorter and shapely. She touched her auburn hair, suddenly feeling self-conscious as she realized how frazzled she must look from the drive.

"Oh, Kate, my darling!" Alice exclaimed in her warm voice

when Kate reached her.

How Kate had missed Alice. Alice was Kate's oldest friend, and sometimes Alice understood her better than she even understood herself. Alice knew her deepest and more profound secrets, and Kate knew that she would be vital in helping her get through this.

"A chapter finally has closed," Alice said, compassionately. "I'm not surprised if you feel some relief. I imagine you have a lot of mixed emotions right now. It's been a long time coming."

They held each other close for a long moment.

"I'm so glad you're here." Kate sighed out a breath of relief. They had a special bond that others couldn't always understand. Even when Alice seemed difficult, Kate knew she loved her unconditionally, like a sister would. And she always showed up when she was really needed.

"Me too." Alice smiled. "This place... I almost forgot how grandiose it is. Max sure did build his very own castle."

Kate watched as Alice twirled her hair, a habit she'd had ever since Kate could remember. The gesture was childlike, but Kate got the familiar feeling that there was a mysterious side to Alice, something else she couldn't quite grasp. Kate never pried, though—Alice had stood by her during those first months after Lacie went missing and hope was still something they were all clinging onto. It had been so difficult for the entire family to process the loss, and Alice helped Kate bear it in a way no one else could, not even Charlie. Kate felt she owed Alice a debt of gratitude forever.

Looking at the house, another memory bubbled up: the looks of despair as the hours slipped further and further away that day, her mother crying while her father pounded his fists on the kitchen table. Kate knew that her mother had always blamed her for Lacie's disappearance, even though she never actually admitted it, just the way she never admitted her obvious preference for her younger daughter. Kate had been the last one to see her sister that day, and for months, her mother would ask her over and over if there was any small detail that she had missed. Her drinking became more frequent as the days passed, and the questioning became more and more belligerent. *"What did she say? How did she say it? What was she wearing? Did she speak to anyone? About anyone?"* The questions were endless. Every day, it was all they ever talked about. *"Do you remember any details that could help us?"*

The search parties had been intense at first. After the fourteenth night, Kate was beyond exhausted, drained, and no longer wanted to search for her sister. She had just wanted to run off and disappear herself. She had left the group, determined never to go back. That was when she met Alice, who was in the woods close to the cliff. She had been searching for Lacie too.

"Are you the missing girl's sister?" Alice had said, her bluntness catching Kate off-guard. Kate knew most of the summer kids in town, but she had never seen Alice before. She must be a townie, someone who didn't come to the wealthier end of Aria. When she spoke, one side of her mouth went up a bit more than the other.

"Well, are you?" Alice had asked again, this time louder.

"So what if I am?" Kate had snapped.

"So, nothing. It just doesn't make you special, that's all." Alice had said coyly, shrugging her shoulders.

"What?" Kate's face had grown hot. How dare this girl say

that to her? Kate would have traded places with anyone right now. She didn't feel special; she felt cursed.

"Who the fuck are you?" Kate hardly ever swore but it felt good, stronger somehow.

"Everyone has shit they deal with," Alice said defiantly. *"Not just you and your missing sister."*

Kate felt the anger boiling up inside her.

"Who the hell are you anyway?"

"Just a girl who's telling you the truth. All this town is talking about is you and her. It's boring," she had scoffed. *"Your picture is in every newspaper."*

Kate hadn't wanted to admit that she was bored too; it would sound awful if she did. But hearing someone else say it had made her feel better, it unleashed something. *"Yes!"* She had finally admitted out loud. *"I am. I fucking am tired of it."*

"Then just stop looking," Alice said.

"What?"

"Stop looking for her. Just stop. If you do, we all can. Maybe she doesn't want to be found, ever think of that?" Alice said it so easily, and Kate realized how badly she wanted things to go back to normal.

"Maybe she ran away? Teenagers do that all the time. Maybe she found a prince and ran off!" Alice had smiled. A princess and a prince in a castle, Kate thought. Maybe she did run off on some great adventure, and nothing bad happened to her. It didn't seem likely, but the thought made Kate hopeful.

Kate had looked at the girl as she scrunched up her button nose. *"Do I know you? I mean I thought I knew everyone from around here."*

"I'm Alice."

And that's how Kate and Alice became friends. They were inseparable those first few months. Kate had been able to tell Alice how she honestly felt about Lacie, the disappearance, and even Charlie, without being judged or maligned. It was like taking a deep breath of ocean air after being stuck underground.

As the fall leaves had begun to shed and the air had become crisp, Lacie had become more and more of a distant memory. A shadow, a story parents told their kids, a cautionary tale. The town had not wanted to tarnish their reputation and risk losing summer tourism, so they painted the narrative of a sullen teenager with an overbearing mother who ran away. Lacie was just another one of the millions of teenage runaways lost within the United States. Slowly the searching had diminished in fervor and by winter, all searches had come to a deafening halt. Without a body, there was just nothing to go on. Kate and Alice seldom discussed what had happened that summer, but Kate knew that when she decided to come back, Alice would be here for her. She needed her more than she even needed Charlie, although she would never admit that to him. Alice was truthful to her in a way no one else was.

So here was Alice, stoic as ever, standing in front of the villa. She and Kate turned when she heard Molly calling her name.

"Kate, honey. Which room should we take?"

Alice shook her head slightly and came back to life, her hair ruffling in the warm, sticky breeze. She looked fresh in her summer dress, not a hair out of place. Kate was happy Alice was here.

* * *

After showing everyone to their rooms upstairs, Kate met Charlie outside as he was unpacking the last duffel bags. He turned to Kate and smiled.

"This is great, sweetie, Sam is just being an asshole. That seems to be his M.O. lately."

Not only were Charlie and Sam friends, they were business partners as well. They met in their freshman year of college, when they had sat next to each other in their Intro to Economics course. They were longtime friends, but lately their connection seemed to be fraying.

"This trip may help you guys sort all your stuff out," Kate said hopefully.

"We'll see, but he's already not starting on a good note," Charlie muttered as he lugged the bags to the door.

Kate looked up at the house. A slight movement in the second-floor window caught her eye. A curtain moving in the wind, she guessed. Maybe it was Susan or Doug tidying up? She looked again, the curtain now still. She must be tired, she thought. Besides, that window was in Lacie's room. No one ever went there.

6

"Ah, my dear children, come indoors and stay with me,
you will be no trouble,' said the wicked witch."
—*HANSEL AND GRETEL,* GRIMM BROTHERS

Kate entered the house and was immediately hit with a strong but familiar odor. She had been too preoccupied before, but now, taking a deep breath, the foyer brought back waves of nostalgia. It still smelled like it had when she was a kid, of burnt wood and cedar oil—a musty smell. She clutched the entryway table, dizzy with the emotion of being back after all this time. She had to catch her breath as she looked around. It all looked the same. The foyer was wide, with an enormous wooden staircase in the center and a table with a big bouquet of blue and white hydrangeas. Kate regained her bearings and noticed an envelope on the table, standing up against a family photo. It was labeled *Katie.* She opened it.

HOUSE RULES & REMINDERS.

Please ensure all windows are closed and secure before activating the alarm.

The electric panel is in the box at the bottom of the basement stairs. Please only open in the case of a power outage.

The pool is functioning and ready for use, May through September.

Use the stairs to the beach on the far side.

Caution when entering the woods. Check for ticks each night.

Stay away from the cliff.

The room on the second floor, to the right of the stairs, is closed. Do not enter.

WiFi password: VillaMagda87

Welcome to Villa Magda

Kate read through the note and remembered how her mother had always had so many rules. By that last summer, she and Lacie had memorized them. They would mock their mother and her rules behind her back on the car ride up. Now they were neatly written in Susan's handwriting. *Caution when entering the woods.* It sounded so innocent.

"*The woods could eat you up and never spit you back out,*" Susan would say eerily to a young Kate and Lacie. Of course, as they got older, they tried to defy the rules any chance they could, but getting scolded by Susan or their mother was no fun. Now, Kate was slightly bothered by Susan's note; after all these years, she was still treating Kate like a child.

Kate re-read the line about the closed room. Why would it still need to stay closed, now that her mother was gone? And did they lock it again after finding her mother there? Kate felt a tingling shoot down her spine. She had not set foot in Lacie's room for almost twenty years, and even though she felt that her mother's passing had lifted some of the foreboding that clung to the house, she still didn't consider that room anything other than off limits. She probably never would.

"Welcome home," Kate muttered to herself as she looked up at the second-floor landing, images of her sister running down the steps coming back to her.

* * *

Kate entered the room Charlie had chosen upstairs with her suitcase, happy to finally be putting it down. The room he'd picked had been her room growing up. Her mother had turned it into a guest room with a nice queen-sized bed. The room overlooked the backyard, with a great view of the pool and the lawn leading to the cliff's edge. Kate looked around at the white furniture; she could tell it was high-end, but there was a coldness about the way the room was decorated. It felt more like a hotel room than her childhood bedroom. The pale yellow walls she had loved as a teenager had been painted over and were now a stark white. Kate wondered where all her old things were. Probably in the attic somewhere. Her mother must have put everything she could out of sight.

Stepping into her old room reminded her of the first summer that she and Charlie had been together. It was the first time they had made love. It had been a warm July evening during one of her mother's famous dinner parties. Everyone had put on their best summer clothes and arrived full of expectation for a beautiful evening. A full moon had lit up the sky, and Susan had cooked her delicious lobster and corn dinner. With a touch of Charlie's hand and a brush of his leg against hers under the dinner table, Kate could feel herself get excited and all she could think of was him.

After blueberry pie and vanilla ice cream, everyone had left the table to go look at the moon from the beach. Swiftly, without saying any words, he had led her up to her room and had locked the door; the secrecy and feeling of danger had excited her even more. She had felt his strong, firm hands caress the small of her back in the opening of her summer dress, awakening her skin, and she had let him take her clothes off. At that moment, she had felt a desire she didn't know she possessed. She would have gone with him anywhere as her desire became his desire, or was it his desire that became hers? He had kissed her all down her body, and in that childhood summer room of hers, he guided her and she had completely let go and become his. He knew what he was doing. It hadn't been his first time, but she had never felt this way before.

They had stayed on the bed looking at each other afterward until they had heard voices from the lawn coming closer. She had peeked out the window and had seen the dinner guests with Gail up front coming back to the house, shoes and glasses in hand, laughing, singing, and ready to party on without a care in the world. He had quickly pulled on his clothes and helped Kate zip up her dress, and in a flash, their first time had been over. Kate had dreamt about it in the following days. She knew she loved Charlie then and that she would forever. She only wished she could have held on to that moment longer.

7

"The witch led them into her little house.
And there they found a good meal laid out,
of milk and pancakes, with sugar, apples and nuts.
They thought they were in heaven."
—HANSEL AND GRETEL, GRIMM BROTHERS

Doug was waiting for Kate in the kitchen, his face jovial but weathered with deep-set wrinkles embedded from years of working outdoors and on the water. Doug was a big man, tall and sturdy, even as age had begun to sap him of his energy.

"So great to see you, Katie," Doug said as he came close and smiled. "And that boy of yours, so tall."

Doug embraced her, his big arms engulfing her, making her feel like a little girl again. Kate could smell fresh seawater on him.

"How's the boat doing?" she asked.

"Rusty, but she still does the job." Doug smiled. "She's weathered more storms than I can count."

Kate nodded. "I'm sure she has. Thank you so much for taking care of my mom. I don't know what I would have done without you and Susan."

Doug handed her a tall glass of homemade lemonade. Unlike her old bedroom, the kitchen was remarkably the same after all these years; tall white cabinets with glass doors and their summer china in blue and white peeking out. Her mother used to call the kitchen the heart of the house.

"You know how Susan and I both felt about your family all these years." His eyes grew watery as he spoke.

"I know. It was always a comfort knowing that Mom wasn't here alone." It was a comfort she hadn't realized she needed until this very moment.

He handed her a white, sealed envelope. "This is from your mother. She wanted me to give it to you once she realized that she wasn't getting any better." He looked down at his hands. "She took a really bad turn after the last bout of pneumonia."

"Did she still smoke?" Kate asked.

He nodded. "Afraid so. Bad habits sometimes never go away."

She took the envelope from him.

"Thank you. Was she comfortable when she died?" Kate wasn't sure why she asked, but it seemed like the right thing to do. Her mother had been difficult to her for so many years. Her being gone somewhat lifted a burden.

"We, uh, we found her in your sister's room," Doug said, avoiding her gaze. "She hadn't opened that room in years."

"She never went in there," Kate said. Ever since Susan had told her, Kate couldn't stop thinking about the fact that her mother died in her sister's room. It was spooky.

"Why did she pick that room, that night?"

"She felt better that day. She didn't want breakfast, but Susan was able to convince her to take a little soup for dinner. And then she asked for the key." Doug explained. "As you know, she wouldn't let anyone in there, not even Susan for cleaning. Your mom was afraid someone would mess up Lacie's stuff. So we were shocked when she asked. But she said Lacie was okay with her going in there now. She wanted her to." Doug continued slowly, his eyes still not meeting Kate's.

"She said that Lacie wanted her to open her room?" Kate asked, her heart in her throat. "Are you sure? Why would she say something like that?" Her hand was trembling. Alice walked in and Kate glanced at her.

"Musings from an older woman. Nothing to worry about." Doug cleared his throat and tried to lighten the mood. "It is wonderful to have people in the house again. You all did enjoy your time here," he said as he turned to the sink. "You will again."

"We did," Kate admitted.

"Susan's got all the groceries you asked for, and she'll take care of dinner. You must be tired from your ride up and being back here for the first time."

"Thank you," Kate replied, smiling. Alice watched them both, her eyes all-knowing.

* * *

Kate went back up to her room. After the car ride and the overwhelming coastal humidity, she needed a cool shower. She watched through the window as the others hung out by the pool and the tennis court in the background. Even though it had probably been years since it was used—Kate's mother wasn't a fan of tennis—the tennis court was in great shape. Maybe she could practice her serve with Charlie, she thought, smiling to herself. He was a much better tennis player than she was.

She turned on the cold water in the shower and let it get to the perfect temperature as she put her mother's letter away in the nightstand on her side of the bed. She wasn't ready to read it right away. The cool water was a shock to her body as she stepped into the shower, but it felt nice. It would be good, being here. They would relax, celebrate, and then Kate could focus on selling the house. There would be nothing more than that. Lacie was in the past and would stay there. Soon the house would be, too.

As Kate let the water flow over her, she heard a shuffling in her room.

"Charlie?" she called out. After several moments with no answer, Kate turned the water off. She grabbed the towel from the rack and wrapped it around her cold, wet body. "Charlie, is that you?"

But the room was empty. She walked to the window and saw them all still lounging by the pool. Even Alice was on one of the lounge chairs. Kate smiled. They were enjoying themselves; it was what she wanted.

Suddenly, Kate heard the noise behind her. She turned and gasped as she found herself face to face with a large man hovering over her, blue eyes wild and rimmed with red. Kate tried to scream, but he placed his hand firmly on her mouth.

"Shh," he whispered. "I'm not here to hurt you."

He loomed over her, his gray hair sticking out on all sides. He looked like he could have been someone's grandfather, but he had a dangerous presence to him. Who was he? Kate's eyes darted around the room, her mind racing. She whimpered, adrenaline making her heart race as he pressed his hand on her mouth, making it hard for her to breathe.

"Please, please don't scream, Katie. I'm not going to hurt you." Kate pushed against him and tried to scream, causing his grip to go even tighter.

"Please, I'm not going to hurt you. Now, I'm going to move my hand, and you won't scream, now will you, Katie?" Kate shook her head, and he slowly took his hand away.

Kate gasped, finally able to catch her breath.

"How... How do you know my name? Who are you? What do you want?" she blurted out, acutely aware that she was naked under the towel that was still wrapped around her.

"You can't stay here. It's not safe," he urged. "You have to leave. It's not safe here, in this house."

She wanted to run downstairs, but he was cornering her against the wall. "Charlie!" Kate called frantically.

The man grabbed her arm roughly, his eyes fiery. Kate tried to pull away but he was surprisingly strong for his age.

"Please, you have to listen to me. I know what happened to her... to Lacie... I have something of hers. I couldn't bring it here, but if you come with me, I'll show you."

"Show me what? Why do you have something of Lacie's? Who are you?" Kate stammered, her pulse racing.

"You don't remember?" He asked, leaning in.

"Let go of me!"

She tried to pull away, but his grip tightened. Without thinking, she kicked him in the shin as hard as she possibly could, causing him to double over in pain. *What did he know about Lacie?* Kate thought as she ran out of the room and down the steps. She was desperate to find out but her instincts had already overridden her curiosity. As she sprinted through the kitchen doorway, she ran into Doug.

"What's wrong?" he asked, his brow furrowed in concern.

Kate's hand trembled as she pointed towards the staircase.

"Upstairs, there's a man in my room! He attacked me!"

"A man?" Doug asked. "Who?"

Kate suddenly noticed that behind Doug, sitting at the kitchen island, was a police officer. He was slightly familiar, but Kate had no time to register who he was as he jumped up and raced out of the room.

Kate was shaking. She turned to Doug.

"I've never seen him before. He said he knew something about Lacie." They moved to the hall as they listened to the loud voices upstairs.

Doug still hadn't answered her as they watched the police officer walk the man down the flight of stairs. The man stared at her angrily. The officer gripped his arms firmly as he nudged him down.

"That's Darien," said Doug, nodding toward the officer. "You remember, my nephew."

"Darien?" Kate echoed, trying to search through her memories.

"Katie, I'm really sorry about this," Darien said, a flush coming over his attractive face. He was handsome, Kate noticed. Probably in his late thirties.

"I don't understand. Who is he?" Kate asked. "And why was he in my room?"

"Carl Warren. He took care of the gardening for your mother years ago. You don't remember him? He's harmless, but he is not well," Doug said quietly.

"Harmless? How the hell did he get in here?" Kate asked.

"The back door probably," Doug said, turning to Carl. "Carl, you know better than to pull something like this. This is not okay. You scared Katie."

Carl looked down at his shoes. Doug turned to Kate as Darien led the man outside.

"His brother takes care of him. Early-onset dementia. He hasn't wanted to put him in a home just yet. He wanders around a lot. Not the first time he ended up here. He thinks he's back at work twenty years ago. I wouldn't take anything he says seriously."

Darien came back in alone.

Doug continued, "Good thing Darien was here. He came by to say hello. Susan told him you were in town."

Darien gave her a chagrined smile. "Sorry about this, but it must have triggered something hearing that you were here. He does show up here sometimes. I put him in my car to calm down. I will make sure he gets home safely. No need to have his brother drive all the way out here."

"Well, I wish someone would have told me. He was in my room when I was in the shower, he started telling me I should leave and that it's not safe to be here," Kate said, her heartbeat slowly returning to normal. "Why would he say that?"

"He doesn't know what he's saying. Please don't be upset. I will have a talk with his brother and suggest he keep an extra close eye on him this week," Darien promised.

Now that her mind was no longer racing, Kate suddenly felt embarrassed she was standing there half-naked.

"Sorry I'm running around like this." She shrugged and fiddled with the top of the towel.

"Glad I was here to help. Looks like I'm always saving you, Katie," Darien said as he smiled. "I'll be back soon for a proper hello. I just came by to bring you some muffins from Harbor House Bakery. I remember how much you liked them."

"Thank you, I was hoping to pick some up this week," Kate said, surprised that he remembered. As she tried to pull memories of Darien, she turned to Doug and murmured. "Let's not tell the rest of the house about this. It's just…"

"Of course not. No need to upset anyone," Doug replied.

Kate nodded. She couldn't shake the thought that maybe Carl was telling the truth. What if he really did know something?

Molly walked in just as Doug was walking Darien to the front door. Her eyes followed him as he walked toward his car.

"Who was that?" Molly quipped.

"Oh, that's Doug and Susan's nephew. He just came by to, um… say hello," Kate said, trying to keep her voice level. Molly saw the muffins and took one.

"Just to say hello?" She smiled. "There's a story here, spill," Molly took a bite.

"Nothing to spill; we used to be friends a long time ago," Kate explained, finally remembering him and smiling to herself as she thought about the kiss between the two of them in the garden one summer.

"Well, he can come and say hello as often as he wants," Molly joked.

Kate grinned in spite of everything. She could always count on Molly to lighten the mood. She felt guilty not telling her the whole truth, but it had been a long day and Villa Magda was already beginning to creak under the weight of new arrivals.

* * *

Kate bent over and rested her hands on her knees as she tried to catch her breath. She regretted letting Molly talk her into an evening jog. It had sounded like a good idea after being in the car for six hours. Molly continued jogging for a few feet before she noticed that Kate was no longer beside her.

"Come on, Kate! We aren't going that fast!"

"I just need a minute," Kate gasped. They had only gone about two miles, and she was cursing herself for agreeing to go.

"We can switch to walking, as long as we keep up a good pace. I need to make sure to get all my steps in," Molly said, jogging in place. "Being on vacation is no excuse."

Kate playfully rolled her eyes as she caught her breath. "Thanks," she said dryly.

They walked alongside the empty road that stretched from the center of Aria and passed Villa Magda. Kate had suggested that they head away from town; she didn't want to risk running into someone who knew her while Molly was around.

"Are you sure you want to sell the house?" Molly asked as they walked. "This seems like an idyllic place to spend the summers. And it would be the perfect rental property. I bet Susan and Doug could manage the guests just fine."

Kate looked down at her feet, watching the gravel road pass as she tried to formulate a response. She knew Molly meant well, but she wasn't in the mood to explain her decision. Molly wouldn't truly understand unless she knew what had happened, and Kate wasn't ready to open that chapter.

"I think it's best if we sell it. Charlie and I haven't been back in so long, and with Andrew leaving soon, I don't want to take on such a big responsibility that would tie us down anywhere.

I'll have enough on my mind when Andrew's in college. I don't need to worry about a house three hundred miles away."

"You don't have to worry about Andrew. He's a good kid. I know he and Ben will be just fine off at school. But you–you will need something to keep busy. And it is really nice here."

Kate chuckled. "Maybe I'll take up gardening, or finally get my degree. I always wanted to go to college. Besides, you're the one that needs to keep busy. How are you and Sam doing, by the way?"

Molly's face scrunched up, and she took a few moments before responding. "Honestly, I don't know. He seems so distant. He spends all his time at work, and he's always on his phone. Every time I walk into the room he's talking to someone quietly on the phone."

"Do you think he's…"

"I don't know. An affair seems so cliché, but I don't know what else it would be."

"Maybe this weekend will help. It might be good to spend some time together."

"You're lucky you don't have to worry about this with Charlie," Molly said, walking ahead.

Kate followed. She knew Molly had a tough job and an even tougher relationship with Sam. But she also knew when to press Molly, and a conversation about Sam was not one of those times.

They walked in silence until they reached the sign announcing, "You are now leaving the town of Aria—come again soon!" Kate was gearing up to start running again when a truck sped past them, leaving them no room on the narrow road. The truck honked as it sped by, causing Molly and Kate to stumble back into the brush. Kate tried but couldn't catch the face of the driver.

"Well," Molly breathed, regaining her balance. "I guess not everyone is so friendly to out-of-towners, huh?"

"I guess not," Kate said, watching as the truck disappeared around a bend.

PRESENT DAY

POLICE FILE—ARIA, MAINE

CASE 1583

Q: *Do you know Chloe well?*

A: *No. She just showed up one day. She and Andrew were getting close.*

Q: *Did that bother you?*

A: *Maybe a little.*

8

TUESDAY

"'Be quiet, Gretel,' said Hansel, 'do not distress yourself,
I will soon find a way to help us.'"
—HANSEL AND GRETEL, GRIMM BROTHERS

The next morning came quickly. Charlie was still sleeping when Kate left to wander the grounds. Andrew and Ben were off playing tennis, and Sam and Molly had gone into town. After the flutter of activity the day before and the effort of keeping up her cheerful hostess façade, Kate was grateful to have a moment alone.

One of her favorite spots was the maze. It had been designed by a famous landscaper, based on labyrinths built during the Renaissance. The maze always helped her sort stuff out when she was a kid, and the incident with Carl had shaken her quite a bit. She wanted to believe Doug and Darien, that it was just the musings of a dementia-ridden old man, but when she looked into Carl's eyes, she had recognized something clear. Was he lucid? she wondered. Did he know about Lacie? Was he responsible somehow? She tried to call up memories of Carl from when she was a child, but nothing stood out. He'd been just another adult in the background that she hadn't really noticed.

The sun was already starting to grow hot as it beat down on the grounds, but it was cooler inside the maze. When they were kids, Susan told them that the maze was where the fairies hid. Kate smiled thinking about how excited Lacie would always get hearing these stories—she had wanted so badly for it to be real.

"I had a feeling you would be here," a deep voice said behind her. She turned and saw it was Darien, smiling as he caught up with her. Kate remembered that smile.

"You did, did you?" Kate smiled back.

"You used to be here a lot when we were kids," Darien said.

"I was. I loved getting lost in here sometimes. I don't think I appreciated how beautiful it was."

"It's pretty remarkable." Darien looked around the garden. Then he eyed her closely.

"You okay?"

"Yeah, it's just…well, you know."

"I do." He paused. "Do your friends know about what happened?"

"No, they don't," Kate admitted. She knew she would have to tell them sooner than later, but she just couldn't do it this morning. Not yet. As she spoke, a blue butterfly settled on top of a nearby hedge.

"I understand."

"Not many people would."

"You never came back to visit," he continued.

"I'm sorry. It was easier to move on, I guess, and forget this place."

"Easier to forget all of us," Darien said wryly.

"I could never completely forget the boy who saved my life," Kate said with a teasing smile, and for a moment their eyes locked.

Kate could feel the awkward, wet kiss on her lips as if it were happening to her right now. A younger Darien with floppy hair stood before her in this very garden late one summer, the year before Lacie disappeared. He had followed her; Kate knew he liked her. She noticed that he was always around, watching her. It made her feel wanted. So she let him kiss her. One innocent, simple kiss. She liked it when he kissed her. He touched her face gently, and she let his tongue find hers. Then she pulled away, afraid that someone might see them. She ran off and pretended it never happened. But by the following summer, Kate's heart belonged to Charlie, and she hadn't given Darien a second glance.

Kate looked at Darien now, his lips still the same, save for a few wrinkles in the corners of his mouth. She suddenly felt exposed, being in the garden alone with him again.

Darien's smile faded, his face somber. "I was just doing my job," he nodded. He had been the lifeguard at the town beach that summer. "Besides, I would have done anything to make sure you were okay." Breaking the palpable electricity between them, he said, "Listen, did you, uh, ever remember anything more from that time, other than what you said?" His voice suddenly had an edge to it. "About her?"

"No, I never really have. It's not something I try to remember, either."

Kate and Darien had been such good friends before that summer. She remembered he'd had great aspirations to leave Aria, but instead it seemed he had followed in his father's footsteps and become the chief of police. She wondered if he was happy.

"Do you mind if I join you on your walk?" he asked as they walked around the maze.

"No, please." They were quiet for a while before she finally asked, "How is your dad?"

"He passed away a year and a half ago. I moved back in with him for the last six months and have been there ever since. I sort of took over where he left off, I guess. Both the house and the job," Darien joked. "Never left town," he added, as if reading Kate's mind. An awkward silence hung between them—he the local, she the summer girl turned stranger, now indistinguishable from any other tourist.

"I'm sorry. I remember you talking about how excited you were to leave."

"It's okay. Not everyone is lucky enough to escape Aria," he said, and Kate thought she could detect a hint of bitterness in his tone.

"So, how's Charlie been?" Darien changed the subject.

"I'm so sorry to hear about your dad. And he's good. He's, you know, Charlie."

"He certainly got lucky with you, Katie."

Kate blushed. "Oh, I don't know about that." Kate paused, the silence resurfacing between them.

"Why don't you come to my birthday dinner, later this week... bring your, uh, wife?"

"Thanks, I will. I'm not married though, well, not anymore. Got divorced a few years ago."

"Sorry to hear that."

"Was for the best." He smiled. "So your birthday, huh?"

"I've avoided celebrating it since that summer, but this year I've decided to reclaim it," Kate said.

"I'd be happy to celebrate with you, Katie," Darien said. His teeth looked so white against his amber skin. She felt guilty being here alone with him.

Darien dropped his gaze and rubbed the back of his neck. Changing the subject, he said, "You have a son. My aunt tells me he's a really nice young man."

Kate beamed. "We had him the spring after Lacie…"

"Yeah, sort of surprised me when I heard. Thought the two of you had maybe broken up after, you know… I didn't know about…"

"It changed everything," she whispered. And then quickly she added, "Charlie is a good man and father." She wasn't sure why she had said that or felt she needed to.

"I'm sure he is." Darien softened.

She wanted to ask Darien more questions. Had he taken over Lacie's case? Were they still looking for her sister after all these years? Did it ever cross his mind?

"I'm sorry we never did find her. My father tried all he could," he said, again intuiting what she was thinking. "He was obsessed, you know, as if she were his own daughter. I don't think he slept many nights after that summer. As the police chief, he felt responsible for Lacie, and he couldn't believe this had happened in his town. He tried every angle. Took a search team to neighboring towns and counties. He practically turned this place upside down looking for her. But she just disappeared into thin air. Not a trace. Except for you, no one else even saw her that day…" He stopped.

She took a deep breath. "I know. We never blamed your father. My mother was so grateful. And so am I." Kate smiled and then looked at him, not sure she should continue, but she asked anyway. "Have you ever considered reopening it?"

"The case?" Darien asked, his brow furrowed.

She wasn't sure why she said it. She had promised Charlie she wouldn't try this, and yet here she was, asking questions. She knew she was going down a dangerous path, but she couldn't help herself. Not after what happened earlier with Carl.

"I'm sorry, but my father and his guys really did everything they could. There was just nothing. It was almost as if she never existed." He shifted his weight back and forth as his tone suddenly changed. "But, I promise if anything should ever change, or there is anything that makes it seem like the case should be reopened, I'll let you know."

Kate nodded, realizing they had walked deep into the maze.

"What about Carl? Was he ever a suspect?" Kate asked, unable to keep her suspicions to herself.

"So many people were suspects, but if there's no actual evidence—well, it just doesn't hold up. Even you…" He stopped himself.

Kate sighed. She knew she had been a suspect—they all had—but was it more than that? The incident with Carl was making her think that maybe she needed to dig a bit deeper.

"You know some believe that the labyrinth symbolizes the relentless pilgrimage toward salvation or enlightenment, that involves a long, difficult, and usually solitary journey," Darien said, breaking the silence. Kate looked at him.

"And who told you that?"

"I think I read it in a book once," he admitted, smiling. Kate could not help but smile. She felt lighter all of a sudden.

"I'm glad I'm back, Darien," Kate said and meant it. "I'm surprised how much I missed it. I've been avoiding coming back for so long, but it feels good to get this stuff out in the open. I wish I had done it sooner."

"I am too." Together they found their way back toward the exit. As Kate exited the garden, she saw Andrew in the distance by the pool, with Ben. They were talking to someone, a girl with long tan legs and flowing blonde hair. Kate blinked. Her mind was playing tricks on her again.

"Who is that?" She asked.

Darien stopped short and a look flashed across his face.

"That's my cousin," Darien said, but his voice sounded strained.

Kate's head whipped toward him. "Since when?"

Darien scratched the scruff on his neck. "They adopted her not long after you and your dad left. It took them a while to find her, but when they did, they just knew that she was their daughter."

How had Gail never mentioned that Susan and Doug had a daughter? She racked her brain, searching for anything that would help her remember, but she came up short.

"I'm sorry she's here. I told her not to bother you."

"Nonsense," Kate said quickly. "Aren't you going to introduce me?"

Darien smiled and nodded. He put his hand on the small of her back and led her toward the group, where Andrew was talking animatedly with the girl. Kate approached them and put her hand out.

"Hi, I'm Kate," she said.

The girl looked at her with large blue eyes.

"I'm Chloe. Nice to meet you. My cousins have told me so much about you," she replied and quickly turned back to Andrew and Ben with a smile. "Hey, how would you guys like to come to a bonfire on the beach tonight?" she asked.

"Mom... is that okay with you?" Andrew asked carefully, but Kate could tell he was delighted.

Kate didn't want them going, but she could practically hear Charlie's voice, saying *Don't be so paranoid, Kate*. She wanted to prove she was the cool mom, who trusted her kid to take care of himself, not the neurotic mom still damaged by her own childhood fears.

"Uh...sure, why wouldn't it be?" she said breezily. "Go ahead."

"I just know how you feel about the water," Andrew said quietly. Chloe cocked her head.

"Yeah, didn't Darien save you one year? He tells the story a lot. Sort of a cautionary tale—you know, stay out of the water when the waves are too big." There was a sudden, strained silence.

"It was a long time ago," Darien muttered, looking at the ground.

"Yes, it certainly seems like forever." Kate forced a laugh.

"Well, I should get going," Darien said, turning back toward the road. "And Chloe, you need to get back to the house, I am sure these folks have plans for the day." A silent hum of tension still hung in the air as Darien walked toward his car, and Kate felt uneasy.

"Okay, nice to meet you, Mrs. Williams," Chloe offered.

"Kate. Call me Kate." She watched as Darien walked Chloe back to the cottage. She knew it was ridiculous, but she couldn't help but be bothered by Chloe's comment. Why had she brought up the day at the beach? Was she trying to unnerve her? And why was this the first she had heard of Chloe?

"I like this place, Mom," Andrew said, grinning.

"Yeah you do, because of the hot girl," Ben muttered, and Andrew smacked him.

In the distance, Darien and Chloe looked to be in deep conversation. Kate wasn't sure, but she thought Darien seemed tense as he talked to her. She had an odd feeling all of a sudden, but it was a feeling she couldn't place.

* * *

Kate entered the bedroom where Charlie was relaxing in bed, checking his email. She sat down on the bed and massaged her neck, trying to work out the kinks. She had forgotten how uncomfortable an unfamiliar bed could be.

"What have you been up to?" Charlie asked as he rolled over and tenderly kissed her shoulder.

"Oh, I just went for a walk in the garden." She didn't want to mention Darien. She felt bad for not telling him, but she didn't want to have to explain. He and Darien hadn't gotten along as teenagers. They were so different. Darien was the quiet kid from town, and Charlie was the rich city kid. But Kate knew it was more than that; she had been close to Darien and then she met Charlie and all that changed. She could not help but wonder if that was why Darien disliked Charlie so much.

"Come here." He motioned for her to get in bed with him. His gaze was sleepy. She let herself be seduced by her husband, sinking into the bed and letting him kiss her while he touched her hot skin.

"Something about being here reminds me of when we were kids," he said, his breath hot against her neck. "Remember how forbidden it felt just to kiss each other in this house."

"Mm-hmm," Kate murmured, shivering as he slipped her underwear down. His touch still made her feel like she was seventeen. Everything was so simple then. She closed her eyes, wanting to savor the moment, but she couldn't stop her mind from wandering. She kept thinking back to the maze and her conversation with Darien. As they spoke, she had realized how desperately she wanted him to reopen the case, to finally learn what happened to her sister. She knew there was no going back if they pursued it. Charlie would not be happy about it, that much she knew, but she also knew that she could not let the mystery surrounding Lacie lie dormant any longer.

"You're right," she replied. "It does feel like no time has passed at all."

9

"The witch's eyes were red, and she could not see very far,
but she had a keen scent, like the beasts.
'I have them and they shall not escape me!'
The witch gave a spiteful laugh."
—HANSEL AND GRETEL, GRIMM BROTHERS

Charlie stepped out of the shower and threw on a pair of shorts and a t-shirt. He looked so boyish, Kate thought, already with some color in his face that accentuated his blue eyes.

"Do you want to play some tennis this afternoon?" he asked.

Kate hummed, stretching out on the bed. "Maybe tomorrow?"

"Being on vacation suits us, even if it is here," Charlie said, as he leaned down to kiss her cheek. "See you downstairs."

Kate smiled as she watched him close the door. Her eyes drifted over to the nightstand. She took a deep breath and then took her mother's letter out from where she had stored it in the nightstand drawer. It felt heavy in her hands. Kate wasn't really sure she wanted to read it, but she couldn't stop herself from wondering if it held some clue as to why Gail had gone into Lacie's room the night she died. Images flashed in her mind of the garden filled with hundreds of volunteers, all feverishly searching for Lacie. On the tenth day, the police chief had returned to Villa Magda, his face solemn but hopeful. Kate remembered how her mother's tired face had been transformed that day, when she thought there might be hope.

"We think we may have found strands of Lacie's hair in the woods," Kate remembered he had said quietly, handing her mother a plastic bag to look at. She had taken the bag and studied it closely. The once silky, yellow strands now mangled and dirty from being on the wet ground.

"This isn't Lacie's. It doesn't prove anything at all. I mean this could be anyone's hair, right?" Kate's mother had insisted. "She never goes into the woods; it is a rule. My girls never break the rules."

"Gail, we'll certainly get DNA samples to be sure and send them off to the state crime lab. And yes, you're right, it doesn't prove anything more than that she may have been in the woods at some time. We will continue our search in any case," he had said gently. "See, if we find anything…if we find her." He had taken the bag with the hair from her in silence.

Her mother had retreated upstairs quietly, while the police chief remained, the strands of hair held tightly in his hands as the rest of the house remained still, frozen.

A few weeks later, the DNA test came back with almost ninety percent certainty that it was indeed Lacie's hair. They surmised that she had been in the woods that week. But why?

Why would she go there alone? It made little sense to anyone what a sixteen-year-old girl would be doing by herself deep in the woods. The police searched the area for any drifters that may have been there during that time. They questioned the kids in town and their parents, but nothing ever panned out. There was never enough information for them to decipher anything more than that she had been in the woods at some point. And they couldn't find a single trace of anyone else.

The heat had been unbearable and stifling the days before, and the rain that day had provided some relief. They had all been inside—Lacie in her room, Kate waiting for Charlie to pick her up. Gail was in a foul mood after having to cancel Kate's birthday lunch due to the rain. Instead, Charlie was going to take her to see some new blockbuster. Gail asked Kate to take Lacie with her, but she didn't want to take her sister with her on a date. She and Charlie had only been dating a few weeks. But Lacie was upset. Even all those years ago, Kate wasn't sure if it had been her fault.

In Kate's hazy memory, Lacie had stepped into the backyard and turned to look at Kate. She said nothing, just shut the door behind her, and that was the last time anyone ever saw her. It wasn't until late that evening that anyone even realized she was missing. As planned, Kate had gone to the movies with Charlie, and when she came home, her parents asked her if she had seen Lacie because she wasn't in her room. Kate had shrugged it off. She never told them about the look Lacie gave her as she left. What secrets was Lacie hiding from them? What had been so terrible for her to leave the house in the middle of that stormy day? And more importantly: why the hell had Kate not stopped her?

As the days dragged on, Villa Magda had become quieter

and quieter until finally only the three of them remained. Kate's parents hardly spoke to her during that time, and they certainly didn't speak to each other. Kate's father tried to help her mother cope, but his frustration got the best of him and he demanded they return home to Connecticut. But Kate's mother wanted to stay; she wanted to wait for Lacie to return. So Kate went back with her father, only seeing her mother on holidays and some weekends.

A few months after Kate and her father returned home, Kate had received a horrifying call. Her father had been found dead in his office. The official cause of death was a massive heart attack, but Kate thought it was from a broken heart. His funeral was one of the last times she and her mother had seen each other.

Kate took a deep breath and looked at the envelope. She opened it carefully. There was a letter and, as she suspected, a key. It felt cold and harsh against her warm skin. Kate unfolded the letter. Her mother's delicate but shaky handwriting was familiar and immediately jolted her back to being a small child, watching her mother transcribe a recipe out of a magazine onto an index card. As she played with the key in her hand, she read:

April 20

My Dearest Katie,

I do hope you and Andrew are well. From what you tell me, he seems to have become such a fine young man. Please tell him that for me. I am not one to write emails, as you may have gathered over the years, and we never did like phoning each other. Too many long, awkward silences. I wanted to write this to you from my heart. I am so very sorry that I could not be the proper mother you needed and wanted all of these years. A mother should never have to lose a child, and losing Lacie and then your father was more than I could bear. Grief is like a wild storm on the ocean, and at times the waves were drowning me. When you told me about Andrew, I was scared. You were so young, and I wasn't ready to be happy. I reacted with anger when I should have reacted with love. I hope you find it in your heart to forgive me for not being able to move on and give you and your family all the attention and love you deserved. I have missed you. I realize now that the day we lost Lacie, I lost two daughters. And you lost your mother. I am so sorry. She was always a special girl, with so much imagination. Those weeks before she disappeared, I knew she had a new friend or someone she had been talking to. I tried so hard over the years to figure out who she might have left with or gone to see. I am sorry I was so relentless at times. I regret that it has consumed me and ruined our relationship in the process.

I can feel that my time is running out. My flame is very low, and I can see the other side at times. Oh, how I wish I had done things differently, but I am leaving you with the key to Lacie's room. She is calling out to me. I know this will sound crazy to you, but I feel her sometimes and I know that she is still here. Some things are too painful to discuss or admit and I wish I had the courage to do so. All I can say is listen and keep your eyes open, you will discover what you need to. She is still here, listen. Keep her memory and know that I love you.

Love always,

Mother

Kate walked slowly out of the room, almost in a trance. She held firmly onto the cold brass key. It felt foreign to her. *Listen and keep your eyes open.* What was she talking about? Listen to whom? Ghosts? Kate didn't believe in any of that anymore. At least she didn't think she did.

Her great-grandfather Max had died in this house with a broken heart, and so did her mother. Neither of them ever did get closure. Kate felt so much sadness for the two of them. Tears welled up in her eyes. All these years, she thought her mother had despised her, blaming her for her sister's vanishing. Now that she was a mother, too, she could see why she had retreated into her own world, shutting everyone, including Kate, out. She could see that it was just the relentless grief that had pulled her mother away from her, not malice or anger. But Kate couldn't blame her mother for being consumed by the loss of her youngest child—if it were Andrew, Kate knew, she would probably do the same.

Kate now found herself at Lacie's locked door. The room on the other side—was it still the pink room of Lacie's dreams? She remembered it filled with books, with Lacie's favorite, *Hansel and Gretel*, always sitting on her nightstand. Lacie had read the fairytale over and over. Each time, Lacie would hope for a completely different ending. She would hope that the witch had a change of heart. She would say the witch was lonely and mis-understood. A happy ending would have been that they forgave the witch and helped her. Kate realized that's how she felt, too: hoping for a different ending in which Lacie would still be here.

"She is still here, listen." The words of a desperate parent, Kate thought to herself. Still here. Here where? She shivered at the thought of her sister hidden in the walls. Kate gently

placed the key in the door and hesitated. She had turned the knob hundreds of times and found her sister on the other side. What would she find now? The rules had clearly stated: *Keep the door closed,* yet her mother had wanted her to have the key. Why? Kate took a deep breath and pulled the key out of the lock as if it were burning her flesh. She would keep it closed—at least for now.

A scream pierced the air, disrupting the moment and her thoughts. It was Andrew. He was calling for her. She quickly put the key back into the envelope and shoved it into her pocket as she rushed toward the yelling, her heart pounding as she ran down the stairs and then toward the kitchen.

Molly rushed into the house and entered the kitchen from the backyard, dripping wet from the pool, just as Kate came into the kitchen.

"What's going on?" Kate shouted as Andrew, Ben, and Chloe frantically swatted at a flying creature.

"Oh my God! What the hell is that?" Molly cried out.

Around the room a creature about the size of a small squirrel flew, thrashing its wings desperately as it squeaked, sounding like a wounded child. The kids ducked and screamed as it flew feverishly around them.

"Get it out of here!" Molly covered her face as it thrashed around her head.

Chloe dropped down as the animal flapped its wings violently. Kate looked at the flying creature closely.

"It's just a bat," Kate said. She couldn't show her fear, not in front of Andrew. "It's way more scared of you than you are of it." She opened both windows, hoping it would fly out on its own. "There are so many caverns along the cliffside. It probably wandered in and is lost." Kate watched it flail its wings in a desperate attempt to flee.

The bat screeched as Chloe swung her arms around, trying to protect her face.

"Do something!" Chloe called out frantically.

Do something, she thought. That was what she was always called upon to do: something. Kate was prepared for a lot of things, but catching flying bats hadn't been high on her list of motherly duties. Kate grabbed hold of a broom from the corner and swatted at the bat. It shrieked and dove toward the kids, who cowered in unison. Molly shooed them aside as Kate took aim once again. Suddenly, she heard Alice's cool voice behind her.

"Don't be so weak, Kate."

Kate then swatted at the bat with all her might, like a protective lioness, killing it. They heard a small thud as the bat fell to the ground. Kate continued to swat again and again at the lifeless body on the floor.

"There, it's dead," Alice announced. Chloe looked at Kate in horror.

"Can we just go outside, Andrew?" Her voice was small. Andrew looked at his mom as if somehow the bat were her fault.

"Bats, Mom? Really? I hope there aren't any more of them around here," he said as he and Chloe walked outside. Kate tried to think back. Had there ever been bats in the house when she was a kid?

"There are probably more." Ben's voice came from behind her, making Kate jump.

"Oh, you startled me, Ben. I didn't realize you were still standing there," Kate said, as she tried to figure out what to do with the bat's body.

"Listen to what I found online about bats: *Bats are commonly said to indicate that the house they frequent is haunted, and an old German myth relates that if a bat flies into your house, the devil is after you,*" said Ben.

The thought chilled Kate to the core. She made a mental note to have Doug call an exterminator.

* * *

Kate watched Charlie as he stepped up to the window of Miss Mable's Ice Cream Hut and ordered. The hut had been a town staple for decades, best known for its rich sundaes and views of the lobster boats in the harbor down the hill.

Kate was grateful to get some alone time with Charlie. Throughout the years, they had tried to make an effort to have date night once a month, but that had been hard when Andrew was so young. During Andrew's infant and toddler years, they had struggled at being young parents. Once Andrew had gotten older, their evenings were full of homework, lacrosse, and swim practice. It had taken a few years for Charlie's venture capital firm to stabilize; when he and Sam had first started the firm, his nights and weekends had been dedicated to work. He said it was something that gave him a sense of purpose. He liked helping others with their dreams. Kate was incredibly proud of him.

"Can you believe we're going to be empty nesters soon?" teased Charlie as handed her a double chocolate cone and sat down across from her, the weathered picnic table bench squeaking under his weight.

"Oh don't say that! Andrew will come home for holidays and the summers."

"He will if he wants to avoid getting an earful from you,"

Charlie murmured, a glint in his eye.

Kate shot him a look, but she couldn't keep the grin off her face.

"He's still going to need us for a few more years."

"Maybe." Charlie shrugged. "We didn't need our parents at that age."

"We didn't have much of a choice." Kate's voice grew soft.

"But we made it through just fine. And now we can enjoy all that hard work."

Kate nodded, not wanting to admit that she was a little nervous about the future. The last eighteen years had been dedicated to their son. For years, she had been consumed by play dates and science projects, and then sports matches and driving lessons. She wondered what their home would be like without him. She would miss the early morning conversations she had with him over breakfast while listening to the news.

They sat in comfortable silence as they enjoyed their ice cream, watching the gulls circling above the water.

"Charlie Williams? Is that you?"

They both turned to find a woman approaching their table. She was about Kate's age, with a bright smile and a natural tan that looked like it came from hours spent out on riding trails.

Charlie stood and smiled, giving her a warm hug.

"Elaine Sullivan. So good to see you."

"It's Brown now," she jokingly wiggled her ring finger at him. "I would recognize you from anywhere." Kate waited for Charlie to introduce her, but he kept his focus on Elaine.

"Hopefully I look a little older from the last time you saw me."

"Of course, and somehow you got more handsome."

A lanky teenager behind the counter hit the sharp bell and called out, "Elaine!"

"I have to get this ice cream home before it melts. Great seeing you!" She shot them one last smile before taking her bags from the cashier. Charlie sat back down, and Kate watched the woman walk away.

"I don't think she looked at me once during that entire conversation."

"She was probably just in a rush."

"Well, you could have introduced me."

Charlie's eyes snapped up to Kate's.

"Do you really want everyone in town to know you're here? If I remember correctly, Elaine was one of the biggest gossips in town. Why drag us into the spotlight?"

At the mention of the town, Kate's eyes darted around the shop. No one seemed to be paying them attention, but Charlie was right; better to keep a low profile.

* * *

After everyone settled in for the night, Kate watched Charlie sleep soundly. It had been a long two days already, and Kate could hardly imagine what the next day at Villa Magda would bring. She hoped she could get started on packing up the house.

Her mind raced as she stared at the ceiling. What had her mother meant by *"She is still here. Listen."* Still where? And listen to what? The words of a grieving mother who had been drinking too much, Kate imagined.

Yes, Kate thought she had sensed something—maybe a presence—within the house when she had first entered, but Lacie? She was beginning to sound crazy even to herself. It was awful that families of missing people wanted a body to prove that the person was real and had existed, but maybe that was what her mother had meant. Did she want Kate to find Lacie's body? It was too morbid to consider and certainly not something Kate wanted to worry about, not this week. But she found herself thinking about Lacie every waking moment.

She remembered that the house had a way of distorting everyone who entered. Kate could already feel a slight change in her. It exposed people's urges and desires, just like it had with Magda. Instead of keeping her there, it pushed her out. Magda had escaped, Kate thought. Kate wondered if that was what had happened to Lacie. Was she just another casualty of the Villa? Kate felt the restlessness, and they had only been there two days.

PRESENT DAY

POLICE FILE—ARIA, MAINE.

CASE 1583

Q: *Who knew about Lacie?*

A: *I'm really not sure. I think only Kate and Charlie. Well, and the caretakers knew, of course.*

Q: *What did you think about Lacie when you found out?*

A: *It was strange if you ask me, her not telling us and having us come here. Really morbid. It makes you wonder what other secrets Kate is keeping from us.*

10

WEDNESDAY

"Nibble, nibble, gnaw,
Who is nibbling at my little house?"
—*HANSEL AND GRETEL*, GRIMM BROTHERS

The next morning, the house was bright as sunlight seeped in. Kate was up early and looked out the bedroom window toward the ocean. The sun was already warm and the morning fog had cleared, leaving not a cloud on the horizon. *A new day*, she thought, smiling, hopeful. It would be a good day. Kate went down to the kitchen and started the coffee, the aroma calming her and making her feel more at home and comforted. She arranged the remaining blueberry muffins on a platter and took out a pan to fry up some bacon. Alice entered the kitchen. Her hair was pulled back, showing the sharpness of her cheekbones.

"Good morning," she said, chipper. "Did you sleep well?"

"Great," Kate lied. "You?"

"I did. Like a baby. That bed is surprisingly comfy. So, what do we have planned for the day?" She was grinning, looking fresh and ready for anything.

"Well, I thought we could just relax today. I was going to do some packing up here."

"Hmm. Sounds all so civilized."

"Sorry, I know I'm boring this week," Kate said.

"It's just been weird, especially since your friends don't know that she existed. Molly is bound to find out. It's just a matter of time, you know."

"Not if you keep silent," Kate snapped. She pinched the bridge of her nose and sighed. "Please, Alice." She whispered. "I just don't want to stir anything up right now. I need time."

"Eighteen years is quite a bit of time, don't you think?"

"Why do you care so much about what I say or when I say it?"

"Because you're not being truthful. Her disappearance haunts you and you know it," Alice said stubbornly.

They sat in silence as the bacon sizzled on the pan. Kate pulled plates out of the cupboard and shut the door with a thud, using a little more force than necessary. Alice cleared her throat. "Did you see Andrew's new friend?"

"You mean Chloe? She's Darien's cousin, or maybe niece. I am a little confused about her," Kate said.

"Doesn't she look…" Alice stopped as Charlie walked in.

"Good morning." He poured a cup of coffee and sipped. "I thought I would take the kids out on the boat later to go fishing. It looks like a beautiful day," he said, looking out over the ocean.

"That sounds like fun. With Doug?" Kate asked, grateful he'd come in when he had.

"Probably. We'll see. Not sure he likes me much." Charlie joked. "But fishing may help us bond."

"Of course he likes you," Kate said, though she didn't sound convincing, even to herself. "He's just not a warm and fuzzy type." Charlie watched Kate. He could always sense when she was upset.

"Are you really doing okay, being here?" Kate nodded and kissed him on the forehead. Charlie raised an eyebrow. "Honestly." Kate insisted. "Dr. Morris is just a phone call away if I need her." Charlie nodded and let it go. "By the way, I spoke to a broker from town before we left home. She mentioned that she may want to come have a look at the house." She went on as she sipped her hot coffee. "She said we don't have to disclose anything about Lacie, since there wasn't a death in the house—well, my mother, but that was natural, and we don't have to say much. It's a relief. I was worried at first, but she'll market it to outsiders, none of the locals. Families looking for a nice summer home."

Charlie started to respond but was interrupted by his phone ringing. "Sorry, it's work," he said absentmindedly. "Hello?" His voice faded as he stepped outside.

Alice waited until the back door was closed before leaning in. "They wouldn't touch this place if they knew all the details," Alice said.

"What's that supposed to mean?" Kate asked, her voice betraying her discomfort.

"Sorry, but you know as well as I do that it's true." Alice shrugged. "You may eventually be able to forget what happened, but then all of the ghost stories, and legends that surround this house? Your sister became everyone's cautionary bedtime story.

Parents used it as a deterrent. There was even a nursery rhyme about her and the woods. I can remember it now:

Into the woods she went to play
Dressed in white that summer's day
But little Lacie said farewell
For off the cliff she fell, fell, fell

Wasn't that the first verse?" Alice's words fell off as Molly walked in.

Kate jumped but was grateful again for the interruption. The last time she had heard that awful rhyme was when a group of teens had snuck onto the property after dark, taunting each other on a dare, just a few weeks after the disappearance. Doug had found them around a bonfire in the woods as they chanted the vile verse. Kate could hear it in the wind. She remembered that she had cried herself to sleep that night—and many nights afterward. She couldn't believe how cruel they had been. They were drinking and laughing at her family's expense, her sister's expense. Kate had hated all of them and wanted them dead. The thought still unnerved her all these years later.

"That smells delicious," Molly exclaimed as she grabbed the last cup of coffee and a piece of bacon. Kate noticed the half-finished bottle of vodka that was still on the counter; she hadn't realized how much they drank last night. Kate knew that vodka was Molly's drink of choice, but she couldn't remember if she had seen Molly drink the night before or not.

"I was up looking at the rooms," Molly continued. "Your great-grandfather sure did put a lot of thought into the details of this house. Extraordinary, really. I mean, some of the stone had to have come from Europe and most of it isn't even made anymore. True craftsmanship. You can tell he hand-chiseled details onto every staircase."

"He wanted to make sure Magda fell in love with the house. He built it to win her heart." Kate explained.

"Ah! So that is who Magda is. I found some etchings of her name throughout the house. Nice touch. He was quite the romantic," Molly said.

Kate nodded. "That he was."

"I found another name etched in as well… another woman's name. A mistress perhaps?" Molly joked, wiggling her eyebrows.

"What name?" Kate asked.

"Lucie, I think, or something like that."

"Where?" Kate's mouth went dry, but she kept her eyes glued to the bacon in the frying pan, trying not to let her thoughts show on her face. Thankfully, Molly didn't seem to notice.

"On the staircase leading to the basement. I was being nosy, and I popped down there for a quick look."

Kate didn't respond. *Who would have etched Lacie's name in the house?*

"Anyway, the good news is I think the house has held its value all these years," Molly chimed. "It has really good bones, plus it is much closer to the water than modern zoning will allow—it's a shame you're going to sell."

"It's what I want," Kate said firmly. Molly would never be able to see the darkness that Kate did when she looked at the structure. To Molly, it was just another house.

"Well, then you may get away with doing some minimal work to get the property value higher, maybe update some of the bathrooms, kitchen, new floors, that kind of thing," Molly rambled enthusiastically. "Oh, and an inspection would be smart, make sure there aren't any carbon monoxide leaks or other issues with the house before putting it on the market."

"Yes, of course, good point," Kate said, forcing a smile.

Lacie was everywhere she turned. A blotch of paint or new furniture could never erase her essence. But there was no need to tell Molly any of this just yet. Or ever, Kate thought wishfully.

* * *

As soon as everyone had finished breakfast and left the kitchen, Kate quietly snuck down to the basement to find the name on the staircase. She stepped off the stairs and crouched down. She traced the letters with her finger. *Lacie.*

Kate jumped when a gust of wind blew the door shut behind her. She took several deep breaths to slow her heart rate down. She turned away from the stairs, her eyes adjusting to the dimness of the basement, boxes stacked in every corner.

The lights abruptly flickered, and Kate found herself in darkness. She spun around, grabbing the railing in the pitch black and called out, "Hello? Is anyone there?" But there was no answer. She carefully took one step at a time in the dark and found her way up to the entrance. She tried the light switch on the wall but nothing. She opened the door and saw Doug down the hall. "Doug?" she called out to him. "Do you know what is going on? The lights shut off in the basement."

Doug appeared in the doorway and started walking down the steps, leaving the door open to let the light in. "What happened?" Kate asked.

He chuckled as he grabbed a flashlight from one of the dimly lit shelves. "Oh, this house has a mind of its own. It turns off the lights when it wants to."

"I got scared, it was so dark down here."

Doug fiddled with several switches on the electric panel.

"This should do it."

Kate sighed with relief as the lights flickered back on.

"I'm surprised you were down here. You and Lacie used to be so scared of the basement."

"I figured it was time to face my fears," Kate joked.

Doug smiled and held out his hand, motioning for her to head up the stairs.

"I was a bit shocked when Susan told me you wanted to come back here," Doug admitted as followed her up. "We thought we would never see you again."

"It felt like something I had to do." Doug nodded and firmly shut the basement door behind him.

"I understand that. There is something about this house. It is hard to break away." Kate glanced over at him.

"I'm sorry it took me so long to come home. After Lacie, it was just too painful. And Mom, well you of all people know how difficult she is…was. I thought it was best for both of us to take some time apart. Before I realized it, so much time had passed, and it was just easier to keep the distance up."

"You know Susan and I would have welcomed you back anytime. You were like daughters to us," Doug said quietly.

Kate watched him as he fiddled with the flashlight, his eyes looking everywhere but her face. She had never realized that he and Susan may have been affected by her estrangement from her mother.

"I'm so grateful for that. It wasn't until I saw how Charlie took care of Andrew that I realized how much you were a father to us during all those summers. It was hard not having Dad around much."

"He was dedicated to his job. We all understood that he wanted to make sure his girls had a great life. And your mother had high expectations for him. He was here when he could be."

"You mean she put pressure on him. Being here for one or two long weekends a month wasn't enough. He worked hard all year. We just wanted him to take some time to spend with us." Kate replied in a small voice. "You were there for us, making sure we stayed safe and had fun. As much as I hate that I can't remember that last summer very well, I am thankful that my memory loss didn't take all my childhood memories."

"Oh, Katie." Doug looked up and sighed as he pulled her toward him and engulfed her in a fatherly hug. "It feels strange to have you here without Lacie, but it's so nice to have you back."

Kate sighed shakily as she pulled away, trying to blink away the tears that were gathering in her eyes. "Well, I should go get ready for the day. Thanks again for your help with the lights." Doug smiled and patted her on the back.

Kate couldn't stop thinking about Lacie as she went up to her room. She knew she should have been getting ready for the boat trip, but she couldn't help herself—she took out her phone and did something she had never had the courage to do: She typed in Lacie's name and "Aria." She quickly scrolled through the search results, past dozens of theories of why Lacie left and where she had gone:

Lacie haunts the woods behind Villa Magda.

Lacie is desperate to get back to the main house because she was killed there.

Lacie waits for anyone to come in and take her home.

Lacie and her jealous sister.
Lacie is seen just outside Aria in the woods wandering... still looking for help.

All the theories, all those voices swirling around Kate. Help—had Lacie needed help? Kate couldn't bear the thought of it. She threw her phone on the bed, sat down, and closed her eyes. And then she felt the hairs stand up on the nape of her neck. She opened her eyes slowly, and there she was, standing there in the middle of the room, smiling—Lacie. She hadn't aged a day. A shadow? A ghost? Regardless, her bright eyes were sparkling, her smile inviting.

Kate blinked, her pulse quickening. She couldn't be seeing her sister standing there. It wasn't real. This was just a memory re-emerging, a glitch in her hippocampus. Her therapist had told her that was where episodic memories are stored and could resurface at any time. This had to be what was happening.

"Lacie?" Kate called out to her, hardly able to say her name louder than a whisper, knowing she wasn't there. She shook as she said her name again, this time a bit louder.

"Lacie?" It couldn't be.

Her grief had brought back all these feelings, and they were manifesting in visions of her sister, forever trapped in the body of a sixteen-year-old. Kate closed her eyes tightly again.

"Go away, Lacie. Please just go away," she whispered, trembling, wishing her away with all of her will. She slowly opened her eyes and saw she was still there, her smile fading. The smell of Lacie's coconut shampoo overtook the room. Kate felt fear like she never had before. Her body froze into place. Her mind tried to make sense out of what she was seeing. She looked desperately at her sister. Lacie's skin was translucent, her lips blue as if she just stepped out of a freezer. Something, water maybe, dripped from her clothes. Kate wanted to hug her, envelop her in her arms and never let go. Kate stood and moved closer, only a few feet away from her.

"Lacie?" Kate asked again, her voice breaking.

But Lacie just stood there, putting her small finger to her lips as if to silence Kate. She then opened her mouth to say something, but no words came out.

"What are you trying to tell me?" Kate said louder this time, her voice desperate. "Please!"

Lacie turned to leave and Kate rushed after her. She reached the door and looked out, but Lacie wasn't there; instead, she nearly bumped into Charlie as he entered the room.

"Who are you talking to?" Charlie asked, eyes searching the empty room. Kate stood frozen in place, her heart hammering.

"Charlie, she was here," she whispered, as her whole body shook uncontrollably.

"Who was here?" Charlie said, peering into the bathroom. "No one is here."

"She was right there," Kate stammered, frantically pointing to the middle of the room, her eyes darting back and forth. "It was Lacie. I saw her." Charlie's eyes were wide.

"Kate, what are you saying? You know that's impossible."

"I know it sounds crazy, but I swear, it was her. I mean, I was awake, and I wasn't hallucinating or anything. I saw a girl here," Kate couldn't help it; she started to cry. She realized he would never believe her.

"It was her. You don't believe me, do you?"

"Kate..."

"No, why would you? It sounds crazy even to me."

Charlie wrapped his hands around her shoulders, edging her toward the bed.

"Kate, look. You're exhausted. Your mother's death, the house—it's just your mind playing awful tricks on you."

"Charlie, I know it was her."

"Do you realize how insane that sounds?" Charlie asked, his voice growing more irritated. "You see your dead sister... like a ghost?"

Kate looked at him, her eyes widening with fury.

"Why would you say something like that? We don't know that she's dead for sure!" Kate cried. "Maybe she did run away."

Charlie took a deep breath. "I'm sorry. I didn't mean to say it like that. It's just... I was afraid that this would happen. You've done so well. After years of therapy, you finally put it all behind you and now this. Coming here was clearly a mistake." Charlie ran his fingers through his hair. "We're only here a few more days. Are you sure you want to stay? We can go. Just say the word," he said, a note of pleading in his voice. He took her hands in his. She shook her head.

"No, I want to stay. Andrew is having such a good time, and I don't want to make our friends leave. I don't want to ruin it for them. You're right; it's my head. I don't mean to sound crazy. I really don't. All the memories—I thought they were gone, but I think they have always just been locked in this house," Kate said, her voice trembling. Charlie took her into his arms, his large frame engulfing her like a small bird. She wished she were telling the truth about being fine. Kate looked over his shoulder and couldn't help but feel as if someone was there, watching them.

***

An hour later, Kate went down to the kitchen to drink something cold while she tried to make sense of her bizarre vision. She had seen something … from the past maybe? Certainly it couldn't have been more than that. But what if it was? What if Lacie's ghost was roaming the halls, trying to tell her something? *Listen*, her mother had written in the note.

"Headache?" Susan asked, interrupting Kate's thoughts when she walked into the kitchen. "Can I make you a hot tea?" Susan smiled. "Your mother loved her tea."

"As long as it had the right amount of vodka or gin mixed in," Kate scoffed, regretting it as soon as she did. "I'm sorry… I shouldn't have said that."

"It's all right. I probably deserve it. Your mother and her tea…" Susan shrugged, seeming embarrassed to be discussing Gail's alcoholism so openly.

"It just seemed like it made her happy. You know how it was when she wasn't happy," Susan said as she fixed the kettle, trying not to look at Kate.

"It's not your fault. You did the best you could," Kate replied, though she wasn't sure she believed it. They had all enabled her mother. Gail was an alcoholic, but no one ever dared tell her so.

"I suppose. This is all getting to you, isn't it?" She said, getting the mugs down from the shelf. "The ghosts are just too overwhelming."

Kate's spine stiffened.

"What did you say?"

"The house, the memories," Susan continued as the kettle began to boil. "It's not so easy being here—she is still a part of this place. No matter how many years have gone by, I see her."

Susan's eyes welled up with tears. "The house is beautiful, but it certainly has its share of ghosts. Just be careful while you're here. Promise me that." She poured a cup of tea and handed it to Kate.

"What do you mean about ghosts?" Kate asked, more pointedly this time.

"I meant our ghosts from the past. The memories." Susan quickly replied. "The older you get, the more of them you have rattling around up there."

Kate nodded and took a sip of the tea, hot and strong. "Of course." She wasn't sure why she needed to be careful, but she took Susan's words to heart anyway.

Suddenly, Susan mumbled under her breath, "She's not supposed to be here." She was glaring through the window to the backyard. Kate looked and saw Chloe by the edge of the pool, setting down her stuff and waving to Andrew.

"I can't believe I never knew about Chloe."

"It happened so fast. We had wanted a child for so long, so when we finally got the call, we jumped at the chance," Susan said, looking nostalgic. "I'm sorry if she's interrupting your week."

"It's fine. Andrew and Ben seem to like her," Kate waved Susan off, but she secretly agreed with her. Why had her mother never mentioned Chloe to her before? It seemed like such a huge oversight. Kate wondered if her mother kept it from her purposely, but why would she have done that? Doug and Susan deserved to be parents and had been so good to her and Lacie. It was only right that they would have a child of their own. "I'm happy for the two of you. I wish you would have shared her with me over the years." Kate said.

Susan smiled. "Thank you, she is a good girl."

"I'm sure she is," Kate said and walked outside to join the

group sitting by the pool. They were so unaware of everything that happened here. For Kate, Lacie's story was a blemish on the house forever, a dark mark on a sunny place. Villa Magda would forever be tainted no matter how many wonderful summers came and went.

But Kate's guests were not from here, and they just relished the summer sun without a care. Kate worried they would look at her differently if they knew about Lacie.

Sure, they would pity her at first, feel sorry for her loss, and then, eventually, doubt would slowly creep in. As they learned more, they would undoubtedly think that she knew more than she let on. Just like her mother had. Like the town had. It made Kate sick to think that anyone had implied she would ever do anything to harm Lacie. She loved her sister more than anyone could imagine.

Still, they deserved to know, Kate thought. Especially Andrew. She would have to tell them eventually.

Kate startled when Andrew jumped into the pool, water splashing on her face. She looked over and saw Ben by himself, reading in one of the hammocks.

"How are you doing, Ben?" Kate asked as she met him under the trees.

"Fine," Ben responded, but his eyes darted to the pool. Kate followed his gaze to where Andrew was splashing water on Chloe.

"He has a tendency to make himself the center of attention," Kate acknowledged quietly.

Ben snorted. "You could say that." Kate wasn't sure, but she thought she heard a touch of jealousy in his voice.

"Charlie was the same way at his age," Kate confided.

Ben opened his mouth to respond when Susan called them all to lunch.

"I'm starving!" Andrew exclaimed. He grabbed a towel, quickly dried himself off, and rushed to the table. The others joined and gathered around the outdoor table that had been set with fresh salads and Susan's famous crab cakes. They sat down, and soon everyone was eating and drinking chilled water and white wine. The crab cakes were as delicious and delicate as she remembered.

"Doug will take you all out on the boat after lunch," said Susan as she brought a fruit plate for dessert.

"Yeah, that was my idea," whispered Charlie in Kate's ear. "But I'll be a good boy. I'll let him be the captain." Kate kissed him and blinked a silent thank you, grateful everyone was getting along.

*   *   *

Kate had always found a sense of freedom when she was out on the water in Doug's fishing boat. As a child, she loved watching Villa Magda get smaller and smaller in the distance. Lacie, on the other hand, would start to panic as soon as the house disappeared from view.

Like most of Villa Magda, not much had changed since the last time she had been out on the water. Doug's boat was sturdy despite all the storms it had weathered. Kate felt as if she were a child again as she boarded the boat. She fondly remembered the hours she and Lacie would spend with Doug on hot summer days, finding a bit of relief thanks to the cool sea breeze and an escape from their mother and the house, which at times both felt a bit oppressive. Doug had taught both them how to steer the boat and how to fish during those trips out on the water.

Chloe sat next to Doug as he steered the boat across the dark blue surface, cold water spraying Ben and Andrew as they sat near the bow. Kate could hear Doug and Sam talking about how far out they were going to go; Kate wondered if Doug still had the same fishing spots a few miles offshore; close enough to keep the cliff in sight, but far enough that Villa Magda wasn't visible.

Kate sat at the stern of the boat, between Molly and Charlie. Alice had decided not to join them—she'd never been a fan of the water, she said. As the boat rocked along, Kate's eyes started to feel heavy and her head began to nod; the salt air, the sun, and the stress of the week catching up to her made for a combination that Kate couldn't fight, and she gave up trying to stay awake.

* * *

"You know, I have fished before," Charlie snipped, his low voice standing out against the rhythmic slapping of the waves against the boat.

Kate jerked awake. She wasn't sure how long she had been asleep, but it must have been awhile. The boat was anchored near the inlet on the other side of the cliff, away from the house, and she could see Andrew, Charlie, and Doug standing at the bow, fishing poles in hand. Molly was still next to her, engrossed in her book. Kate watched as Doug handed a pole already baited to Charlie and explained to Andrew that having the right bait was the most important part of fishing.

"That and patience," he joked.

"Having upgraded equipment seems like it would be impor-tant," Charlie quipped. Doug gave Andrew the other pole and looked over his shoulder at Charlie.

"Fishing should be relaxing, not a competition," he muttered, straightening his hat.

"You need to fish more than just once a summer to know what you're doing."

Kate could see Charlie's shoulders tense and he rolled his neck. Kate knew he was holding back a searing reply.

"Charlie," she called out to him, hoping to ease the tension. "Do you want something to drink?"

Charlie looked back at her, and they shared a knowing look that came from years of marriage. Without saying a word, he handed his pole to Doug and walked back toward Kate and Molly.

"See, I told you he hates me," Charlie whispered as he took a gulp from the bottle of water Kate handed him.

"Shh, he'll hear you. It's not you. He likes being in charge of fishing trips. And he is having fun teaching Andrew."

Kate didn't want to admit it, but Charlie was right. Doug had never liked Charlie, and she had never understood why. As a teenager, it hadn't bothered her much. To be honest, it made dating Charlie feel a little dangerous. But Kate didn't understand why Doug was still so dismissive of Charlie. By now, Charlie's devotion to Kate and their family should have been clear to everyone. Doug wasn't standoffish with her, or with Andrew, or even Sam. Doug and Susan had both welcomed Andrew with open arms. It made Kate wonder if she had made the right decision to stay away for so long, when it meant that Andrew had been deprived of knowing this side of his family. Doug and Susan were all he had, now that both of Charlie's parents had passed away.

Charlie turned around to the cooler, but Molly was already

huddled over it. Her back was to them, but Kate could tell she was adding more vodka to her tumbler. Kate couldn't stop the angry flush that pricked her neck. She knew Molly was an adult, but her mind kept replaying that winter night over and over. Molly's cries on the other end of the line, as she sat in a cold jail cell, begging Kate to save her.

Molly tiptoed uneasily back to her seat, cackling as she almost lost her balance. She noticed Kate's eyes on her.

"I'm going to need more of this if I have to spend the next two hours with that jackass," she explained, gesturing to Sam, who was dangling his legs overboard.

"It's either this or I throw him off this fucking boat."

Kate started to reply but was interrupted by a shout, followed by a splash. She sprang from the padded bench seat and looked around, trying to get a headcount. Sam was standing up, looking for the source of excitement. Ben was near the bow, looking down into the water. And Andrew, where was Andrew? Someone was crouched down beside Ben, but Sam was in the way, and because of the sun, she couldn't tell if it was Andrew or Chloe. The wind and waves had picked up and the boat was rocking back and forth.

"Andrew!" She yelled, her heart racing.

Then she heard giggling from the water.

"Geez Mom, you don't need to yell. I'm right here," replied Andrew as he grabbed hold of Chloe's hand and helped her back into the boat.

"What's the problem? Chloe just lost her footing; she's fine."

"It's no big deal, Mrs. Williams. I am a great swimmer," Chloe chimed in.

"Andrew," called Doug. "You better get back to your pole,

I think you may have caught something."

Andrew jogged toward Doug, his feet barely touching the bottom as the boat rocked against the strong current of the waves, making Kate wince. Doug handed Andrew his pole and helped him reel it in, grasping onto the rod along with him as he had so many times with Kate and Lacie.

"Dad, look." Andrew laughed as a medium-sized flounder squirmed at the end of the hook.

The fish flopped furiously on the deck. Kate had a flashback to Lacie squealing whenever Doug or Kate would catch a fish. She would turn her head away as the fish struggled. Kate hated when she did that. Lacie would cry until Doug had no choice but to throw it back into the water. Lacie would watch the fish as it regained its breath and then swim away in a flash.

"Nice catch, Andrew," Charlie said. Doug smiled. "Should we just throw her back in, Katie?" Doug asked, "Like we used to?"

"No way!" shouted Sam. "A catch like that needs to be taken home."

"Yeah," chimed in Andrew. "Where's the fun if I have to throw it back in? I want to be able to say I ate the first fish I ever caught."

Kate's stomach churned as she watched the fish take its last breath.

* * *

By the time they got back to Villa Magda, the buoy bells were clanging in the wind. They had just finished dinner when large raindrops began splattering on the patio.

"Let's get inside, everyone," Kate called out, as dark thunderclouds rolled across the sky.

After drying off, Charlie suggested they watch a movie, and Kate popped popcorn as the group collapsed on the living room couches. As she walked back to the living room, snacks in hand, she heard the familiar notes of the *Jaws* opening song echoing faintly from the living room TV.

Kate had never been a big fan of scary movies, but she had to smile as she sat curled into Charlie's chest. Even though their evening had been interrupted by the rain, it was nice to have a moment of normalcy among friends. Kate wished she could hold onto this moment forever.

Just as Chief Brody's face filled the screen and uttered the line about needing a bigger boat, the lights flickered as a bolt of lightning illuminated the sky. A few moments later, a booming crack of thunder rattled the walls and the house went dark. Kate's heart stopped, and Molly let out a small shriek. Charlie stood and opened the flashlight app on his phone.

"Sam, I bet there are some candles and matches in the pantry. Let's go find them." Kate was relieved that Charlie was taking charge. She knew that he would make sure they were safe.

Charlie and Sam quickly returned with two hurricane lamps, a handful of candles, and two big red flashlights. Andrew and Ben helped them place the candles on the mantel and the lamps on the coffee table.

"Who's up for a ghost story?" Sam said conspiratorially. Molly shook her head.

"Absolutely not."

"Oh, come on. It's barely 9 p.m. What else are we going to do?"

Kate sighed, but Ben and Andrew had already pulled their chairs into a circle.

"You guys go ahead. I'm going to make sure our window is closed," Kate said, picking up a flashlight. Alice followed her, and they climbed the stairs to the second floor, muttering under her breath, "Two power outages in one day. That seems a bit odd, don't you think? Maybe the house is trying to tell you something."

"It's an old house. I'm sure the power will be back on by the morning."

Alice made a murmuring sound, and Kate could tell she disagreed, but luckily she didn't press Kate on the topic.

They entered the pitch-black room, the flashlight beam tracing a path across the floor. The window was wide open, rain blowing in and soaking the carpet. Kate rushed across the room to pull it shut.

As she yanked the window down, another flash of lightning illuminated the backyard. At the end of the pool, Kate saw a figure dressed in white. She gasped, but when another flash lit up the yard, the figure had vanished. Kate shook her head. She must have imagined it; nobody would be outside in weather like this. But when she blinked, the outline of the white dress flashed across her eyelids.

As she watched, waiting for the figure to reappear, Alice's voice came from the doorway.

"Kate, I think I'm going to bed. I'm still feeling a bit off from my headache earlier today."

Kate paused. She wanted to spend time with Alice, but it seemed like Alice was pulling away from her today.

"I understand. If you change your mind, you know where to find us."

* * *

Charlie was finishing his story by the time Kate got back downstairs.

"Rumor has it, the witch was burned by Colonel Buck. And to this day his grave is haunted by her foot, it keeps coming back. It doesn't matter how many times the grave is cleaned, the outline of the foot is always there." Charlie held the flashlight to his chin, letting the light cast eerie shadows across his face.

Andrew rolled his eyes. "You've told that one a million times, Dad."

"Charlie has about two stories he cycles through," Sam joked.

Charlie's eyebrows shot up. "Why don't you tell one then?"

Sam shrugged, taking the flashlight from Charlie. "Let's see. Okay, the story starts at a prep school in Connecticut," he murmured, lowering his voice dramatically. "The school was full of spoiled kids who spent their parents' money on drugs and cars. One day, there was a boy—" Sam paused, eyes flickering over to Charlie. "We'll call him Chuck."

The kids snickered, and Charlie shot him a look, but Sam continued. "Chuck was quite the ladies' man. He always had a few girlfriends at a time. He even dated a pair of sisters."

"That dog," Molly teased, but Charlie had his eyes narrowed at Sam.

"Well, Chuck also had a bit of an anger streak in him. He s known for starting the most fights out on the football field."

But how many did he finish?" Andrew jokingly called out across the circle.

His tackles were even said to be *deadly*." Molly "oohed" stically.

m became more animated as he continued his story, but

Kate's eyes were glued to Charlie. His body was growing rigid, and even in the dim candlelight Kate could see that his face had paled.

"Sam, stop," Charlie warned.

"Chuck wasn't too happy when another teammate got the scholarship he wanted," Sam continued. "And rumor is he got a bit violent."

Charlie stood up abruptly, his chair scraping against the wooden floor.

"I mean it, stop."

Sam threw up his hands in fake defeat.

"What's the problem, Charlie? It's just an urban legend, right?"

"You're a jackass," Charlie muttered under his breath, and he stalked upstairs.

Awkward silence followed him, and Kate's head swam. Sam had to be making the story up, she thought. She had never known Charlie to be physically aggressive. But was it true? Was that why Doug and her mother hadn't liked Charlie?

Molly cleared her throat, breaking Kate's train of thought.

"I think it's about time to go to bed."

* * *

Despite the storm, Charlie fell asleep as soon as his head hit the pillow, leaving Kate to ponder the day alone.

"*Good bones,*" Molly had said. Yes, the house did have some really good bones, but Kate could not help and wonder if Villa Magda had a soul as well. If it did, it was certainly dark. She felt the house drawing them in, ready to reveal something soon. Maybe they shouldn't have come, Kate thought. The dark memories seemed to be seeping out of her mind and infecting everyone around her.

* * *

"What do you think is in the woods?" Lacie asked. Kate looked at her. She was smiling, wearing that white dress their mother had gotten for her. "Do you think that's where you'll find me?" she continued.

Kate knew she was dreaming. Her voice didn't come out. She wanted to tell her sister not to leave. But she couldn't.

"Come find me," her sister taunted. "You know where."

Kate woke up drenched in sweat, the thunder now far off in the distance.

PRESENT DAY

POLICE FILE—ARIA, MAINE.

CASE 1583

Q: Had you heard anything about Charlie's past?

A: No, not until Sam brought it up at dinner. It was just old drama—something about Charlie in high school. But it really set Charlie off.

11

THURSDAY

"When Hansel and Gretel came into her neighbourhood,
she laughed with malice, and said mockingly:
'I have them, they shall not escape me again!'"
—HANSEL AND GRETEL, GRIMM BROTHERS

A loud pop echoed across the tennis court as Kate's racquet made contact with the yellow tennis ball. The sun was burning through the last of the morning fog, and she felt a single bead of sweat drip down her back.

Sam let out a loud grunt as he sent the ball flying back to Kate and Charlie's side. Kate had spent the first match fighting off yawns and trying to wake up. Her night had been filled with strange dreams, dreams that were so real they scared her at times. She was happy to be awake and rid of them.

"I can't believe we're in Maine. It feels like we're in a swamp in Florida," Sam said, wiping his face on his sleeve. "Although if we were in Florida, we would have a working AC!"

"I'm not sure what you expect, Sam," Charlie grunted as he missed the ball. "The house was built a century ago."

"Then maybe it's time for a facelift," Sam joked. "Isn't that what you told me last night, Molly? Good bones and all; just don't look too closely!"

Molly glared at Sam and started to respond when a shrill siren pierced through the quiet morning. A flock of birds scattered from the nearby treetops. The two couples glanced at the house. Charlie dropped his racket and sprinted toward the house. Kate followed him closely, her heart in throat as she imagined the worst. Was there a fire? Had someone broken in? And where were Ben and Andrew?

By the time they got to the kitchen, Susan was already at the alarm control panel, trying to get the alarm to turn off.

"What's wrong?" Kate yelled. Susan stepped back to let Charlie take over.

Finally, the noise stopped; Kate's ears rang as she adjusted to the silence.

"Well, that will surely wake you up," Susan said, letting out a nervous chuckle. "I haven't had to use this thing in years."

"Where are the boys?" asked Molly, barely out of breath as she rushed through the door.

"I sent them out to the bakery to pick up some goodies for brunch; they seemed a bit eager to be out of the house." Susan responded.

"What the hell is going on?" Sam huffed, a few paces behind Molly. Kate looked to Susan, who shrugged.

"I didn't set the alarm. It must be malfunctioning. Maybe there's a short somewhere."

"I don't smell any smoke," Kate said, but her body was tense.

"That was the burglar alarm. The fire alarm sounds different," said Susan.

"Are the windows still open?"

"I shut them all this morning."

"We should check the house anyway, just to be safe." Charlie was already opening the basement door.

"I'll check upstairs."

"Sam and I will take the first floor," Molly called out to Kate.

As she ran up the stairs, Kate prayed that this didn't have anything to do with Lacie's room.

But when she scanned the floor her eyes were drawn to the door of her mother's room. She had been avoiding going in, not quite ready to see where her mother had been living for the last eighteen years. But now the door was slightly ajar. She could have sworn it had been closed earlier that morning. Kate pushed it open slowly.

Curtains fluttered as a gust of wind blew through the open window. Kate breathed a sigh of relief.

"It's okay," Kate called downstairs. "It was just a window!"

Glancing around the room, Kate could see that it had been cleaned up. The nightstands were bare, all of the photos gone. She opened the closet; all the clothes were gone, too. A life erased. Doug and Susan had done a thorough job of cleaning. Even though it was as if Gail had never existed, Kate was grateful. She would have to do the same with Lacie's room, but not yet.

Still left on the wall was a painting that Kate had always liked. Max had commissioned a local artist to paint it, and the house looked happy in that picture, filled with promise. There were children playing in the front yard, a small dog with a stick nipping at their ankles. As she looked around, she noticed Lacie's name carved into the bedpost, similar to the etching on the staircase Molly had found yesterday. Kate realized sadly that her mother must have been the one etching Lacie's name all over the house. She felt sadness for her mother as she never had before; it was clear she had been lonely in this big house, mourning a daughter and a life she could have had. She left the room, shutting the door behind her. There was nothing here for her anymore.

* * *

Alice was waiting at the top of the stairs.

"Well, that was dramatic."

Kate responded with a small smile, not in the mood to deal with Alice's snark.

"Do you realize that we've hardly spent any time together?" Alice sneered. "You asked me to be here with you, but now it seems like you are avoiding me."

"I'm sorry. It's just overwhelming being here, I didn't realize how much attention the house would need," Kate said, suddenly worried Alice would leave. "I'm only here to help," Alice said.

The air was starting to feel stifling.

"I know you are. I promise we'll spend some time together later, just you and me. Just like old times," Kate said and she meant it. She had been pushing Alice away on this trip and realized that it was because she didn't want anyone to judge her, especially not Alice.

"Okay, I'm holding you to it." Alice smiled, gave Kate a quick kiss on the cheek and headed down the steps.

* * *

Charlie found her in their room, sitting on the edge of the bed with her head in her hands, "Andrew and Ben are back. I already filled them in on what happened with the alarm. And you know, I hate to take Sam's side, but what's going on with the air conditioner? Are we all just going to roast up here?" He was chuckling, but Kate could tell he was only half-joking. "No, really, are we?"

"Don't be so dramatic. It's not that bad. Doug said they are going to fix it."

"So incredible that they don't know how to work the alarm system after living here all these years." Charlie remarked, looking out the window. "Still living in that little cottage."

"It's as much their home as it's ours," Kate replied quickly. "My mother needed them."

"You don't find it a little strange? I mean after all that happened."

"Why would you say something like that?" Kate asked.

"It's just, they knew you both best," Charlie said defensively.

"They have always been like family to us," Kate protested. "People say and think lots of things, doesn't make them true. People thought I had something to do with it too. Terrible, awful rumors are just that. Let's just not bring it up again, okay? They mean a lot to me." Kate turned and sat on the bed.

"Sorry, I just don't think they ever liked me," Charlie continued, not letting up. "Remember how they always gave me such a hard time whenever I came over?"

"You were a little cocky as a seventeen-year-old." Kate smiled. "Besides, I'm sure they like you now, so many years have passed." She playfully kissed him on the cheek, trying to lighten the mood as best she could.

"I don't know about that. Susan has hardly said two words to me since we got here."

Kate laughed despite herself. She thought back to the boat trip. Kate had spent most of the time trying to ignore Chloe and Andrew's laughter from the back of the boat.

"Why did she have to join us on the boat? I thought this was going to be a family vacation." Kate commented out loud.

Charlie's brow furrowed. "Who?"

"Chloe. It seems like she is always lurking around the house."

"Kate, she lives on the grounds. Of course she is around."

"I don't know; she just rubs me the wrong way."

"She's keeping the boys company, that's all. Don't make it weird," Charlie said.

He wrapped her in his arms and held her tight, kissing her on the cheek. His cologne engulfed her—it smelled like summer, salt, and wood. She smiled, longing for more of this.

"I guess so. It's just that I caught her looking at me before, like she was studying me. And I've barely seen Andrew this entire trip. Do you remember Mom telling us about her? For the life of me, I can't."

"You're sounding a bit paranoid. She's a kid, who's probably just grateful to have some new friends. She's harmless, just like we were, remember? And you and your mom probably weren't talking when they adopted her."

"I know," Kate sighed. "Sorry, I think I'm just stressed. My whole body has been so tense lately. I wish I could just relax and enjoy the next few days." Kate wanted to be light for once. Charlie rubbed her lower back, and Kate delighted at his touch. He kissed her. His lips were soft. It felt nice, comforting. She could always count on him to take her out of the dark moment.

He still had the power to do that for her.

"Oh, and I had Doug call an exterminator to check the house for any more of those nasty bats," Kate said.

"I thought I heard some noises in the attic. That should be checked out. Old houses, gotta love 'em, but they make a lot of noise…"

Noise. Kate wondered if he'd heard the whispering too. Based on how their last conversation had gone, she figured it was better not to ask.

He kissed her forehead, bringing her out of her thoughts. "I'll be downstairs if you need me." Charlie turned at the door. "By the way, just a heads up: Sam and Molly are fighting again. Same old shit, different place, different day. Stay out of the line of fire."

"I thought they were doing better?"

Charlie shrugged. "Who knows with them."

"And are you guys okay, you and Sam?"

Charlie's face darkened. "I don't know. I'm waiting on a few phone calls."

Kate hadn't expected him to be so upset.

"I didn't realize it was that serious. I'm sorry, I'm just—"

"Not now, Kate. Okay?" He turned and left before she could respond.

* * *

Why had Charlie snapped at her? After he went downstairs, Kate vowed that she was going to have a better day. She was looking forward to dinner. A slew of Maine specialties was on the menu, and she went into town to go to the local farmers market for sweet corn and fruit. She was happy to be having some time by herself. Kate had loved the quaint town of Aria when she was a kid. She and her family had known most everyone. And after all these years, it looked as if time had stood still. Memories that had been locked away started to come back. A few specialty shops and the diner where she and Lacie had gone when their mother needed the house to herself were all still there. The movie theater where she had her first date with Charlie had sadly closed. She did notice a small Starbucks on the corner and chuckled to herself—somehow it had made its way even here. The police station, smack in the middle of town, was next to the only bank. And next door was the local bookstore, Barry's, where she and Lacie would spend hours getting their summer reading done. It was there that Lacie had bought *Hansel and Gretel*.

At the farmers market, Kate walked through the stalls and picked up ripe tomatoes and corn for dinner and blueberries and strawberries for dessert. Carrying her basket, she crossed the street to go back to the car and nearly collided with another woman. She was slightly heavyset, with long reddish hair tied back in a messy ponytail.

"I'm so sorry," Kate apologized, taking stock of all her bags and items. Instead of waving it off, the woman stared at her, scrutinizing her for a moment. Kate tried to sidestep to get out of her way, but the woman stopped her with a hand on her arm.

"Katie? Is that you?" The woman's glasses were perched way too high on her nose and she reminded Kate of a red hawk.

"I'm sorry," Kate said, unable to place her. "Do we know each other?"

"Barbara, remember?" Her expression softened and she took off her glasses. "Is that any better?"

She still couldn't place her.

"Barbara Anderson. Darien's sister."

It was obvious now that she'd said it.

"Yes, of course!" Kate exclaimed. Barbara was the chief of police's daughter and Darien's younger sister. They had all been friends that summer. A group of them—some from Aria and some from out of town, all so different but so alike in their youth—had all hung out together, just wanting to enjoy their time off as best they could during the Maine summer. Looking at Barbara, she saw the eager young girl who followed Darien around like a puppy.

"Darien told me he saw you the other day at Uncle Doug's— well, at your house, I mean. You were gone for so long. Eighteen or so years, right? Time does fly, doesn't it?"

Kate smiled and nodded. "Sure does."

"He couldn't stop talking about seeing you." Barbara smiled, but her voice was hard. "He's right—you look great."

"Oh, well thank you." Kate felt a little thrill at the thought that Darien had been talking about her.

"I heard about your mother. I'm so sorry. She never did come to town much," Barbara continued. "Not ever really that I can remember; she just stayed tucked away in that house all these years. Sad."

"Well, it's very nice to see you again." Kate looked around, uncomfortable rehashing the past and talking about her mother with this woman she hadn't seen in so long and never really knew that well. She was suddenly desperate to move on.

"I met Chloe. She and my son Andrew have been getting along well."

"She reminds me of us at that age," Barbara said. "Always

playing with boys' hearts, that one. Something you would know about, huh?"

"Well," Kate blinked, surprised at how quickly Barbara's tone changed. "I better be going. I need to get these in the fridge."

"Wait, I know this may sound like a strange thing to ask, but would you mind if I came by to visit you at the house one of these days?"

Kate stood up a little straighter at that and noticed sweat had formed on Barbara's upper lip. She didn't know what to say, but the words just spilled out.

"Sure, but we're only here a few more days and the schedule is a bit tight."

"It would be a short visit. I write for the blog *Aria Today* and I'm writing a piece on the anniversary of Lacie's disappearance," Barbara shifted awkwardly from one foot to the other.

Kate wasn't sure she had heard her correctly.

"Excuse me? Why?"

"I write about the anniversary every year. Usually just a few lines, but with you here, I would love to interview you for it. And you haven't been back since that summer. So, people will want to know all about those missing years. It'd just be a personal interest piece, but it's something to write about nonetheless." Barbara was babbling a little now, her eagerness palpable. "Really harmless. Just lots of crime buffs you know, actually a lot of tourists come here because of Lacie, believe it or not."

"I don't think that I feel comfortable with that. We're just here on vacation." Kate was getting antsy.

"I get it. It is brave of you to come back here after everything, especially on the anniversary," Barbara said.

"What do you mean by brave?" Kate challenged, feeling scrutinized by Barbara's beady eyes.

"Well, since everyone thought you knew something when she vanished. I mean, not that anyone thought you could have... just us silly kids..." Barbara blurted, flustered.

Kate felt the world spin, her vision blurring, like the whole town was whirling around her. She felt the heat rise in her throat and her cheeks flushed.

"What are you saying?"

"Come on, we all knew how you felt about your sister." Her head cocked to the side.

Kate could hardly keep her head up; it was pounding.

"You don't even know me." Her voice cracked, feeling her face flush with anger.

"But I do. It's all anyone talked about that summer. They still do. Tell me: What happened to her?" Barbara prodded. "You must know something."

"She was my sister. I loved her. I still do."

"She was so beautiful. Some thought it was obvious. I mean, especially after that incident at the beach. We could have sworn you were purposely taking her out farther in the storm so she would drown. We saw it all." Barbara smiled, her teeth showing, a bit like an animal hungry for its prey.

"What you saw was me trying to save her, not to drown her," Kate said. She didn't want to admit her memory was hazy, but she knew she would not have tried to drown her own sister.

"Really? Is that what that was?" Barbara's tone was incredulous. "Ask Charlie what he thought about it. I'm sure you'll be surprised at what he really thinks." She spat out.

"You have no clue what you're talking about. This is all just small-town gossip for people with nothing better to do." Kate's words were meant to sting, and she could tell she had hit a nerve.

"Well I guess you think us townies should be grateful that you've finally graced us with your presence," Barbara muttered.

"I don't think I should have to defend myself to anyone in this town."

As Kate started to walk away, Barbara called after her, "Why did you come back anyway?"

Kate wondered how true what Barbara said was. There were always people out there who thought the worst, no matter how little they knew the people involved. Barbara had said that the kids, Kate's friends, had suspected her. Did the kids, now adults, still think that? Maybe that was why Chloe looked at her the way she did, as if she were some killer. After Lacie disappeared, there were so many blurry days of searching. Kate left that summer without seeing any of her local friends after that day. Had Charlie been part of one of the groups who doubted her and believed the rumors? Or Darien? Kate's head pounded, pain searing through her temple. If she let it go, the doubt of her innocence would forever taint her.

12

"The woman led the children still deeper into the forest,
where they had never in their lives been before."
—*HANSEL AND GRETEL*, GRIMM BROTHERS

How well do we ever really know the person we are married to?
Kate wondered, as she drove on the winding roads back toward
Villa Magda. She thought about how she had always assumed
she knew all there was to know about Charlie. He was the darling and charming only child of Walter and Maddie Williams,
a renowned lawyer from Boston and a beautiful debutante from
North Carolina. Walter and Maddie had met on a semester
abroad in Europe and married young, then tried and failed to
have children for many years. When they had all but given up,
Charlie arrived, all curls and sea-blue eyes. He was perfect, and
his parents spoiled him. Charlie had gone to one of the top

boarding schools in the country, and he was good at almost any sport he tried, the star of the football team and always had a group of friends around.

When Charlie and Kate first met, it was at a bonfire on the beach near Villa Magda. Kate had been there with Lacie. Gail only allowed them to go if they both went. For their first date, they walked around the grounds. He listened to Kate, and she liked that. She remembered seeing her mother looking down at them from her window. "What does such a good-looking boy want from you, Kate?" she had asked later, implying that Lacie was the real catch, not Kate. Her mother had never actually said Lacie was the prettier of the two, but Kate knew how her mother felt. Children always know if their parents have a favorite child and it isn't them.

Kate wondered if she was enough for him. But for some reason, he loved her, and she reveled in that love and protected it with all her heart.

* * *

Back at the house, Kate drove up and saw her handsome husband and son standing outside in the blazing sunlight. They were both so perfect, Kate thought. She sometimes felt she didn't belong with them at all. Charlie smiled, and his dimples and intense blue eyes still worked their charms. Would he hide something so important from her—believing she was capable of something horrible? Maybe Charlie, like the house, only seemed familiar and was harboring secrets from her.

Kate parked her car in the driveway and turned the ignition off. She slumped back in her seat and closed her eyes, still reeling from the encounter with Barbara. If she went inside and

Charlie came in, he would immediately know something was wrong; she was never able to hide her emotions from him. But she wasn't ready to tell him everything yet. As she lugged the groceries in, she hoped she could slip in and quickly unpack the bags without having to explain herself. But Susan was busy in the kitchen, humming and running the blender. The counter was covered in mixing bowls and crab shells.

Susan smiled as she looked up at Kate.

"Hi, Katie. The food will be ready soon. I wasn't sure if you had a plan for lunch, but I was worried that the boys would get hungry and you took longer getting back than I expected, so I went ahead and whipped something up."

Kate knew she should be grateful for Susan's help, but she couldn't help feeling annoyed at Susan taking complete control. Susan was acting as if this were her home, not Kate's.

Alice walked into the kitchen and whispered in Kate's ear, causing her to jump.

"Wouldn't want to mess with Susan. She's clearly the boss around here…" Kate shot Alice a look. Susan's voice brought her back.

"I was thinking about packing up the study after lunch, while you all enjoy some pool time."

"I'll do it!" Kate blurted, surprising herself. She hadn't been looking forward to packing up any of the rooms, but the thought of Susan rifling through more family items from the house didn't sit right with her.

"Are you sure? I'm happy to do—"

Kate waved her off.

"I'm not very hungry anyway."

She could feel Susan's eyes on her as she unpacked the

groceries. It was rare for Kate to be so dismissive, but she was desperate to end the conversation, and she was grateful that Susan didn't press it.

* * *

Kate opened the door to the study, a musty smell immediately wafting into the hallway. Dim sunlight filtered in through the curtained windows. In the center of the room stood her father's desk, barely touched from the last time he was here more than eighteen years ago.

The family's computer—where Lacie spent hours IM'ing friends—was noticeably absent. Kate wondered if the police had taken it for evidence. It seemed like their home had been raided in the weeks after Lacie's disappearance.

To the right of the desk loomed a large bookshelf, filled with old family photo albums and boxes of mementos. Kate picked up the box closest to her and peeled away the lid, sticky from years of neglect. It was filled to the brim with loose-leaf photos, some newer than others. She started flipping through them and sighed. It would take hours to decide what was worth keeping.

As she dug through the box, one photo caught her eye. Two men stared back at her, Villa Magda in the background, their wide smiles beaming through the faded sepia tone. Kate remembered seeing this photo as a child. Although she never met him, she recognized her grandfather instantly. He had piercing blue eyes and light blonde hair, the spitting image of Magda. Paul was the eldest child of Max and Magda, and had inherited Villa Magda on his eighteenth birthday. He and his sister Rose had been taken in by their aunt after Magda's abandonment and Max's death. Their aunt had refused to live in the house—she claimed it had bad energy. But Kate had never seen the man standing next to him. She flipped the photo over, and noticed in shaky handwriting the words "Paul and Ted."

Kate sifted through the remaining photos, until her hand caught the edge of something hard. Her fingers grasped onto a soft, leather cover. She pulled out a small, weathered journal, the bottom right corner engraved with her mother's name. Kate sat in her father's old chair and flipped through the journal. The pages stopped on an entry halfway through the book, the words scribbled in haste.

September 12

Dear Diary,

Today I saw Dad angry for the first time ever. I was playing in the woods when I heard shouting. A teenager from town, I think it was Carl, was near the edge of the cliff, and Dad was pushing him away, screaming that he shouldn't be there. Dad doesn't let anyone near the cliff. But then he saw me and started yelling at me, telling me he was going to ground me for a month if I played near the cliff again. I don't know why he worries so much about the cliff. Oh well. Next year when I turn 13, Dad is sending me to a boarding school anyway. But I know I'm never playing near the cliff again.

September 13

Dear Diary,

I helped Mom cook dinner tonight, and I told her about Dad yelling at me. She's never heard him yell either. I asked her what the big deal is about the cliff and she wouldn't tell me, but she did say that Dad had a friend who got hurt there. I know a caretaker named Ted lived on the grounds, but that was before I was born. I might have to ask Mel. She always knows everything.

September 15

Dear Diary,

I was right, Mel knows the full story. I asked her when we were at the movies tonight. She says it's easy to hear things around town. All you have to do is listen. I guess she heard people talking about Dad and the caretaker Ted. She says they were friends, and never left each other's side. But some people in town thought their friendship was too close. Even whispers of love. And then one day, Ted was dead. I don't know if this is true. I want to ask Dad about Ted, but he'd probably just yell at me again.

Growing up, Kate remembered her mother dramatically telling the story of Ted's death at dinner parties. According to Gail, as Paul puttered on the roof trying to replace some rotted shingles, Ted had taken one of the younger horses out for its morning ride. The air was thick with the notorious Maine fog, so thick you couldn't see two feet in front of you. As Ted was bringing the horse back to the stables, Paul stepped through a weak spot in the roof, causing a loud crack to echo across the grounds. Spooked, the young horse took off, hurtling away from the house through the fog. Ted didn't even have time to register that they were nearing the cliff until it was too late. Their bodies were flung over the edge, airborne as they fell fifty feet into the water along the rocky shoreline.

Paul, still injured from his fall, had spent all morning searching through the fog. It wasn't until the fog cleared that afternoon that rescuers were able to recover Ted's body. Some people in the town swore they could hear Paul's mourning from miles away.

A few years later, Paul met Edith, Gail's mom. Edith was a lovely young girl from the neighboring town, and when they met, she had just turned nineteen. She was kind and sweet and loved Paul from the start. Her family continued to support her, so she didn't expect too much from Paul. They had a gentle and soft relationship, but Paul had closed down after Ted's death. A secret locked away.

Villa Magda had once again crushed the love that had been blooming there.

* * *

Kate shut the door of the study behind her. The sounds of chatter and silverware against plates drifted up from the patio. She knew she should go join them, but right now she just needed to be alone with her memories.

She lay down on her bed and shut her eyes. Stories from her mother circulated through her head, the faint images from her own childhood playing in her mind like an old movie.

That day was so long ago. They were at the beach. Music was playing. The smell of the sea and peanuts—Lacie loved peanuts. "Why do you have to eat those when you know that I'm allergic? It's like you do it on purpose or something."

The sounds changed, the memory fog shifted away, and images came into view, slightly out of focus. It was as if Kate were looking down on the scene playing out on the beach.

"A storm is coming," Kate warned. "Mom said we should go back in if it rains."

Lacie was excited.

"I love it when it storms. Come on, let's go for a swim, Katie, please." Lacie begged relentlessly.

Kate looked at her warily. "Are you crazy? Look at those waves. They're like ten feet high and will drag us under. Stop asking me." Kate was firm.

Lacie frowned. "You're just being a total bitch because he's here."

Kate glared at her. "Shut up. Don't say that. Mom hates it when we curse. Not ladylike at all. I knew I should've left you at home." Like all sisters, Lacie knew how to push Kate's buttons.

"He doesn't really like you, you know. It's just a silly game for him, like the ones we used to play. But in his game, he pretends he likes you," Lacie insisted as she chewed peanuts.

"I wish you didn't exist," Kate snarled, slapping the peanuts out of her hand.

"You're just jealous," Lacie hissed as she turned on her side so she didn't have to look at her sister. And then she got up and walked off. "And maybe I won't exist."

Kate had been furious at her mother for making her take Lacie to the beach, and Lacie was acting brattier than usual. But Kate

was not going to enable her sister's behavior, not this time.
The picture went black again, but the sound seemed amplified.

"Lacie!" Kate called out.

Kate remembered the feel of the cool water as she rushed into the ocean. She swam against the waves as hard as she could, going after Lacie. Eventually, Kate struggled to keep the water from getting into her lungs as the high waves tossed her back and forth. She swallowed salt water as she called out Lacie's name.

"Lacie, get back here!" Kate screamed. She could hardly see her sister as her head bobbed up and down in between the thrashing of the waves. Lacie was gasping for air as the waves slammed into her small frame. Kate's hand made contact with Lacie's shoulder and she tried to grab hold of her sister. But Lacie's arms gave up and she sank under the wave. The next thing Kate knew, an arm was around her, jerking her body back.

Kate looked up, unsure who it was at first, finally seeing that Darien had saved her. Once on shore, she coughed up salt water and debris from her lungs, convinced her sister had drowned when she saw Darien drag Lacie's small body onto the shore. Everyone had been staring at them. Barbara was there; she remembered her now. They had all formed a wide circle around them, Charlie's face as white as a ghost. They were all gawking, some pointing. Whispers. What were they saying? Kate couldn't remember.

* * *

Kate jerked awake. Her hand went to her neck as she gasped for air. The sea breeze had picked up, and the curtains fluttered. She was confused. Had Barbara been right? Surely Kate had been trying to save Lacie and instead been caught by the waves herself. The scent of sweet blueberries and dough filled the house. Kate got up and went downstairs, and found Susan diligently working in her apron in the kitchen.

"There you are. Smells good, doesn't it?"

Kate didn't have the heart to tell her that she felt nauseous from the sickly sweet smell.

"Your mother would have loved to see all these people here giving the house some life. Nice to hear some laughter for a change." Kate returned Susan's smile, but her mind was still reeling.

"Doug said it might take a day or two to fix the air unit. It blew out some years ago, your mother never cared much about those things. Sorry about that; we should have had it fixed professionally before you all got here."

"It's not your fault, she didn't care about much except Lacie," Kate said quietly.

"She did the best she could, it wasn't easy all those years. Lacie was a special little girl, with so much imagination. The two of you spent so much time playing make believe in the cottage. Your mother meant well, but the cottage was a place where you two could be what you wanted to be." Susan said, taking a deep breath.

"It's awful how scrambled my memory is," Kate said. "Some memories seem so clear and others are barely there, feelings mostly, especially leading up to that day or the day itself."

"I remember that day and the day before. I can't ever forget it. I noticed a lot. It was like most days at first. Nothing much felt different, except—" Susan stopped herself mid-phrase.

"Except?"

"I don't think it's the time to dredge up old memories and

issues, dear. It won't bring her or your mother back, for that matter." Susan turned to the sink and rinsed out the bowls.

"What was different that day?" Kate probed. "Please, Susan." Kate was suddenly struck by how old Susan looked. Her hair was pulled back neatly, her hands wrinkled from years of doing laundry and housework. She looked tired. Kate wanted to hug her and pretend she was a little girl again. Susan sighed.

"There was that awful fight when you two got back from the beach. We tried to break it up. Even Charlie tried to help. Each of you said the nastiest things to each other. It broke my heart. I hadn't heard you fight like that before. It just wasn't the normal sort of way siblings fight, it was brutal. Your mother was so furious with the two of you. She pulled you apart and sent you to your rooms."

"I don't remember any of that," Kate said, shocked.

"It was terrible, what Lacie had... implied that day," Susan shook her head. "She could be quite the terror when she wanted to be. That girl was all beauty and terror, I used to say. She hid it well, but when she wanted something, there was no stopping her."

"Implied?" Kate asked, going back to that word. "What did she imply?" She was afraid to hear the answer.

"She said you took her out into the ocean and tried to drown her. She insisted that you had been trying to kill her." Susan looked away. "Of course, we didn't believe her, which only made her more furious."

"She said that? That I was trying to kill her?" Kate asked, her voice shaky. She was trying to save Lacie that day, so why were they all trying to say otherwise? Kate's head swirled, and the smell of baked blueberries and cinnamon made her dizzy.

"Oh honey, of course you did. We all loved her. I'm sorry.

I told you that it was something we shouldn't talk about. Let it rest. Carl is a crazy old man; he upset you and started this. Don't let him ruin this week for you," Susan declared, as she carefully checked on the pie.

"Susan? One more thing?" Kate looked at her reluctantly. She was not sure if she should say anything, but she needed to hear it from someone who had spent so much more time at Villa Magda. "I know this might sound crazy, but… I thought I saw her the other day."

Susan wiped her hands on her apron and candidly said, "Why, of course you did. She is here, you know. I told you so. You feel it too, don't you?" She turned back toward the oven, fussing with the rest of the food preparations. "We've all seen her at one point or another. She's just a part of this house, like any room here. Your mother was always blaming Lacie's ghost when she couldn't find something she swore she had left in a certain spot."

Kate stood still, a shiver going through her as Susan carefully held out a bowl.

"Here you go. The best blueberries in the world."

Kate's eyebrows scrunched together.

"Why did she say I tried to drown her? Why would she make that up? I don't remember that at all!" Susan looked evenly at Kate, the way an adult looks at a child who's just old enough to grasp something fundamental for the first time. "It was because of Charlie. She said that you saw them together. But I always assumed she was making up stories again. Creating her own little fairy tale. We all know you wouldn't hurt your sister."

* * *

She couldn't trust which memories were real and which were not. She didn't want to admit it to Charlie, but chunks of their marriage were also hard for her to remember. She could recall every second with Andrew, though—she stored that in a place where everything was happier and easier. But her recall from that summer, that part of her brain was scarred and jagged. She had always assumed, as her therapist had explained, that the intensity of the trauma of Lacie's disappearance and her family's dissolution had wiped out some of her recollection. The more she thought this, the more comfortable she became with it as an explanation. But of course, even if she believed that, it didn't account for the other pieces of her past that she couldn't easily recall. She tried to push those questions out of her mind, but now they all rushed toward her at once, unleashed by Susan's simple explanation.

Kate shut the back door behind her and walked past the pool area, with its blue and white hydrangeas, and down toward the beach. As she took the stairs, the wind from the ocean caressed her face and she felt a surge of emotion. She thought about what Barbara and Susan had told her, and their revelations clouded her mind. Charlie had been here that day and heard her huge fight with Lacie, but had never mentioned it to her? Why couldn't she remember? She had tried doing memory recall in therapy, but it hadn't helped. Some of the memories were buried. Certainly, it would have helped if Charlie had told her—could they have discussed it at some point, and she blocked that out, too? Was this why he didn't want to come back here? Kate couldn't help but wonder what else she would discover if she went digging for answers. Maybe she should talk to Darien and see what he said.

* * *

Kate returned to the house and entered the kitchen to find Alice already there, sitting by the kitchen table, sipping on white wine and nibbling on some of the leftover berries.

"There you are!" Alice smiled at her, but her expression was scrutinizing.

"I need some coffee; my head is pounding." Kate looked in the pot and poured herself a cup, ignoring Alice.

"You've not mentioned her to me since we got here, you know. Your mother," Alice added.

"I just don't have much to say about her, I guess." Kate took a deep breath and sipped her coffee. "I guess it's strange to be here without her. And now, being here with Andrew... I see why Lacie's disappearance affected my mom so much. She left me a letter, mentioning that she thought Lacie was here."

"Here in the house?"

"I know, and Susan told me the same thing. It's actually unnerving. Part of me is glad Susan mentioned it, because I think I saw her too." Kate paused and looked at Alice, who appeared stricken. "Do you remember anything about that time that's significant, something I'm missing? Did I say anything about her that stands out? About our relationship or anything about..." Kate paused.

"Charlie?" Alice finished the sentence for her.

Kate was shocked. Did everyone know about this except her? And why couldn't she remember?

"You did. You said you suspected that there was something going on between them."

Kate's heart bottomed out.

"Something like what?"

"I don't know. I thought you were so upset you just said anything you could think of." Alice shrugged.

"Maybe I was right."

"Don't go down this road again, Kate. I think you just have Molly's worries on your mind. Charlie's always loved you. Anyone who saw the two of you as teenagers could see that he was completely smitten with you."

A cold breeze blew in through the kitchen, and Kate hugged herself. It was getting darker outside, the clouds increasing. Suddenly, the door flung open, and Susan bustled into the kitchen carrying bags of groceries, interrupting their conversation.

"Doug brought us some groceries. I thought we'd make some good ole' shepherd's pie for everyone tonight."

"I already bought some stuff for dinner today. I had planned on making it myself," said Kate, her voice pinched. "But that's okay; I am feeling quite exhausted. I can make it tomorrow. Shepherd's pie sounds lovely, thank you."

Alice may have been right—maybe Kate was letting Susan take over her house. Kate was grateful that she wouldn't have to cook, and she could use some comfort food. But she also didn't want to be bossed around. This was her home, after all. She needed to start putting her foot down.

PRESENT DAY
POLICE FILE—ARIA, MAINE.
CASE 1583

Q: Anything you can tell us about last night?

A: I just can't believe it.

Q: Where were you?

A: I was mostly in the kitchen, cooking, and cleaning up. I just went outside a few times, I don't like when there's too much drinking or arguing.

Q: Arguing?

A: I heard voices raised quite a bit.

Q: Do you know who was arguing?

A: They all were.

13

FRIDAY

*"And when the full moon had risen,
Hansel took his little sister by the hand, and followed the pebbles
which shone like newly-coined silver pieces,
and showed them the way."*
—*HANSEL AND GRETEL*, GRIMM BROTHERS

The next day, Kate slept in. After waking up, she pulled the curtains to find the day was overcast, and the air was cooler. She looked at the ocean from her window. The waves were high and choppy, and she could hear the crashing against the rocks. Opening the window, the salty air that breezed in was soothing. She went downstairs to get some coffee and found the kitchen already full. Molly and Sam were having bacon and eggs, and Susan was making pancakes. Kate felt guilty that she was hardly spending any time with her friends. Her time was being sabotaged by Lacie. Doubt had seeped in and was infecting her by the minute. She caught a glimpse of her reflection in the china cabinet; her eyes were dark and sunken.

"Good morning, sunshine," Molly said, and opened her arms to hug Kate. Kate thought she smelled wine on her breath, but Molly pulled away quickly. "I'm planning to go paddle-boarding today, I thought it might clear my head. Do you want to join?"

"Maybe?" Kate said unenthusiastically.

"You seem a bit out of it. Is it because of your mom?" Molly continued.

Kate paused, "No, not just about my mother… I wasn't sure how to tell you this, but do you remember the name you saw on the stairs? Lacie?"

"Pancakes are ready," Susan called from the stove, interrupting Kate.

"You might want to check on Charlie first, Kate," Sam said through a mouth full of food. He gestured out the window with his fork.

Kate shifted her gaze out the window and saw Charlie and Darien in the backyard, glaring at each other. She stood up quickly, the legs of the chair scraping against the floor. "You guys stay here. I'll see what's happening."

"What the hell are you doing?" Kate heard Charlie yell as she rushed onto the patio.

"What's going on here?"

"I just found this creep snooping around the house."

Darien backed off and raised his hands in mock surrender.

"I just came by to bring you this." He handed her a file. "I thought you should have it. I know what I said in the maze about the case being closed, and others in the department do not agree with me, but I am chief of police now, so it's my call ultimately. Anyway, you looked so lost before, and I thought this could help. I'm sorry," Darien said. Kate could see he meant it.

"In the maze?" Charlie asked, eyeing Kate.

Kate ignored Charlie and took the file from Darien. "This is the file on Lacie?"

He nodded. "Yes. Apparently Charlie didn't want me to give it to you."

Charlie turned to Kate. "I just don't think it will do any good, drudging this all up now."

Kate barely heard him as she opened the file; on top of the stack of papers was a photo. The image was slightly blurry, but Kate could clearly see that it was taken at one of Gail's garden parties. The photo was of Gail smiling with friends, but in the background, a young Charlie and Lacie were standing at the entrance of the maze. Their faces were inches apart, and Lacie's hand was placed delicately on Charlie's arm. Kate's heart hammered in her ears. As she turned to Charlie, she noticed his face turn white.

"Mom, who's Lacie?" Andrew asked.

Kate realized she was getting more confused but all she could focus on was this new information. Nothing else mattered—even Andrew's pleas were muffled.

"I've never seen this before. Why didn't I know anything about it?"

"Your mother never wanted my father to ask you about it. She thought it might upset you too much." Darien sounded apologetic.

"Why bring this all up now?" Charlie said, teeth clenched.

"He's trying to help, Charlie. Just please stop," Kate's voice was thick with tears.

"You said you wouldn't do this," Charlie snapped, the hurt and desperation evident in his tone.

"I think Kate deserves to know the truth about her sister," Darien said.

"Thank you." Kate clutched the file to her chest. Her heart was heavy as she realized that now she had no choice but to dig deeper. Charlie would just have to deal with it.

* * *

"That no-good son of a bitch." Charlie seethed as he slammed the door to the study closed. "I don't trust him or anyone in this town."

"You're overreacting; this isn't like you at all."

"You asked him to reopen Lacie's case and didn't bother telling me?" he yelled. "Since when do we keep things from each other?"

"I didn't think it was a big deal. He came by to see Doug and said hello. He's the chief of police now, so I just asked him about the case. It was a normal thing to ask, don't you think?" Kate babbled while still trying to calm Charlie down.

"Don't you realize none of this is normal, Kate? You want to act like it is, and that you just came here to pack up the house, but I think that you came here with an ulterior motive and you wanted to dig into the past." Charlie lowered his voice. "Have you even thought about Andrew?"

"Of course I thought of Andrew." Kate was insulted by his tone. "He's all I ever think about."

"Kate, Darien bringing you the file doesn't mean anything. You know that right? I don't want you going down this endless rabbit hole to only be disappointed or, worse, traumatized all over again."

"What were you and Lacie doing in that photo?" Kate

challenged him, distrust seeping through her voice.

"I have no idea what you're talking about." Charlie stormed out of the room.

The house felt like it was closing in on Kate and she needed some fresh air.

Kate walked out into the hall and realized that Molly was standing there and had heard their entire conversation about Lacie.

"Were you ever going to tell me?" Molly asked with tears in her eyes.

"Molly…"

"I'm your friend, Kate, I wouldn't have judged you."

"Please Molly, I'll explain everything. I'm just not ready. Can you give me some time?"

"Of course. I just feel so confused. I get it that you have trauma in your life that you didn't want to share, but this is a big thing. This is not something we can push under the rug. I just wanted to be here for you; you need to let us in." Molly sniffled and then turned and walked away.

It pained Kate that Molly was doubting their friendship. She wanted to run after her friend and reassure her, but she wanted to read what was in the file even more. Kate might finally have the answers she was looking for, even if it meant upsetting those around her to get the truth.

Alice stood there, her arms crossed, a smirk slapped across her face.

"What?" Kate said defiantly.

Alice shrugged. "I told you that this was all going to go to shit, yet you insisted on inviting Molly. It could have just been us." Alice raised her eyebrows.

"I can't just hide; it's my truth. And quite frankly, it's past time that she knew."

"But now you worry, don't you, that she will judge you or wonder if you're hiding something else?" Alice persisted.

Kate did worry about that, but she didn't want to admit to it.

"She's my friend, Alice. She can help me," Kate said, but she didn't really believe it herself. Kate turned and saw Chloe, in the doorway of the kitchen watching her suspiciously.

* * *

Jealousy started seeping into Villa Magda shortly after Max and Magda's wedding day. Max had built so many rooms that finding his wife most days was a challenge. She would hide from him, he said. The only time he saw her smile was when Marshall, the farmer from down the road, came to drop off some of the crops. Magda would be in the kitchen waiting, fresh and excited. Max would watch them from the second floor as she talked to him. Her eyes were bright. Jealousy had no place in Villa Magda, no place at all.

14

"Gretel began to cry and said:
'How are we to get out of the forest now?'
But Hansel comforted her and said:
'Just wait a little, until the moon has risen,
and then we will soon find the way.'"
—HANSEL AND GRETEL, GRIMM BROTHERS

Kate held the police file tight as she walked into the library. The room was dark and smelled of old books. Kate opened the curtains, letting the morning light shine in. She sank into the large leather couch and set the file down on the table beside her. The back of her neck tingled, and she had the overwhelming sense that she was not alone in the room. Her eyes were drawn to the wall opposite her, where the pair of Max and Magda's portraits hung high, studying her. As a child, Kate had always looked at Max's portrait and felt sorrow, but now, his cold gaze just felt intimidating. Magda, with her long, blonde hair and bright blue eyes, reminded her of Lacie, making Kate's heart ache.

A loud creak from upstairs made her jump, and Kate remembered the file. She had never seen an actual police report before. There were newspaper clippings, photos, and dozens of statements from witness interviews. Kate scanned the pages, looking for any detail that would feel new or relevant to her.

ARIA POLICE DEPARTMENT

FULL RECORDED INTERVIEW: KATE CAMBRIA.

AGE 18. SISTER OF LACIE CAMBRIA

CONDUCTED BY: DET. TOM ANDERSON

Q: Please state your name for the record.

A: Kate Cambria.

Q: How do you know Lacie?

A: She's my sister.

Q: I know how difficult this is for you, but can you tell me how you found out your sister was missing?

A: Um… it was late and my parents said she was missing.

Q: Were you home all day?

A: Yeah, it was raining and Mom had… we weren't supposed to go out. Until I went to the movies.

Q: I see. So, can we back up to that morning? Did you see her leave the house at all that day?

A: I saw my sister that morning in her room. She was writing in her journal like always.

Q: She keeps a journal?

A: Yes.

Q: Have you ever read it?

A: No, she'll kill me if I do.

Q: Kill you?

A: I mean, she's private.

Q: Do you know where it is?

A: No.

Q: Do you have a good relationship with your sister?

[pause]

A: [Family Attorney] Kate, you don't need to answer that. Can we get a glass of water?

Kate felt sweaty under her arms, she couldn't believe what she was reading. She skimmed through the rest of the interview. She didn't know if her younger self had been lying on purpose or if her memory problems were already starting to manifest; what she remembered now didn't match what the police transcripts said. Kate knew that she had had problems with her memory since Lacie's disappearance. Sometimes she would lose big chunks of her life. But this seemed specific. Her journal? Kate remembered it vaguely; Lacie had it with her a lot that summer. Did it hold any clue to what happened?

Q: Let's pick up, shall we? So, you don't recall anything about your sister from that morning or the days before?

A: I mean there was nothing different about her if that's what you mean. In the morning it was raining really badly. I told her Mom hated us going out in the rain and she should stay inside. But...

Q: But she went outside anyway?

A: She didn't say a word, she just left. She didn't listen to me.

Q: Did you try to stop her?

[pause]

Q: Do you remember anything else? Was she carrying any luggage with her?

A: I'm not sure. It's all I can really remember right now.

Kate leafed through pages and pages. It was overwhelming. She stopped when she flipped to Barbara's report.

ARIA POLICE DEPARTMENT

FULL RECORDED INTERVIEW: BARBARA
ANDERSON. AGE 17. FRIEND OF LACIE CAMBRIA.
CONDUCTED BY: DET. MORRIS

Q: So, you're a friend of Lacie's?

A: No, not really. I mean I know of her. No one really is friends with the Villa Magda girls. They're strange. I mean we hang out with them, but because we're all a little curious.

Q: What do you mean by strange?

A: Well, the house is supposedly haunted.

Q: That sounds like just a rumor.

A: Maybe.

Q: Okay, let's move on then. Did Lacie ever say anything to you that made it seem she would ever run away?

A: She said she hated her sister once. She wished Kate were dead. She said she didn't need her anymore.

Q: When did she say that?

A: The day Darien saved them from drowning. They were fighting with each other.

Q: What do you think she meant by that?

A: Who knows? Like I said, they're weird.

This was news to her. Kate was hurt. She thought they had all been friends but from the sounds of Barbara's interview, the other kids thought Kate and Lacie were weird. Kate kept looking for other statements. There were dozens, and most of them provided little or no insight. And then she found Charlie's.

Kate could hear voices, breaking her concentration briefly. She looked at the yellowed pages, their edges deteriorating. It probably hadn't been looked at for years.

ARIA POLICE DEPARTMENT

FULL RECORDED INTERVIEW: CHARLIE WILLIAMS.

AGE 18. BOYFRIEND OF KATE CAMBRIA.

CONDUCTED BY: DET. TOM ANDERSON

Q: How do you know Lacie?

A: [Lawyer] You can answer.

A: She is a friend. My friend Katie's sister actually.

Q: Not a girlfriend?

[No answer.]

Q: Look, we just need to find this girl. And if you can help, then we need you to be honest with us. Do you speak with Lacie?

A: Sometimes. Not a lot. I mean, I say hi.

Q: Look, we know that the girls had a fight, and it was over you. We have witnesses from that day at the beach who said so.

A: They fight sometimes. [pause] Sometimes over me.

Q: And why do you say that?

A: [Lawyer] I think we have been very cooperative. If there is any reason to believe my client will be charged with anything, then we will be back. Otherwise, it's getting late.

Q: One more thing. Has she ever mentioned her friend Alice to you?

A: Alice? Um… maybe, I mean I can't be sure.

Q: So, this message we found on her computer to you doesn't mean anything? For the record, I am showing a printout of emails from the family's computer.

A: Like I said before, I don't know.

Kate flipped through the file to see if the printouts were there, but she couldn't find them. So Charlie. And Alice? What did Alice have to do with this? Kate had met Alice that day in the woods, weeks after Lacie went missing. But she was mentioned in the interview? None of it made sense. Kate read Doug and Susan's statements; they were working in the cottage most of the day and the house was quiet. They had cooked for the girls that morning and then gone back in the evening for dinner, when Kate's father realized that Lacie was not in her room. Doug was the one to call his brother-in-law, the chief of police, who came over within the hour.

Charlie walked into the library, startling Kate. She slammed the report closed. She had more questions than ever, and now, her best friends from all these years seemed to be lying as well. She didn't know whom she could trust. Darien—she would have to talk to him and figure out what pieces of this puzzle she needed.

"I'm sorry about before, with Darien," Charlie said sincerely. "I overreacted."

She knew that he meant it. But she also knew that he hadn't told her everything about that summer. She did love Charlie, Kate now knew that. Did he do something to Lacie? Was Alice involved? Kate's head was spinning. She gathered all the papers together. She would have to get back to it later, in the meantime she would find a safe spot for the report. The old gardener, Carl, had said he knew something about Lacie. Doug said that Carl had dementia, but Kate still wanted to know what he was going to say. Maybe he had seen her that day or knew whom she was meeting? In any case, he could be her only shot at getting some answers.

15

"They fell asleep and evening passed,
but no one came to the poor children."
—HANSEL AND GRETEL, GRIMM BROTHERS

Everyone was by the pool when Kate emerged from the house. She watched them for a few minutes, thinking how she wished she could be relaxing with them. Instead, she was losing herself in the past.

She worried they were judging her. What had she been thinking, keeping this from them? She would have to apologize to Molly and Andrew. She wasn't sure how much she wanted to divulge, but she couldn't keep pretending everyone was okay. The cat was already out of the bag and she had to do damage control.

She saw Molly looking at her. Kate waved and Molly looked quickly away, the awkwardness lingering in the air.

Kate sat down in the lounge chair that was next to Alice. She looked at Chloe. She looked like a young Grace Kelly, Kate thought.

"Chloe seems to have fit in perfectly," Alice said.

Kate shifted in her seat uncomfortably. "I ran into Barbara, her cousin, in town. It was weird," Kate whispered.

"Weird?" Alice asked.

"She seemed aggressive, accusing me of horrible things," Kate said.

Alice looked at Kate. "You really don't remember, do you?"

"What did you say?" Kate asked, her blood chilled as she watched Alice put that smile on her face.

"Oh, nothing dear."

Secrets have a very strange way of chipping away slowly at the soul bit by bit. Festering like an open wound. Kate knew that all too well. She wanted to be honest with her friends, to tell them the whole story and lean into their love and support. But, especially after reading the police file, she was afraid no one would believe her. Right now her memories of Lacie before she disappeared seemed as unreal as the ghost she must have dreamed up yesterday in her childhood bedroom.

* * *

As Kate walked upstairs after dinner that night, she heard whispers echoing through the hallway. The light from Molly and Sam's bedroom filtered through the crack in the doorway. Kate paused at the top of the landing as her attention was drawn to Sam's whining voice.

"Do we really have to stay until Monday?"

"It's only a few more days. Kate needs us." Molly reasoned with him.

"Does she? It seems like Kate is spending most of her time avoiding us. And there is something strange about this house. Didn't you hear those noises last night? I could barely sleep."

"It's an old house. Of course, there are noises. Besides, it's the least we can do, Sam. We can't leave before her birthday."

Sam murmured something indistinguishable in response before Kate heard something shift. A shadow passed under the doorway, and Kate jumped slightly, remembering where she was. She hurried to her room, stepping inside just as Sam yanked open his door and huffed down the stairs.

Kate's mind reeled. Had Sam heard the same whispers? She let out a long breath. She felt a strong sense of relief that it wasn't just her, but then guilt twisted her stomach. Molly and Sam were arguing because of her. She moved to her bedroom window, catching sight of Charlie smoking by the pool. The flickering light of his cigar comforted her.

Later, Charlie stumbled into bed. His hands searched for her body. For the first time, she felt as if he could be a stranger. He quickly fell asleep after two vigorous but failed attempts at trying to rouse her. Once Kate could hear his steady breathing, she shifted in the bed, wide-awake and staring at the high beam ceiling. She tried to compartmentalize all that had occurred in the last few days. Running into Barbara had shaken her to the core. She needed to dig more to find out what secrets her sister had. Her head pounding from too little sleep and too much wine, she looked over at Charlie. She realized that over the years, any time she tried bringing up that summer to him, he would quickly change the subject. He would always say that he didn't want to mention Lacie or that summer and that it wasn't healthy for her. But what if there was another reason he didn't want to bring up that summer? What if he was guilty of something? She heard whispers again. For a moment, she thought it was Chloe, Ben, and Andrew, and got up and put her robe on. The moonlight accentuated Charlie's body on the bed as Kate tiptoed toward the door. The voices were louder now. She opened the door quickly and looked down the hall—it was empty. Terrified, Kate closed the door and went back to bed. Kate was worried that maybe, like her mother, she was losing her grip on reality. She lay there until she finally drifted off to sleep, wondering what the whispers were trying to tell her as she pondered the thought of her husband being the biggest secret keeper of them all.

PRESENT DAY

POLICE FILE—ARIA, MAINE.

CASE 1583

Q: Tell me about Chloe. Do you like her?

A: I don't know her that well. We just met. But she seems great. Although I think she was looking for something here at the house. I am not sure what.

Q: Looking for something?

A: She was curious about this place, she said. I guess there were ghost stories she had heard. Something about the Villa being cursed. We just thought it was weird at first, and that she was just trying to scare us.

Q: And now?

A: We should have believed her.

16

SATURDAY

"The witch led Hansel to a little stable and shut him in.
'He must be fattened up. And when he is fat enough I will eat him,'
she said to Gretel."
—*HANSEL AND GRETEL,* GRIMM BROTHERS

Kate woke up feeling groggy, having been unable to sleep for most of the night. She would go for a swim, she thought—that might help her feel refreshed. The sooner she got rid of this awful place, the better.

From her bedroom window, Kate saw Chloe walking toward the house. She thought about how much Susan and Doug had wanted their own child, and realized she was happy for them despite her feelings for Chloe. Kate shut the curtain and opened the dresser drawer, settling on a pair of shorts and a T-shirt. As she started down the stairs, she practically ran into Chloe, who was on her way up.

"You startled me," Kate said. "What are you doing here? I think Andrew and Ben are already outside."

"I could ask you the same question," Chloe said with an air of cool defiance.

"I'm sorry?" Kate looked at her, feeling a bit awkward on the stairs, blocked by Chloe.

"Why are you here?" Chloe asked. "I mean all these years, you never came back, my parents missed you, your mother missed you. Now, you come here and act as if you cared."

"You don't know anything about it, you're just a child—it is actually none of your business."

"You took the easy way and stayed away until it was convenient for you to come back. You don't know what it's like to live here with everything that happened, just like a typical out-of-towner."

"You mean everything that happened with Lacie."

"No one ever said her name out loud," Chloe said mournfully.

"I didn't realize how difficult it still was," Kate admitted quietly.

Chloe looked at her. "What was she like? I mean I know what she looked like, but…"

Kate swallowed. "She was my little sister. We all loved her."

Both Kate and Chloe paused, an awkward silence growing between them.

"I was walking down the driveway on the night your mother died, and I saw her looking out of Lacie's window. I told my mom she was in there. It was weird, you know, because she had it locked all the time. My parents made sure she stayed out of that room. It was too hard for her heart, they said."

Kate took a deep breath. "I didn't know you saw her that

night. I'm sorry you had to see her like that."

Chloe shrugged and shifted on the stairs. "This place is beautiful, you know, but sometimes it can feel..." Chloe stopped. Kate looked at her.

"Feel like what?" Kate asked, probing.

"Nothing," Chloe turned around and headed back downstairs.

"Mom!" Andrew called from the bottom of the stairs. "What is this?"

"What is it?" Kate answered. "Are you okay?" Kate followed Andrew's voice and saw him standing next to Chloe. The expression on her face was unreadable. Sam and Charlie came in to see what the issue was, crowding around.

"Do you know about this fucking blog?" Andrew demanded, but he sounded confused. Sam took Andrew's phone and started reading aloud.

ARIA TODAY

LACIE'S SISTER RETURNS

BY BARBARA ANDERSON

Kate Williams, née Cambria, sister of missing Lacie Cambria is back in town for the 18th anniversary of her sister's disappearance. She has returned to sell the Villa Magda estate. The sighting has brought up a very dark page in our town's history. The disappearance of Lacie. Those among us who were here could never forget that day that turned so dark. For those who weren't there, here is a brief summary of the events.

It all started on a hot August summer day. The town's kids were enjoying the usual joys of summer in Maine, the freedom longed for all year. Beaches and boats, strawberries and camp, swimming and bonfires. The week had been unusually hot and most were

161

down by the beach. Then, that day, it rained heavily. Katie and Lacie were home. The events then become fuzzy. The police never figured out what happened exactly, but it is believed that Lacie and Kate were out in the woods and only one of them came back. And that night, the searching began. The whole town took part in a search that went on for days, weeks, even months. Every inch of the forest was combed and every corner of every beach. Not a trace. Not a clue.

Since then, there have been rumors and sightings, even crazy rumors like the one of the jealous sister trying in every way to get rid of her pesky sister or the haunted house where the two sisters lived, but nothing has been proven.

After that, the girls' mother withdrew into the magnificent Villa Magda and just recently passed away. We have gotten news that the house is to be put on the market very shortly. Will anyone buy the house with the cursed past?

We are all hoping to hear more from Kate Williams and learn if she has discovered any more details of that fateful night.

"Let me see that," Kate hissed as she took the phone from Sam. Kate looked to Charlie for help.

"That author has nothing better to do than to make up crazy stories about your mother," Charlie said.

Chloe shifted.

Some of the tension in Kate's neck unknotted with the relief that Charlie came to her aid.

Andrew pouted. "How many other people know about your sister?"

"Just ignore it. This was written by a busybody in town."

Sam rolled his eyes. "I'm going to go outside; this is clearly a family issue."

"You've acted weird since we've been here," Andrew stated once Sam was out of the room.

Kate knew he was right, which left her with no idea of how to respond. After a few moments of silence, Andrew and Chloe walked off.

That article had made it seem like she had had something to do with Lacie disappearing. She'd seen the doubt in her son's eyes, and it killed her. She was aware that she shouldn't have used them to buffer her feelings. Maybe she should have just come here alone—or told them all the truth.

"Kate," Charlie said, bringing her back to the room and her current predicament. "Please talk to me. Don't worry about that stupid blog."

"Easy for you to say."

Let's pack up and leave today," he said, pulling her toward him. "Please Kate, come on. I have a bad feeling."

"No" Kate shook her head. "I can't now, don't you get it? Darien—"

"Darien? What about him? He's the reason for this," Charlie said. "He followed you around like a puppy dog."

"He was here for Susan and Doug, helping them a lot. She's his aunt. We were friends," she insisted.

"Lacie was positive that there was something going on between the two of you," Charlie blurted.

"What did you just say?" Kate looked at him, her mouth agape. "Lacie? When did you speak to Lacie about me and Darien? Or at all, for that matter?"

Charlie backtracked. "I remember once she said something, maybe that day at the beach."

"You told me that you hardly saw Lacie, yet she was talking to you about me?" Kate said, raising her voice. "You don't see how that seems strange?"

"Kate, what is the big deal? So, maybe I talked to her when I was waiting for you outside, or that day at the beach. Does it matter?"

"Of course it fucking matters," she snapped, furious. "How could you act like it doesn't? Every little detail matters when someone goes missing. No one knows what happened to her, where she went, or what her frame of mind was. You don't think that could be a big deal?" Kate asked, her voice trembling with anger.

Charlie looked at her. "I don't know if any of it matters anymore."

"Do you remember when the police questioned you that summer? You told me they had come to your house." She could feel her heart race, afraid of what she was thinking.

"Questioned me?" Charlie shrugged. "They questioned all of us."

"About Lacie? Do you remember what you said to them?" Kate continued.

"It's been nearly twenty years. I just remember they came to the house and asked me if I had been with you. And then asked a ton of questions about Lacie and if I had noticed anything unusual," he said. "I just told them I had been with you and that no, I hardly saw Lacie much, especially during those last few weeks. I was a kid."

"Stop saying that." Kate clenched her teeth.

"What?"

"Stop saying you were just a damn kid, or that we were kids. Kids do stupid things all the time. Things that have consequences." She was afraid to probe but was also desperate to get to the bottom of it. Heart pounding, she asked, "Are you telling the truth, Charlie? I need to know."

"This is exactly what I was afraid of coming here. It's not healthy, and this is your bullshit to deal with, that's the truth. None of us here care about Lacie. And none of this will ever bring her back. Do you get that?" He spoke in a tone she had never heard before, his face turned away from her and his body tense.

Kate looked at him as if for the first time, and fear took over. She was afraid of him, of what he was capable of. Had he lied to her? And was he still lying?

"What about the day we almost drowned?" Kate pushed. "Susan said that Lacie thought I was trying to drown her that day. I was trying to save her."

"Maybe you weren't, Katie. Maybe you just thought you were," Charlie said, his voice quieter now.

* * *

The house was agitated. Stirring up trouble again as it always had. The arguing, the jealousy, and distrust were all too familiar to Villa Magda. It riled things up and then spit the bones out. Being back here made Kate realize feelings she had never been able to articulate as a child. She wished that Max had never built the house for Magda. There was no love here. She sensed that now. She just needed to put her own doubts to rest, and she would wipe her hands of Villa Magda once and for all. She and Charlie could return to Connecticut, where everything made sense—where she didn't see people who weren't there, and didn't have to wonder if her husband was lying to her. She didn't care, in that moment, what the truth was. She just wanted to have her life the way it used to be.

She tried to focus on what she had read in the police file, to keep her terror of the house and of Charlie and of the unknown at bay. She had forgotten all about Lacie's journal until she read about it in her own statement. Why hadn't the police looked for it, or mentioned it to her mother? Of course, maybe they had and Kate just didn't know or remember. Had Lacie taken the journal with her? Or maybe her mother had found it and kept it a secret? It would have been in the report if they'd found it, wouldn't it? She would have to ask Darien later.

* * *

After her fight with Charlie, Kate found Andrew outside by himself. She didn't know what to say. He looked at Kate with different eyes, his adoration of her wavering.

"I don't understand why you wouldn't say anything about your sister to me." His big brown eyes were soft and tender.

She looked at him and wanted to hug him but knew he would withdraw. He was too big for that now, she thought sadly. And at the moment, too upset with her to let her do the comforting.

"I was going to tell you myself," Kate said quietly. "I just wanted to find the right time."

Her tidy world was a mess now. She couldn't admit to Andrew that she had never truly gotten over the disappearance, or that she now blamed herself for it more than ever. She certainly couldn't tell him that maybe his father knew something.

"Who would hide something like that from their son?"

Andrew asked, obviously upset. "What happened to her? Did you know something?"

Kate could hardly speak, her voice trembling. "Of course not," she said, defending herself—although a small part of her was beginning to doubt that was even true anymore.

"Chloe has been researching the house and your family," Andrew said. "She found old articles online. All about you."

"She did what? Which articles?" Kate asked, tears welling up in her eyes. She wished she'd never come back to the house. Wherever Lacie was, she was enjoying this. The attention was all on her again.

"Articles that make it seem like you had something to do with all of it. You were the last one to see her, Mom," Andrew said, his eyes welling up with tears. She could see the little boy in him. "That's what everyone in town thinks."

"Tell Chloe to mind her own business," Kate said. All she wanted to do was get as far away from all of them as she could. She slammed the door and ran across the lawn, heading toward the woods. She wanted to lose herself there and never turn back. The last time she had been in these woods, she'd met Alice.

Kate walked through the woods, as far from the house as she dared, and sat down. She wondered if her sister had met someone here that day. Who? Kate wished she could just shut her brain off completely.

Kate was more determined than ever to prove everyone's theory about her wrong. She wasn't some crazy jealous sibling who wanted her sister to be gone. She needed proof that something happened to her sister that had nothing to do with her. What had Chloe found? Kate glanced at her phone and was grateful when she noticed she still had one bar of wifi. She typed in her sister's name on her phone and waited impatiently as the results loaded. Kate scrolled through the articles, and pictures of Lacie popped up. There were so many crazy theories, one even mentioned that she may have been abducted by a cult or aliens. Kate was looking for more than half an hour without finding anything useful. She was exhausted, her eyes were weary when she found a Reddit thread titled *"What happened to Lacie Cambria?"* It was dedicated to Lacie's disappearance. Pages and pages went over Lacie's life, Kate's life, their mother, the sad history of Villa Magda, and the days leading up to Lacie's disappearance. She scanned through the numerous threads looking for something new that she might have overlooked in the past. Kate hoped she could find something that made sense to her. Kate's eyes watered as she read the small print. One post jumped out at her:

r/laciecambria

the boyfriend did it: I think it was the sister's boyfriend. He got the sister pregnant and there was for sure something going on between him and Lacie.

Posted by Adrien_A_69 7 hours ago 30 Comments

Seven hours ago. Kate read through the comments. They each had their theory about Charlie. But one was different, Kate noticed:

Meg123321: No way! He was so in love with Katie. He wouldn't have ever looked at Lacie.

Adrien_A_69 there was something going on there. He was

seeing both sisters. We all knew it.

Kate's heart felt like it was beating out of her chest. She jotted down the user's name. Who was this person? How would anyone know about her pregnancy? It hadn't been in any of the newspaper articles, and Kate had gotten pregnant after she left Aria. The only people in the town who knew about it were her parents and Susan and Doug.

The threads continued, but nothing else popped up that seemed as important. Kate went back and clicked on Adrien_A_69 and a page appeared.

Kate felt like she was finally onto something. There were dozens of photos of Lacie she couldn't recall ever seeing before. Lacie at the beach. Lacie at the ice cream shop. Lacie in her room. Where did these photos come from? It had to be Barbara, Kate thought. Who else would have photos of Lacie? She seemed to know a lot about the case, and she would have access to all this information through her father. Kate hoped it was her. She googled Barbara's name, and her website appeared. On the front page was a blog post titled "The Mystery That Shook Aria." Kate's breath quickened with each post she read—Barbara was using this as a platform for a true crime book she was in the process of writing. The thought of her exploiting them like this made Kate furious.

She clicked on an entry and there was a photo of her, from the day they almost drowned. The entry was titled, "*Sisters Almost Drown. Accident?*" In the post, Barbara claimed that everyone overheard the two of them bickering loudly on the beach.

"Lacie ran into the ocean and her sister followed her. We could all hear Katie screaming at her. That's when my brother jumped in, and good thing he did or they would both be dead. Well, maybe one of them ended up dead at the hands of a spiteful sister?"

A spiteful sister? Had she been and not realized it? As she scrolled, another photo from that day appeared. She looked closely, zooming in, and saw herself sitting on the beach, her head down. Lacie was standing a few feet away, talking with Charlie. And that's when Kate noticed it. It was so slight and hard to pinpoint at first glance, but when you looked close enough, you could see the dainty butterfly locket around Lacie's neck. Kate's chest tightened. She could hardly breathe. Why had she not remembered it before? Lacie was wearing it that day. Did Charlie give it to her? Back then, had Kate suspected that Charlie and her sister were having some sort of secret relationship?

Kate felt her hairs on the back of her neck tingle. She whipped her head up, fully expecting to see Lacie standing in front of her, but instead, she found Charlie standing there. A shiver of fear slid down her spine. At that moment, she wondered if the father of her son was hiding something about her sister.

"Kate! What are you doing?" he asked.

"I'm just working." Kate lied. "Putting together the menu for my dinner."

"Well, everyone is out by the pool, it would be nice if you would join us. After all, they all came to be with you and now I find you in the woods? It's getting embarrassing," he said, annoyed. "If this continues, I'm going to pack up and leave tonight. I mean it."

"Sorry, I have to run some errands in town. Would you mind just holding down the fort a little while longer?" Kate asked as she got up. "I just want everything to be perfect. And I know

I've been acting a little crazy, but…"

"Kate, I mean it. No more of this, I think you need to call your therapist. Maybe she can help?"

"She can't help. She hasn't helped me regain my memory, she just tells me to dig deeper, and that's what I'm doing here." Kate felt desperate, but she just couldn't muster the courage to confront him about Lacie yet. It would have to wait until she found out more.

17

"Early in the morning before the children were awake,
she was already up, and when she saw both of them sleeping
and looking so pretty,
with their plump and rosy cheeks
she muttered to herself: 'That will be a dainty mouthful!'"
—HANSEL AND GRETEL, GRIMM BROTHERS

Kate hoped Charlie believed that she was running errands. She had never outright lied to her husband before. It was time to confront Barbara about the article and find out exactly what she knew, and she knew Charlie would have been upset if she'd told him that. Kate had easily found Barbara's home address online, and thought about how scary it was that it was so simple to track people down these days. A quick name search and you could find out all sorts of things—their age, political affiliation, sometimes even what car they drove. There was no hiding in the era of the internet.

Pulling her SUV across the street from the address, Kate looked at the small saltbox Cape across the street. It had been neglected—the bushes were sparse and the lawn dried up, and the front door had the wear and tear of years of harsh weather and no upkeep. A small Ford was in the driveway, and Kate could hear a dog barking. She hoped it wasn't a big one. She went over her prepared speech for Barbara and took a deep breath. She would ask her point-blank about the post and if she was "Adrien_A_69" and what she knew about Lacie.

Kate turned off the ignition, hesitating as she saw a police car pull up. It was Darien. Kate slouched down, fearing that Darien might see her. He had been so helpful so far, but if he thought that Kate was going after his sister, he may not be as forthcoming. He approached the front door, and knocked, a disheveled Barbara answering fairly quickly. He walked into the house, slamming the door behind him. Kate lowered her window. She couldn't make out the words but could tell they were arguing. Barbara looked like a wounded animal. Darien was angry. She had never seen him so upset.

She would have to wait or come back later. Kate drove away, trying to figure out her next step. She thought about Carl, the old man who was in her home. Hadn't he said he knew something about Lacie? Maybe it was the ramblings of an old man, but maybe not. Kate would pay him a visit.

A few blocks away, Kate looked up "Carl Warren" and "Aria, Maine" on her phone and found his address in the White pages. She hoped that her hunch was right and that Carl hadn't been delusional when he said he knew something about Lacie. Kate arrived at the small house on the other side of town. As she approached the house, she looked in the window. A man who looked a lot like Carl was sitting on the couch next to Chloe. Kate assumed this was Carl's brother, but she was surprised to see Chloe. Kate approached the door and rang the bell.

The man answered the door. His surprised look turned to anger once he recognized her.

"Get the hell off of my property or I will have you arrested," he said firmly as he tried shutting the door on Kate's face.

"I'm sorry, I'm just here to see Carl," she replied. "My name is..."

"I know who you are," he snarled.

"He came to my house. Please, I just wanted to talk to him," Kate begged.

"I don't think that is a good idea. You have upset him enough. I think you should just leave him alone."

"I'm sorry, I didn't mean for that to happen."

"He dedicated years to your family up at that house. He spent weeks looking for your sister and then did all he could to be there for your mother, and this is the thanks he gets?"

"I realized he was trying to tell me something about my sister. Please, if there is anything he knows, then I would hope you could tell me," Kate pleaded.

"Why don't you ask your husband?" The man sneered.

"I'm sorry, what was that?" Kate said, her hands shaky.

"Charlie isn't it, the Williams boy, his father sure did a good job of covering up what he did to his classmate back at that school of his."

"I'm not sure what you're implying," Kate said, trying to catch herself from faltering. This man was lying about Charlie.

"Why are you here, dredging all of this up again?" He slammed the door before Kate had a chance to interject.

Kate stood in shock. As she walked to her car, she wondered if maybe it was time to pack up and leave Villa Magda.

As she drove away from the house, movement in her rear-view mirror caught her eye. In the distance, she could have sworn that she saw Chloe watching her from the porch.

* * *

When Kate returned home, she sat in her car, trying to decide what to do. She looked at the house, sitting there menacing, the windows like eyes judging her. Her eyes were drawn to Charlie as he jogged over to the car, her mind replaying the fear that she had been the one to hurt Lacie and Charlie had known all along.

She looked up at the house again, at Lacie's window, and jumped out of the car, slamming her door behind her. A figure stood in the window watching her. Her heart fluttered with fear, and she looked back at Charlie.

"Do... you see that?" Kate stammered as she pointed to Lacie's window. "Don't tell me you didn't see that?" she said, her voice shaking.

"See what?" Charlie looked up.

The trees next to the house created just the right amount of shade, but the sun was dizzying nonetheless. Kate looked up again and there it was—a slight figure, a woman, she could tell by the curve.

Alice's voice startled her as she came out to join them. "What's going on?"

"Someone is standing there, in Lacie's window," Kate whispered, suddenly wishing she hadn't.

"No one is there," Charlie said, his irritation evident in his voice. He was looking at her as if she were insane.

"The door to that room is locked, Kate. Remember? It is just your imagination." Charlie took a long, deep breath. "I don't want to hear another word about Lacie. You can't change anything. There's nothing to discover. Lacie is gone."

Alice's face was creased with worry as she looked intently at the window. She saw the figure too. Kate could tell.

"Come, let's go upstairs," Alice murmured. "I'm tired, and it's hot out here, and I think you need a nap." Alice waited for Kate.

They walked to the house together, and Alice whispered in her ear, "I told you so."

Kate looked at her with her brow furrowed. She wasn't sure what Alice meant, but she hated being told she was wrong. Kate wasn't quite ready for the entire truth just yet, she thought, though her mind slipped to the key sitting at the bottom of her nightstand drawer.

* * *

Upstairs, Kate stood in front of Lacie's door, her heart beating wildly in her chest. She turned the knob, expecting the door to swing open and reveal someone in the room. But nothing happened. The handle wouldn't twist. The door was still locked, Kate realized with a sigh of relief, her shoulders relaxing. It must have been her imagination, just like Charlie said.

Alice suggested that Kate lie down for a while. She didn't argue. She would tell Charlie she wanted to leave, that he was right all along. She shifted restlessly. This place was making everything worse. She couldn't trust anyone—not even herself.

As Kate closed her eyes to ease her building migraine, a quiet chanting began to fill her ears.

Little Lacie went to run
All she wanted was some fun

She disappeared into the woods
Now little Lacie's gone for good.

"Who's there?" Kate cried out as she jolted from her bed. But the chanting was only in her head. It was just a dream. Kate sighed. She lay down onto the bed again, waiting for her heartbeat to slow, memories playing in her mind. She could hire a lawyer to take care of selling the house and make sure that Doug and Susan were taken care of. Yes, tomorrow they would pack up and leave this place and Lacie behind once and for all.

* * *

Kate and Lacie were playing "Secret Language" for the first time. It was a game where the letters were all jumbled up. Lacie picked it up right away, but it took Kate a little longer to understand the game.

"What is a short sleep and something you cook with?" Lacie had asked, eager for the answer.

"I don't know. Can you give me a hint?"

"Nope. You have to practice, Katie. It's gonna be our language."

Kate had finally guessed. "A nap?"

"That's it, Katie. Come on. You know it."

"Please, just tell me!"

"Nope. Those are not the rules," Lacie had teased. "You have to follow the rules."

"Fine. I'll figure it out."

"Jumble the words for a nap, something you cook in?"

"A pan."

"See, those two are connected. Anagrams PAN and NAP."

They had spent hours on these riddles until the language had become second nature.

18

*"Just keep your noise to yourself," said the old
woman, "it won't help you at all."*
—HANSEL AND GRETEL, GRIMM BROTHERS

Suddenly, there was screaming, and Kate sat up in bed, disoriented. For a moment, she wasn't sure if the scream had been real or if she had been dreaming about fighting with Lacie. Then she heard the angry voices coming from somewhere in the house. She rushed out of her room and followed the voices downstairs to the hall.

"You were too!" Chloe shrieked. "You're a freak!"

Andrew was caught in the middle. Kate could see him struggling.

"She's only hanging out with you because she's obsessed with your mom anyway." Ben's voice was higher now.

Chloe lunged toward him. "You little shit!"

"Hey, hey!" Kate put her arms out. "Stop it!" She pushed against Chloe and Ben, breaking them up.

"Ben?" said Molly, as she and Sam rushed in. "What's going on?"

Chloe started crying. "He had my phone," she sobbed. "He was snooping around. Creep."

"She's been taking pictures and snooping around the house, like a stalker. I found her going through a box in the study the other day. And you—" he turned to Andrew. "You're letting her do this to your mom, what does that make you?"

"Ben! Stop it." Molly's voice was stern.

Andrew lunged at Ben.

Kate shrieked. "Andrew!" She rushed toward her son, instinctively making a barrier between them. Then she looked at Andrew as if she hardly knew him anymore. "That's enough!" Kate said. "No one is doing anything to anyone! Is that clear?" Her heart was beating loudly in her ears. She wondered if anyone could hear it. Déjà vu has a strange way of appearing. Like a shadow. Images flashed as if she had seen this scene once before. Only Chloe wasn't Chloe, but Lacie.

Kate turned to Chloe and looked at her. "Is any of this true?" she asked.

Chloe stood there and looked her directly in the eye. "You're the crazy one. Who doesn't remember anything about a missing sister?"

"Chloe," Andrew said, a warning tone in his voice, and looked at his mother. He felt bad; Kate could tell.

"It's true. People think she had something to do with this. It's all over the internet, not to mention the town. She's trying to blame anyone else, but she's the one to blame. Even my family thinks so. And she kept you in the dark." Chloe's words rang like a sharp pain in Kate's ears. She turned to Kate, her eyes shooting daggers into Kate's chest. "What happened to Lacie?"

* * *

Kate went looking for Charlie. She found him in the study, on his laptop, typing frantically. She could tell he was deep in work; his shoulders betrayed his stress. Lately, it seemed like something serious was going on at the firm. But at this moment, Kate needed the old Charlie, she needed her rock.

"Did you hear all the yelling?" Kate demanded, but he continued typing, ignoring her, which only made Kate more irate. She wanted to shake him. "I told you she was a bad influence, but you wouldn't listen."

Charlie's eyes never left his laptop, and Kate felt something in her deflate. "Say something," she whispered. If loud didn't work, she would try going quiet.

"What do you want me to say, Kate?" Charlie looked at her. "This is all your doing."

"Andrew yelled and tried to hit Ben! You heard him. And you heard Ben—she's obsessed with me and Lacie!" Kate was unable to control herself; she was livid.

"You're not the only one who's having problems now, Kate!" Charlie yelled, suddenly inches away from her face. He put his head in his hands and took a deep sigh. "Kate." She could see sweat on his brow. He was fidgeting. "I was afraid of this. I hate to say I told you so."

"Why didn't you ever tell me about you and Lacie?" she asked. "Please just tell me the truth."

"We were… We were just kids. I know you don't want me to say that anymore, but it's true." Charlie's eyes were watering as the words flowed out of him.

"What else happened?" Kate asked, afraid to hear more.

"It's not what you think. She—" Charlie ran his hands through his hair. "Kate… Do you remember the night I asked you out?"

Kate nodded.

Charlie, usually so confident and collected, now looked pained as he tried to get the words out. "I haven't been completely honest with you. My friends and I were idiots…" He cleared his throat. "Everyone thought that you and Lacie were strange, so my friends dared me to ask you out." Charlie swallowed, eyes meeting Kate's for the first time.

Kate's head swam. All of her feelings growing up—feelings of insecurity, unworthiness—were they valid after all? "I don't understand," Kate whispered. "What does this have to do with Lacie?"

"I didn't think anyone had heard us make the dare, but a few weeks later, Lacie started messaging me, telling me that she knew about the dare and she was going to tell you. But by that point, Kate, I had fallen for you."

"Even though it was all a lie."

"No, it wasn't. I realized how amazing you were that night when we started talking. But Lacie never believed me. She always assumed I was just using you. She became obsessed, threatening to tell you if I didn't. At first it was just little things she would say to me, but then she followed me, showed up at my house, my summer job, the beach, my tennis games. That photo that you saw in the file? I confronted her at your mom's party. I was trying to get her to back off, but she was being so unreasonable. You know how she was."

"So, you thought you would just never tell me?" Kate accused. She suddenly felt nauseous. Kate knew she was over-reacting, but she couldn't help it. The room was spinning. Too many memories had come to light over the last few days; she felt unhinged.

"I was going to, but it was your birthday and then…"

"She disappeared," Kate finished his sentence. The reality of it was hitting her.

"Kate, I told you she was troubled. I was afraid of what she would say or do," Charlie explained. She remembered the lengths her sister would go to to get her way.

"I just thought she was being a dramatic teenager like we all were at times, but then you were fighting that day and both went into the ocean and swam far out like that. I was terrified. You both almost drowned. You have to believe that I would never hurt anyone."

"Oh my God," Kate cried. "How could you not tell me any of this?"

Charlie shook his head. "She's gone. It's neither of our faults, Kate. Don't make this a bigger deal than it needs to be."

"If you had told me what was happening, maybe I could have talked to her. She wanted my attention, don't you see? It had nothing to do with you. She was angry with me. For ignoring her, for choosing you over her. She had no one. My mother was busy and my father was away. I was all she had, and I abandoned her for a boy."

"Calm down, Kate. You didn't abandon her," Charlie said.

"You keeping this from me makes me wonder what else you

are hiding from me," Kate said. "What if…"

"What if?'"

"Did you… did you do something to her?" Kate asked, her hands shaking.

"What? How could you even think such a thing?" Charlie said in shock. "I love you. You know me. I would never have hurt her or anyone."

But Kate wasn't so sure about that anymore. For all she knew, Charlie wasn't who she thought he was.

He grabbed her, hard.

"You are the one hiding stuff, Kate. I've always just tried to protect you."

"You're hurting me," Kate whimpered, her strength gone.

Charlie let go. Defeated, he looked down at her wrists. They were red from his rough hold.

"Believe what you want. I'm telling you the truth." He sighed heavily. "I'll stay here tomorrow, for you, but I'm tired. It's this house, Kate. It's gotten to you. And I don't know how much more I can protect you." He said, leaving her alone in the room.

She heard bustling outside the window and looked down. Doug had turned on the barbecue and was grilling burgers. Andrew and Chloe sat on pool chairs with drinks in their hands while keeping their distance from Ben. Sam was waiting for the burgers by the barbecue, as Molly gazed out toward the ocean while sipping on yet another cocktail.

"Kate, join us," called Alice from the hallway. "We're waiting for you."

PRESENT DAY
POLICE FILE—ARIA, MAINE.
CASE 1583

Q: When you first saw the body in the pool, were you surprised to see who it was?

A: Actually, I wasn't. I can't say why, but I sort of expected it.

19

SUNDAY

*"Gretel began to weep bitterly, but it was all in vain,
for she was forced to do what the wicked witch commanded."*
—*HANSEL AND GRETEL*, GRIMM BROTHERS

Villa Magda was definitely purring. Kate could sense it. The soft humming of satisfaction. The energy they had all brought was awakening it. She could tell that the house was thriving off all the fighting. It had been still for too long. The uncomfortable fighting, the questioning looks, it was all familiar; it had happened before. Kate could tell that the house was thrilled that all was coming to surface. She just wasn't sure if she wanted to stay any longer.

The room was still dark when Kate woke up. She was groggy and soaked in her own sweat. It was the middle of the night. The fight with Charlie had been one of the worst they'd ever had. She looked at Charlie as he slept peacefully. How could he sleep after all that had happened? She got out of bed and slipped off her sticky nightgown, exposing her naked body. She reached for the drawer and took a fresh t-shirt out and pulled it over her head. When she pulled it down, she stopped, startled to see Alice standing in the doorway. She hadn't heard the door open. *Had Alice seen her naked?* Kate wondered, a bit embarrassed.

"I could hardly sleep either," Alice whispered. "Somehow it feels like it is hotter at night than during the day."

"Do you want tea? I was going to make some," Kate cut the silence between them.

Alice nodded. Together they walked down the hall as the moonlight began to peek out from behind clouds. Kate fiddled through the kitchen until she found the teapot.

"I don't know that it was a good idea that we all come here," Kate said. "Things seem so tense. You saw what happened last night… It's just, it's better to be alone sometimes. Everyone seems on edge, and I just have a bad feeling, like something terrible is going to happen." She found tea bags and placed one into a cup for her and one for Alice.

Alice shifted in her chair. She was uncomfortable. "I've been hearing things."

Kate looked at her, surprised. "Like what?"

"Same as you, whispers. I don't know—it's not a happy place."

The black teapot started hissing along with Kate who was seething underneath. She wanted to scream at Alice. *What are you hiding?*

"I used to love this house. Summers were so full of promise. And then Lacie changed all that," Kate said.

"Did she?" Alice asked.

Stop it. Kate wanted to scream.

"It does feel creepy, unsettled, sad. It's a sad house," Alice continued.

She looked at Alice. "It isn't just the house. It's us. We're all messed up. Molly and Sam are on the brink of self-imploding. Andrew and Ben are fighting because of a girl, and Charlie and I…" Kate stopped herself.

Alice sipped her tea. "You will tell me when you're ready, I suppose."

Kate looked at her not sure that this time she would.

"You always do," Alice continued. "I mean if it were about you and Charlie, you could tell me."

Kate turned away from Alice as she took a deep breath, trying to remain calm.

"But then again, you have been keeping secrets from me for years, haven't you, Katie?"

Kate jumped and turned to look at Alice, only it wasn't Alice standing there but Lacie, dressed in her white dress soiled with dirt, her hollow eyes staring back at her. Kate felt a scream, but it wouldn't come out. And then she woke up, panting and sweaty.

Charlie was looking at her. "What is it?"

"A dream. It seemed so real."

"I'm so sorry for not telling you about Lacie. It didn't mean anything." He looked worried as he kissed her on the head as if she were a child.

Emotion overcame her then, and she wept—for her sister, for her mom, and for the doubt that she had allowed in.

"It's going to be okay. I promise," he said into her hair.

Kate wanted to believe it all would be, and for this moment as he kissed her and caressed her hair, she did.

20

"When four weeks had gone by, and Hansel still remained thin, [the witch] was seized with impatience and would not wait any longer."
—*HANSEL AND GRETEL*, GRIMM BROTHERS

Kate woke up early and snuck outside before anyone could see her, finding her way to the garden. She would let the others know that they needed to leave by the end of the day. Carl was right—the house was no longer safe for her, for anyone.

She went to the maze and was startled to find Alice sitting in the grass in front of the entrance. "I do love this flower," Alice said, holding a tall, purple bloom. "What's it called again?"

"They're alliums," Kate replied, remembering how much Lacie had adored the giant flowers shaped like pom-poms. Her mother had planted them to make her happy.

"They symbolize prosperity and good fortune. It's funny, I

think my mother actually believed that it meant something."

"Well, they are beautiful."

"Sometimes I feel you like it when I need you so much," Kate admitted in a quiet breath, knowing she would hurt Alice, but not caring anymore.

"Why would you say that?" Alice looked sad.

Kate sighed. She suddenly imagined what life would have been like without Alice all those years. Alice who was there when her sister disappeared, Alice whom she could call in the middle of the night, Alice who was always trying to help.

They sat there quietly, the two of them. The vegetable garden looked lush next to the hedges, with large heirloom tomatoes, cucumbers, and squash. The house looked lovely, even normal, to anyone who didn't know what had happened there. Each generation had its own tragedies, but maybe Kate would be able to break the pattern.

"I'm going to tell the others we should leave," Kate said.

"Are you sure?" Alice asked. "I don't think you really want to."

"I think we have to. It's not safe here."

"I think you have to see this through, for everyone's sake," Alice said softly.

Kate took a deep breath. The house watched. It always did. There was something about being here, almost as if all sense of time was lost, days blurring into the night. She wasn't even sure what day it was anymore. When she thought about it, Kate wanted to leave, to go back to her life and forget all of this again—but there was a need, a pull, to know the truth. She could see that it was slowly being revealed piece by piece. She knew now that Alice had known Lacie; she just didn't know how or why Alice had kept that from her—unless Alice had something to do with Lacie's disappearance. Questions kept swirling in Kate's mind. Nothing made sense yet, except she now realized that everyone had been keeping secrets from her that summer, and maybe Alice and Charlie were still keeping secrets. She hated that Alice was right. She did need to see this through. They had come this far, and she would always doubt Alice, her husband, and even herself if she didn't find out what really happened to Lacie.

"Maybe, you're right. It's just one more day, right? Maybe I need this day to answer some more questions, and if I don't find anything we can close this chapter," Kate said, trying to convince herself as much as she was trying to convince Alice.

* * *

It was Sunday, her birthday, and she had planned a beautiful day for all of them. Kate appreciated how her friends were sticking around, despite everything, to help her celebrate her birthday. After she and Alice got back from the garden, Susan greeted her with mimosas and blueberry pancakes.

By midday, the adults had all been drinking too much. As Kate was relaxing in the cool kitchen, Molly stumbled inside, giggling, almost falling flat on her face. She regained her balance and slurred her words.

"Come on, Kate, come swimming with me."

It will take more than two Advil to help her, Kate thought, looking at Sam.

He shrugged. "She'll be fine in time for the party. Don't worry," he said, watching his wife go outside.

Kate nodded, not wanting to draw attention to it further.

She watched as Molly approached the pool.

"Molly," Kate called out. But Molly was already running toward the pool, peeling her clothes off. "Shouldn't we make sure she's okay?" she said, realizing she was the only voice of reason since she hadn't been drinking at all. Images of Lacie running toward the water that day at the beach suddenly flashed in her mind. A sense of dread enveloped her and just as she started after Molly, they heard a shriek.

Molly was thrashing around in the pool, half of her clothes and one shoe were still on, her top off. She had fallen in and was so drunk, she didn't come back up for air.

Kate's heart was beating out of her chest as Charlie ran past her. He dove in fully clothed and emerged seconds later with Molly in his arms.

Charlie dragged her up and onto the cold blue stone surrounding the pool. They crowded around her as she coughed, heaving. Kate helped Molly to her side, water dribbling out of her mouth. Sam stood over them, his body blocking out the sun. Kate grabbed a towel. Poor Molly, Kate thought as she looked up at the house. The house was only content with chaos. She remembered her mother saying that, and now she could see why. It wasn't a still house. It was just like Magda had been—restless.

Sam swore under his breath. "Look at you. You're drunk," he practically spat.

"Sam, don't." Kate warned, but she couldn't stand looking at him.

"She is! Can't you go one day without embarrassing me?"

"What about you, Sam? You're not Mr. Perfect. Should I tell her?" Charlie challenged Sam, and Kate had never seen such a wild look in his eyes. "Should I tell Molly your little secret?"

Sam was enraged. "I swear to God—."

"Charlie, what are you talking about?" Kate pleaded. But Charlie didn't say anything; he just glared at Sam and shoved him away.

Sam stormed into the house and up the stairs, slamming his door. Chaos had started to erupt in the house, and now there was no way to keep it contained. Kate was terrified of what could happen next. "It's this place," Kate cried. "I'm sorry I brought you all here. It seems crazy for me to continue and have this birthday dinner with everything that has happened."

"We came all this way for you to celebrate your birthday and we're still going to," Alice insisted as she took a bite out of an apple. "Molly is okay. She had too much to drink. And it was about time someone took care of that buffoon. Don't make it tragic," she said. "Now go get ready so we can have a good time."

21

"'I have heated the oven,' said the witch.
'Creep in and see if it's properly hot,'
she said and pushed Gretel toward the oven."
—*HANSEL AND GRETEL*, GRIMM BROTHERS

Even though Kate wanted to crawl into bed and sleep for days, she opened her closet and took out a dress that she had bought especially for her party. It was sexy and sheer, not something she usually wore. She hardly felt festive at all. She took the dark red dress out and held it up against her pale complexion.

Doug had hung more lights in the garden, and the grounds looked lovely, helping Kate forget all of the ugliness from the last week. Kate could suddenly hear voices coming from Molly's room—she and Sam were arguing. Again.

Kate reached under the mattress and grabbed the police file that she had hidden. She picked it up and pulled out Charlie's statement, skimming down to a specific question:

> Q: *One more thing. Has she ever mentioned her friend Alice to you?*
>
> A: *Alice? Um… maybe, I mean I can't be sure.*
>
> Q: *So, this message we found on her computer to you doesn't mean anything? For the record, I am showing a printout of emails from Lacie's computer.*
>
> A: *Like I said before, I don't know.*

Kate shut the file. Alice and Charlie. They both didn't want Kate to know the truth.

Kate opened the door to the hallway, hoping to find Alice, but it was empty. She went into the living room, then tried the library, where she found Alice sitting in a large leather chair reading a book. She noticed the title: *The Missing Girl* by Shirley Jackson.

"Is it any good?" Kate asked.

"I found it here," Alice said. "Have you read it?"

Kate shook her head. She had never seen it before.

"The girl goes missing from a summer camp, and then everyone searches for her."

Kate felt as if she were seeing Alice for the first time. Why would she pick a book about a missing girl? Kate couldn't understand why she had been friends with Alice all these years; she didn't seem as nice and supportive as she had thought she was, at least not now when Kate desperately needed Alice to help her retrieve her memories. Alice was there that summer, and maybe having her as a friend would prompt her to help her with those memories.

She had to play it all very carefully when it came to Alice.

Alice was cunning, and if she let her in on what she was thinking, Kate may never know the truth.

"You never have liked Charlie."

"Why do you say that?" Alice asked as she closed the book and placed it aside.

"Any time I bring him up, it seems you either have something negative to say or you ignore it."

"I have never trusted him."

"But why?" Kate insisted on an answer.

"I don't know, just a feeling, I guess." Alice shrugged. "Sorry. I know he's your husband. I'm just being honest."

"Are you?" Kate asked.

"Am I what?" Alice asked as she got up.

"Honest, are you being honest?"

"What is that supposed to mean?" Alice asked, her tone angry, her face close to Kate's. "I'm the most honest person you have in your life. I think you need to understand that. Remember, Kate, all that happened that summer. With you and Charlie and Lacie."

"I'm not sure I get what you're saying?" Kate said, as Alice looked at her intently.

"But you do. We're here because you knew all along that something wasn't right. Even if you weren't physically here, it's always been brewing, right there under the surface," Alice said, her steel blue eyes narrow and cold, piercing through her. "You know I'm right. Maybe you're the one not being honest." Alice handed Kate the book. She had always thought Alice would never lie to her. Now she wasn't so sure.

"People are capable of a lot more than we think. It only takes a second to do something we may later regret."

* * *

Kate remembered fragments. Her therapist had tried over the years to tie them together. Put the puzzle in a place, she would say. Snippets of memories were coming back. *How well do you know Charlie?* She could hear her sister's voice in her head. *"I heard a rumor that he did something terrible in his town to some boy."* Kate wasn't sure if that was a real memory or a projection of her doubts about Charlie. Lacie's room might hold some answers—she was finally ready to open it.

Kate opened the drawer next to her bed. Lacie's key lay there, untouched. She had held off long enough. It was time to see what was behind the door. Standing in front of the door, she slipped the key in the keyhole and turned it. The door creaked open, and she quickly took a step inside. It took a moment for her eyes to adjust to the darkness. It was a tiny room, with a canopy bed off to the side and a desk facing the window. A low bookshelf crammed with books stood near the bed with a red reading lamp on top. It was just as she remembered it; her mother had not touched it in all those years. The room stood in stark contrast to her mother's room. Her mother's room had been cold and empty, devoid of life. But here in Lacie's room Kate felt as if she had been transported back in time. The bed had been made that day, but some of Lacie's clothes were draped over the back of the chair. Lacie's lamp, Kate remembered, gave such a comforting hue. She pulled the light switch but the light did not turn on. She walked over to the window, and opened the curtain so some light flooded the room.

Kate turned back, letting her hand brush against the heavy curtains. She ran a finger along the bookshelf, leaving a clean trail through the layer of dust. A loud creak caught Kate off guard, and she noticed that the door to Lacie's closet was ajar. She moved toward it slowly, her palms growing sweaty. Kate could feel her heart beating in her chest, and she tried to relax her shoulders, realizing how on edge she was.

She counted down from three and yanked the door open. Lacie's clothes hung neatly in a row, and Kate breathed out, feeling ridiculous for her reaction. Kate could almost smell Lacie's perfume still hanging in the air, and she blinked away a sharp stinging behind her eyes. She ran her hand along the soft fabrics. She saw the striped fabric of one of Kate's favorite dresses, one that Kate had thought she'd lost years earlier. She smiled and rolled her eyes, remembering how mad she used to get when Lacie would steal her clothes.

Her finger caught the sleeve of one of the shirts and it fell to the ground. She crouched down to grab it, and her attention was drawn to the square panel in the back of the closet. Kate's own closet had a matching door, that led to one of the secret passageways that Max had built into the home all those years ago. They would play in the passageway for hours, scampering between their two rooms until their mom would yell at them to come downstairs.

Opening the door, Kate coughed at the cloud of dust that was dislodged. Cobwebs covered the opening and she recoiled, slamming the panel shut. Kate jumped to her feet and shut the closet door with a firm click.

She suddenly felt so incredibly tired, all the years of sadness and missing Lacie overcoming her as she slumped down in the desk chair, her head drooping heavily. She rested it on the desk. She whispered Lacie's name over and over again while tears flowed down her cheeks.

After a few minutes, she wiped her tears and looked at the photos around the room. There was a photo of Kate smiling and hugging Lacie. Despite how difficult Lacie had been, she realized that she missed her so much. She had so hoped to share all of life's best moments with her little sister, but instead she was frozen forever on that day.

The other side of the desk was filled with small knick-knacks under a layer of heavy dust: Lacie's small crystal dancer and her miniature porcelain dog.

Under the desk was one drawer, which Kate pulled open. She found a few cards and a wooden letter stamp set. Kate smiled as she remembered the birthday cards they used to make for their mom with the stamp set. One time, they had spelled out what her mother called vile words, and she'd gotten really angry. Kate chuckled at the memory. She wondered why some memories were so vivid for her while others were buried so deep. The bottom of the drawer was dented. Kate looked at it. She ran her fingers over the surface and noticed that there seemed to be one piece of wood on top of the others making up the bottom of the drawer. She slid this top piece away and felt around inside the gap it left. There was something there—a small notebook with a dusty velvet cover. She took it out. *"Lacie"* was written in beautiful handwriting on the first page. Mom's handwriting. She turned to the next page.

"To my darling Lacie, hope this is the summer of your dreams. Love, Mom."

And there was Lacie's squiggly handwriting. Even though she hadn't seen it for nearly twenty years, the familiar lettering made Kate's stomach turn with the shock of recognition. She didn't think she'd remember this part of her sister so clearly, but looking at her handwriting felt like she was suddenly looking at Lacie's face, or hands, or her favorite stuffed animal. The immediacy of her sister's presence took Kate's breath away. She closed her eyes momentarily, then forced herself to focus on what Lacie had written.

MY DIARY

June 25

I can hear the music coming from her room. I know she is probably drinking her "tea"... Ha. She thinks we don't know that Susan spikes it. She doesn't know that I sneak into the woods some nights with my friend and we get drunk together. I've tried them all, I don't like gin. Today she was mad at Katie for not telling her she was going to another bonfire with Charlie. I told her though. I went into the kitchen and saw Mom's tea. Was it number 3 or 4? Never can tell.

Now it's noon, and she is still in bed. My friend is waiting for me, and I want to get out before any of them notice. Especially her. She would be so mad if she knew I go into the woods at night. The thing is, this place can be a lot scarier than the woods. I am so careful when I sneak out. I am Princess of the Villa after all. I can make things happen. As long as her records are playing, I can get out without anyone knowing.

June 26

I could smell the alcohol and smoke on her breath when she kissed me good morning. I couldn't tell if it was from last night or this morning. I pretended to stay asleep. Katie says Momma oozes sadness. I kept my eyes shut until I heard the door close behind her.

Today will be a good day. Nothing, not even my mother, will ruin my good mood. I'm meeting my friend later. I will wear my pink blouse and jean shorts. Perfect for a picnic in the woods.

June 29

I love the necklace. I have to hide it so she doesn't find it. Katie will be upset. And anyway, I want to keep it a secret. I saw Susan today. She looked at me like she saw a ghost. I yelled "Boo." It made her jump.

July 2

Ghosts do exist. I have seen them. Mom says "It's your imagina-tion, not ghosts." She says that ghosts don't exist, but I know they do and I know they're in the house. This house was built for my great-grandmother who drove my great-grandfather mad. There is a portrait of her in the library, and I think I look like her. Maybe she loved someone else and is never happy, but her portrait changes. Sometimes she is smiling and other times she isn't. Momma swears that the portrait never smiles. This house always feels sad inside, I wish we could spend the summers somewhere else.

July 7

Why are sad songs always the same? I haven't left my room since Friday afternoon. I tried to see if we could talk today but he didn't return my call. I even messaged him. Mom keeps trying to check in on me, but I tell her I'm feeling sick. I am though. A broken heart maybe. It rips me up inside and makes me want to throw up. She tried to give me the tonic she always gives me when I'm sick. It's apple cider vinegar mixed with leaves from the garden. Susan gave me chamomile instead. Susan is such a better mom.

The message, Kate thought. That's what they had shown Charlie during his interview, but Kate hadn't seen it when she flipped through the file.

July 9

He's told me there will be no more meetings. There will be no more talks in the woods or the garden. No more picnics together. I hold the locket. I am not going to give up. I need to talk, to explain. I'm not just any girl. This summer I know what I want. I know that I don't want to be here. I am feeling sick again. I just want to go away and never come back to the house again.

All these secrets her sister had. She had no idea. She thought of Andrew. Her own son—did she know him as well as she thought? When Kate turned the page, she realized that there were clearly pages missing, ripped out, the edges of the notebook ragged. She flipped through the rest of the pages, but they were all blank. A loud bang erupted from the hallway. She jumped up from the chair and slammed the drawer that held Lacie's journal shut. She ran toward the noise; water was gushing from the utility closet, flooding the landing and getting Kate's beautiful red birthday dress was soaked. Sam appeared with a bunch of towels.

"A pipe must have burst," Kate yelled over the sound of the water. "Get Doug." He nodded and ran back down the stairs.

Alice stood in the doorway.

"Lacie's trying to tell me something. I know it." Kate looked at Alice.

Sam arrived with more towels and began patting everything down, telling her Doug was already shutting the water off. Kate looked toward the end of the hall toward Lacie's room. *The water bursting, what does it mean, Lacie? Why can't you let me have my day? Why do you have to ruin another birthday?*

Darien suddenly appeared on the landing, a birthday gift in his hand. "I'll call a plumber. The pipes are so old, I am not surprised this happened. Last year one burst in the attic."

"The attic?" Kate remembered that that had been one of Lacie's secret hiding spots when she'd been younger. She would inevitably always end up there.

"Go get dry," said Darien.

Kate nodded but she went to the back steps and up toward the attic. The attic in the tower was musty and old, just as it had been when they were kids. Lacie had loved the attic. She had pretended for years to be a princess captured and hidden away, waiting for her prince charming to save her. Kate and Lacie spent endless hours playing that game. Kate sat in the corner and looked out the small window where Lacie had looked out a million times when they were playing and saw what Lacie saw each time: those woods. The attic was dark as little sunlight shone through the small windows. She took her phone out and gave the area one last look.

Kate spied Lacie's old trunk. Kate opened it and revealed the dusty play clothes that Lacie used to wear, her dresses yellowed with age. She picked them up, carefully looking at each one as if an heirloom from a time long gone. The dresses were all fit for a princess. Kate put them back and looked around the room. The window. What else did Lacie see when she looked out? She must have been lonely that summer. Kate was with Charlie all the time, and their mother was "busy" most days. Kate saw Lacie's tea set. The one they used to play with when they were kids. Lacie was five when she received it and she'd cherished it. It was white porcelain with tiny blue flowers. Kate looked at it, flashes of Lacie preparing the pretend tea, all dressed up, in her head.

"*Did you know that tea is an anagram for ate or eat? You just have to rearrange things sometimes to make them fit. You have tea in your name, Kate. See,*" she'd said as she circled the letters in the name to spell T E A. "*Sometimes it's all right there, you just have to be looking.*"

The secret language. Their words. They would jumble them… like her memories. She needed to rearrange them as well, like the letters, make sense of all of it. Images of Lacie sitting playing with her tea set. Images of her kissing Charlie at the beach. *No, those weren't real,* Kate thought. Were they? Did she see them together and snap? Kate didn't want to think about something so terrible.

She picked up the teapot and heard it rattle. A clink. She carefully opened the top and inside was a metal chain. She pulled it out, and staring right at her was a butterfly locket.

* * *

Kate arrived back downstairs with her hair still dripping wet. She had to do something about what she'd found. She found Darien waiting for her.

"All patched, but he mentioned you should get an inspector in before you try to sell now," Darien said, then did a double take. "You should get into something dry."

She waved off the comment. "Thank you so much, and sorry for all of this tonight. I should have known better than to try and celebrate this day," she said. "I feel like this evening has been completely ruined. You must be regretting agreeing to come to dinner."

"This stuff happens, especially in an old house. It's just a pipe, that's all. But you look pale. Are you okay?"

"It's just that this week has been kind of terrible all around," Kate said. "Can I ask: Whatever happened to Carl?"

"He's with his brother. He's got Alzheimer's."

She nodded, but something felt off. Hadn't Darien been the one to suggest Carl go to a nursing home?

"Did you know Chloe was visiting him the other day?"

Darien stilled. "Chloe? With Carl? I don't know why she would go see him. Wait, why did you go see Carl?"

"Chloe!" Andrew called out before Kate had a chance to respond. "Mom, have you seen her?"

"No, is she coming to dinner?"

"Yeah, she was supposed to meet me an hour ago. I'm going to call her again."

"I wouldn't worry about it, Andrew. I'll give her a call," Darien said, and he walked out to the patio and quietly shut the door behind him.

First the leak, and now Chloe was missing? None of this was making any sense, and Kate couldn't help but feel that it wasn't a coincidence. She was tempted to show Darien what she had found, but with everyone around, it would have to wait.

22

"The old woman had only pretended to be so kind;
she was in reality a wicked witch, who lay in wait for children,
and had only built the little house of bread
in order to entice them there."
—HANSEL AND GRETEL, GRIMM BROTHERS

By the time Kate had put on a long, blue dress and gone out into the garden, Charlie had returned. He was barefoot and carrying his shoes.

"Where have you been?" Kate was exhausted.

Charlie nodded. "I was at the beach. I needed to clear my head."

"There was a huge leak."

"I'm sorry, I had no idea."

"Did you see Chloe while you were there? No one knows where she went. Andrew is concerned."

He looked a little surprised and nodded. "She came to the

beach just as I was leaving."

"It's just not like you." Kate couldn't let it go. "I mean to leave and not tell us. I'm not understanding anything."

"C'mon Kate, I went for a walk," he snapped. "That's it. I'm human, and this week—this whole trip—has been difficult. I can't wait to get this over with and get back home."

After all that she had learned, she was confused and didn't know if she could just go back home with Charlie and act like everything was like old times. She looked at her husband, her first love, the father of her only child, and didn't know what she believed anymore.

* * *

The lights were all strewn and lit beautifully in the garden, just as Kate had envisioned for this night. The table was set with a white tablecloth and flowers from the garden. She looked at the group all dressed nicely, eager for the festivities ahead—or eager to be done with the week so they could all go back to their lives.

Everyone was drinking cocktails, waiting for dinner, trying to pretend that everything was fine. Even Molly seemed to have pulled herself together. It was as if she had never fallen into the pool. Sam, sucking on a smelly cigar, grunted as Kate passed by. Questions kept swirling around in Kate's head. Chloe's absence, rumors about Charlie and the girl. What was it that happened that got him in trouble?

Susan and Doug emerged from the kitchen with dinner. Smoked salmon toasts, sauteed mushrooms, steak and potatoes, and green salad. They served themselves and sat down to eat and drink wine. Kate couldn't follow most of the conversation, her mind stuck on Chloe, Lacie, and what it all meant to her. She kept a close eye on Charlie. He seemed so calm. Surely, none of what she was thinking about him could be true…could it? Kate felt her surroundings spin as she continued to sip on her drink, fingering the necklace in her pocket. She would show Darien. He would know what to do.

She was so preoccupied that she didn't hear who suggested they all take a swim, but before she knew it, Molly, Sam, and Charlie had jumped in. Alice came and stood next to her, and together they quietly watched everyone else in the pool.

"Why were you looking for me that day?" Kate suddenly asked. "That day, all those years ago, you found me in the woods. What were you doing there?"

"I told you, I liked the woods, I went there sometimes to think." Alice shrugged. "Why?"

"I mean it just seems strange," Kate said.

Kate didn't believe her anymore—or Charlie. She watched as Charlie took Sam aside; both were drunker than usual and she could tell from the way they stood it would not be friendly.

Suddenly, their voices rose, and everyone could hear them.

"You know you're a self-righteous prick sometimes," Sam stammered.

"Don't make a scene. It's my wife's birthday. I told you that next time it happened, I would let Molly know."

"Let me know what?" Molly asked as she dried off. She picked up a glass and took a sip. Charlie looked at her, and Kate could tell he was done protecting Sam.

"That he gambled your fucking savings away and I've been bailing him out this whole time. And now I hear that he's been pulling money from the company, from our clients, to cover his debts."

Molly dropped her glass, shattering it to pieces, glass flying everywhere.

"You'll pay for that, Charlie," Sam grunted. And then he decked Charlie, knuckles connecting with the side of his mouth.

Charlie stumbled backward but didn't fall. In a split second, he reeled back and punched Sam squarely in the face. Sam staggered back, hands flying to his face.

"I've been wanting to do that for a long time," Charlie said, his tone satisfied as he shook out his hand.

"You think you're better than me. Well, I wasn't the one that cost a kid a scholarship that he desperately needed and had his daddy pay the family off," Sam spewed.

"Charlie…" Kate said, her voice trembling.

Everything was disintegrating—friendships, families, and trust. All it took was Villa Magda to expunge all they had worked on for years.

Charlie wiped his mouth and trudged into the house.

She stared after him. She loved him for so many reasons. He was her Charlie, and she knew he would never knowingly hurt her. But she now wondered what lengths he would go to to protect her. She had no other proof than some journal entries, and town gossip, but now she knew that Charlie had dark secrets and maybe he had a motive to silence Lacie.

This was the last night they were here, and Kate still didn't have all she needed. She knew she had no other choice but to let Darien know all she had learned, even if that meant implicating her husband.

* * *

Kate needed to talk to Darien now. He must have noticed something. He was in the kitchen, starting to pack up the leftovers.

"Can I ask you a favor?"

"Sure, anything."

"Chloe said that you all believe that I had something to do with Lacie disappearing. Is that true?"

Darien looked at her. "She's just repeating what some of the locals have mentioned in the past, but I know you, Katie, and I don't think that at all. The people here just want to forget about it. You coming back stirred up some of the gossip, that's all."

"What about Charlie?" She whispered. "Did you know about that, what Sam said?'

Darien looked at her and moved closer to her.

"My father always thought that he may have been hiding something. But Charlie had a lot of lawyers in his corner at the time."

Kate could hardly bear to hear anything else. How could he have kept this from her?

"There had been talk that Charlie thought he deserved the scholarship. So when he didn't get it, he took out his aggression on his teammate during practices. At a party after Homecoming, Charlie got really drunk and started a fight. With the little information my dad was able to find out, it sounds like Charlie attacked the kid pretty aggressively. Somehow his knee got shattered, and he wasn't able to play again. He had to give up the scholarship."

"Charlie was in trouble, the only child of a wealthy family, you know how that is. Kids like that get away with..." Darien stopped mid-sentence.

"Kids like that get away with murder," Kate murmured, finishing the saying.

"You hear stories about things like that happening all the time. The family refused to press charges, so there wasn't anything the police could do."

"Darien..." Kate shook her head.

"Look, you should just ask him about it, Kate. I don't know the full story. I'm just focused on Lacie's investigation."

Kate's mind jumped to the necklace sitting heavy in her pocket. She took it out and showed it to Darien. "I found this. It was hers, Lacie's."

Darien looked at her sharply. "Where did you find this?"

"The attic. It was Lacie's hiding spot. I went up there before to check on the pipes," Kate said.

"Can I keep this? Do some analysis. See if it means anything at all." Kate nodded and Darien slipped the locket in his pocket.

"I was just hoping to understand better... find some closure... anything that maybe was missed. I never expected any of this," Kate insisted. "I really thought I could handle all of this. But now, to suspect my own husband... Charlie has always been the person I trusted the most."

"I know." Darien sighed. "We can't know what anyone is ever really thinking, Kate. It's what my father always said. It's what made him a good police chief all those years; he never doubted that anyone was capable of anything."

He was trying to reassure her, but Kate knew that life as she had lived it for the past eighteen years was coming to an end.

"Do you believe in ghosts?" Kate asked, out of the blue.

He raised his eyebrows. "Literal ghosts?"

She nodded. "Yes. I never did, and this is going to sound

odd, but… I think Lacie is here. I feel her and hear her. I know, crazy, right?"

"I can sometimes still smell my father's balm he used to use for his sore back. It's so strong some days, I could swear he's in the other room," Darien admitted.

Kate took a deep breath. "Maybe it's a part of our memory that presses on." She felt so much comfort standing here talking to her old friend. Darien understood her. He didn't question why she was here.

* * *

After talking to Darien, Kate ducked out and went up to her room. The moonlight filtering in through the open curtain, she put her head on the pillow, closed her eyes, and just wished it would all go back to what it was before they came back. She was happy Darien had been there. She felt comforted by him in a way she hadn't felt with Charlie. He was kind and, in some ways, he knew her more than her friends did.

She could hear everyone quietly retreating to their bedrooms. All was silent when Kate woke up a few hours later. She opened her eyes and pulled open the drawer next to her bed. She looked for Lacie's room key. Her body went cold. Where was it? And who could have taken it? She was dizzy from the knowledge that someone had that key and may have been in Lacie's room.

She went into the bathroom and stopped. Written on the mirror was the word: *"SILENT."* Kate shivered. Her breath caught as she glimpsed a figure standing by the window, looking out. The hallway was long and dark, making it hard for Kate to make out who it was. Long hair flowing over her shoulders. "Alice?" she whispered.

Alice turned and smiled.

"Oh, you scared me!" Relief flooded through her and she moved toward Alice, feeling better having company in the dark house.

Alice pulled Kate in for a hug. "Are you okay?"

She shook her head a little. "Someone took Lacie's room key and wrote on my mirror... Lacie... someone is trying to make me go crazy," Kate said as Alice held her.

"That doesn't make sense. Why would they do that? We can't stay here, Kate. You're falling apart," Alice said as she eased Kate out of her arms.

"No, I can't leave. I told you, she's here." Kate's eyes filled with tears as she spoke. And just then, there was a piercing scream. The kind of scream that changes everything.

PART THREE

AFTER

23

"Ah, how the poor little sister did lament
when she had to fetch the water,
and how her tears did flow down her cheeks!"
—*HANSEL AND GRETEL*, GRIMM BROTHERS

The sound of the scream was sharp. Was it Chloe?

The next words were alien to Kate.

"It's a body! In the pool. Oh my God! Somebody call an ambulance."

Body. Pool. Police. The words ran through her head, but she couldn't put them together.

The voice echoed through the house. In an instant, the quiet of the night turned into frenetic action. Kate ran barefoot, the harsh wood of the flooring quickly replaced by dewy grass.

Body. *Whose* body? Fear gripped at her throat and all she could think of was Andrew. *Please don't let it be Andrew.* The house stirred violently, and everyone was suddenly awakened out of their sleep by the cries. Kate realized with a start that blood was mixing in the pool. The body floated, lifeless.

Charlie. The thought came unbidden, but she knew it was true, his body floating on the surface, a gash on his head. Her body froze. Horror set in as she began to comprehend what was happening. *The body. It's Charlie.*

Kate opened her mouth to let out a scream, but she could hardly breathe. Her body was stiff, but she jumped in the pool. She pulled on him with all her might. Charlie was heavy, like a million bricks. How could he be so heavy?

"Help!" She screamed. She got him over to the side and the others helped her get him out of the pool. She thought of Andrew. Where was he? His father was dead. Her husband. No, no, no, it couldn't be true.

"Andrew!" Her eyes couldn't stop the tears from flowing. "This cannot be happening." She heard her voice, trembling and sputtering, and it sounded unfamiliar to her. Kate wanted to run away and never look back. Charlie dead. How? Not possible.

Molly arrived wearing only an oversized t-shirt and kept repeating, "No, no, no," over and over again.

Sam held his hands on Charlie's chest, attempting CPR, as water dribbled out of his mouth. "Mouth to mouth?" he cried out to Kate.

She put her lips over Charlie's mouth and blew as strongly as she could. She continued several times as Sam did chest compressions, but it was useless. His body looked smaller, like his soul had gone and just left an empty shell.

Sam sat back on his heels, face frozen in shock. Molly put

her hand on his shoulder and caressed it over and over, and closed her eyes.

"I can't believe it's Charlie. No, no, no."

Ben arrived in his pajamas with his hair disheveled. "I've called 911," he stammered. "They'll be here any minute."

"What's happening?" Kate cried out as she cradled her husband's lifeless body in her arms. She turned and vomited. Her whole body shook.

"Is he dead?" Molly asked, her voice a sliver of its regular self.

Doug nodded. "I think he is."

Molly's strong legs buckled beneath her as she fell to the ground.

"Please, Charlie. I'm sorry. Please wake up, we can go home now, please." Kate pleaded. "I believe you now." She did this to him. It was all her fault.

The roar of the ambulance punctured the thick morning air. Kate had lost all track of time, each second felt like minutes, each minute felt like hours. Finally the two EMTs arrived at the scene, but Kate held on tight to Charlie. She didn't want to let go.

"Andrew…" she whispered.

Susan gently led a drenched Kate away from Charlie. She could hardly move.

They checked his pulse carefully, but she already knew. Kate knew he was gone. She looked up. They were all around her. Watching her closely. Their friends who had come for a relaxing week, now all standing there with faces of horror and confusion, wondering why they had agreed to come. Each of them wishing they hadn't and each of them now a possible suspect.

A police car stopped in the driveway. Kate saw it but hadn't heard it approaching. Her ears were still filled with screaming. She would never be able to forget the sound of it. Darien got out of the police car and immediately went over to Kate and put his arms around her. Kate fell into his embrace, comfort washing over her.

"He's gone," Kate whispered. "Just like that. I don't understand."

"Kate," said Darien, calming her down. "Come, let's sit you down. Susan, can you make her something hot, maybe a cup of tea? And Doug, can you bring a blanket, please? She's wet and shivering."

As he spoke, Kate looked down and felt her clothes clinging to her body. She hadn't even noticed that she was shaking. Doug arrived with a blanket and Susan with tea. Kate looked up at Darien.

"It can't be true." Kate choked on her words.

"A terrible, terrible accident," exclaimed Molly, her voice louder than usual. "We were all drinking too much last night," she admitted.

A tall woman appeared next to Darien. "When you have warmed up, we will begin," she said calmly.

"This is my colleague, Officer Christine Mallory. She'll be helping conduct the interviews."

She was older than Darien. She nodded and looked around the grounds.

"We are deeply sorry for your loss, Mrs. Williams. I'm from Aria, and I know this house has seen its share of tragedies." She sighed. "We just need to do our routine investigation, ask some questions. I will be in charge of this crime scene and interviews until the State Police arrive. I am sure Chief Anderson will agree that given his personal relationship with the victim, it isn't appropriate for him to be involved."

"Officer Mallory, you of all people should know my ability to separate facts from feelings during investigations."

"Of course, sir. Still, since you were present this evening, you're now considered a witness."

"Investigation?" Molly said. "He must have fallen when he was drunk."

"I won't ever be ready," Kate cried. "Charlie…" Kate's sobs came in angry waves, her whole body moving with them.

"I'm sure that's what it was, an accident. But by law, we have to. It's just what we need to do. I wish we could wait, but as you know, Chief Anderson," she nodded toward Darien, "it's important to start the investigation right away, when the memories and facts are fresh. And we'll need to check his system for alcohol and drugs."

"Drugs?" Kate said, shocked. "He doesn't do drugs." She sobbed. "This is all my fault. We all had a lot to drink. When I woke up, he wasn't there."

"When can we get out of here?" Sam blurted out.

"Sam," Molly scolded.

"You wanted us all together, Kate," Sam continued, his voice sounding on the edge of hysteria. "I didn't sign up for this."

"Sam, stop!" Molly said sharply. "This is not someone. It's Charlie."

"You were mad at him. Mad that he had accused you of embezzling from the company." Kate cried, her eyes ablaze on Sam.

"Me?" Sam growled. "You're the one that's unstable. He was worried about you, all this talk about your sister."

"I'm sorry, sir, but I'm afraid no one can leave until we've questioned everybody who was present," Officer Mallory said.

"What will they do with him?" asked Kate as she looked over at Charlie's body.

"The medical examiner is on her way, and she'll determine if an autopsy will be needed."

"Autopsy?" Kate's voice was faint. "Is an autopsy really necessary?" Kate repeated, her voice low.

"Usually they are done, just to rule anything else out other than an accident." Officer Mallory spoke slowly. She turned to Molly and Sam.

"Was the deceased acting at all under the influence last night?"

"No. Well, I mean he had a drink or two," Molly said.

"I think it's fair to say that you and Charlie had more than just a drink, Sam." Darien interjected.

"What the hell is that supposed to mean?"

"It looked like there was more going on than just conflict between business partners."

"Mom. Mom! What's happening? Dad?" Andrew's cries were filled with anguish and confusion as he searched for his father. He saw Charlie on the ground and fell down next to him. "Dad. No. Oh my God."

Kate wanted to hug Andrew with all her might and make the pain go away. Her heart broke for him.

The officer began speaking.

"I'm so sorry about your father." She helped Andrew up from the ground and sat him down on the lounge chair next to Kate. Kate held her arms around her son and closed her eyes.

"I'll need to speak to each one of you," Officer Mallory

continued. "We'll do everything we possibly can, Mrs. Williams, I assure you. It won't make the pain any easier, I'm afraid, but at least we can hopefully answer some questions."

"How could this have happened?" whispered Kate. "It's all my fault." She hated this house, every damn inch of it. She should have just burned it to the ground.

"That's why we are here. We will figure it out. I promise," Darien said.

Kate had heard that before, years ago from his father. In a press conference, when they talked about Lacie. But they hadn't figured it out.

Darien put a comforting arm around Kate and squeezed her shoulder. He turned and looked at her with such compassion. "You're a strong woman, Katie," said Darien quietly. "You really are."

Kate sat in the chair, her head pounding. She didn't know how she would ever sleep again. "It's like I am living in someone else's nightmare." Kate shivered. She looked at Darien. She knew in her heart that Charlie's death wasn't merely an accident. Somehow it was all connected. The house, Lacie's disappearance, and now Charlie.

Officer Mallory cleared her throat and motioned toward Kate. "Is there a room I could use? Somewhere for the interviews?"

Doug pointed to the house upstairs. "There's a library inside."

"Yes, that would be fine."

Kate watched them walk into the house, realizing that they would suspect her. She looked at Darien, but his face looked the same. He was clearly empathetic toward her.

"Um, Sam... the officer wants to talk to you first," Doug

said as he returned to the group.

"Why me?" Sam asked.

"I don't think it makes a difference who goes first. They're just doing a routine investigation."

Kate watched Sam head inside.

Where was Alice? Just like her to disappear in key moments. They would need to talk to her too, she guessed. She hoped the police would remember to call her in.

POLICE FILE—ARIA, MAINE.

CASE 1583

INVESTIGATION REPORTS

NOTES TAKEN BY OFFICER MALLORY

SAM EVANS

RELATIONSHIP TO DECEASED: BUSINESS

PARTNER, FRIEND OF THE FAMILY

Q: Thank you for joining me. I just have a few questions.

A: First of all, I want to say that Charlie was one of my best friends, shit maybe my only one.

[Brief pause as witness regains composure]

Q: That's okay. What can you tell me about last night?

A: It was Kate's birthday. We had steak and great wine. Cigars. It seemed normal enough, except…

Q; Except what?

A: This place, the mother, the sister—nothing seemed right. It seemed as if it was all coming to a head. We were all here trying to pretend everything was normal. Just bullshit.

Q: Okay, let's switch gears. How is your business going?

A: What does that have to do with anything?

Q: You said Charlie was your business partner.

A: He was. We were partners at the firm.

Q: And Mrs. Williams said that you and Charlie had been having trouble lately.

A: I mean everyone has had setbacks this year, but we are doing pretty good. There was just a small misunderstanding, but we would have figured it out once we were back in the office. Charlie is a great people person. I mean was. Shit. People trust him.

Q: Did you?

A: Did I what?

Q: Trust him?

A: Sure. But Charlie had his secrets, just like everyone else.

Q: Did he have any enemies or anyone who would want to harm him?

A: Listen, we've both pissed some people off. I'm the first to admit that Charlie and I haven't been great lately. But I loved the guy. Everyone did. I would never hurt him.

Q: We're not suggesting anything like that right now. We just need to get some more information.

A: I just can't… Are we done here?

Q: Just a few more questions, Mr. Evans. Did anything unusual happen tonight?

A: Well, Charlie and I had a little disagreement earlier in the day, but by dinner we were fine.

Q: What was the disagreement about?

A: There was a small misunderstanding with one of our clients. But really, it was nothing. Things got a little physical, but that's how Charlie and I work stuff out. By dinner, we were good.

Q: Physical? Physical how?

A: I was being an ass, and a few punches were thrown. Charlie hit me and I responded. But it was one-and-done on both our parts and we walked away after that.

Q: Did you notice anyone acting unusually during dinner?

A: Not that I remember. I noticed Kate was out by the pool, and it looked like she was speaking to someone. I mean, I just saw her talking, I couldn't see the other person as she was facing in the other direction and it was dark. Maybe the mojitos didn't help either.

Q: Could you hear what they said?

A: No, but she seemed different when she came back. Upset. A lot has been going on though. What with her sister.

Q: Sister—you mean Kate's sister? Who knew about Lacie?

A: I'm really not sure. I think only Kate and Charlie. Well, and the caretakers knew of course.

Q: What did you think about Lacie when you found out?

A: It was strange if you ask me, her not telling us and having us come here. Really morbid. It makes you wonder what other secrets Kate is keeping from us.

Q: Hmm. When did you last see Charlie?

A: *After we had the after-dinner drink. Molly interrupted us while we were having a cigar on the terrace and thought I had had enough to drink. She insisted I go with her to our room. Insisted is a nice word—she was busting my balls. She can be a bitch. And she was probably right. I don't remember even getting undressed. I just fell asleep on the bed and woke up to the scream. It's just horrible.*

Q: *Where were you when the body was found?*

A: *Asleep, in my bed. Didn't I just say that?*

Q: *Anything else you would like to add?*

A: *I can't think straight right now. Sorry.*

* * *

BEN EVANS
RELATIONSHIP TO DECEASED: FRIEND OF THE
FAMILY, SON OF SAM AND MOLLY EVANS

Q: *Hi Ben.*

A: *Hey.*

Q: *So, I know this must seem strange and that you are upset, but do you mind if we ask you a few questions?*

A: *Do I have a choice?*

Q: *I suppose you don't. Sorry. You are best friends with Andrew?*

A: *I guess.*

Q: Why do you say that?

A: He's just been acting all weird ever since he met Chloe.

Q: Can you tell us why?

A: I'm not sure. It's just that I don't trust her.

Q: Why not?

A: She seems obsessed with his mom and I don't know why. I like his mom. She's a nice lady.

Q: Do you know Chloe well?

A: No. She just showed up one day. She and Andrew were getting close.

Q: Did that bother you?

A: Maybe a little.

Q: Have you noticed anything strange the last few days?

A: Lots.

Q: Like?

A: The bat was strange. It was a bad omen, and I told them so. But the way she killed it.

Q: Who killed it?

A: Andrew's mother. It was like she took out so much anger on it. I told her it was bad luck.

Q: Anything else?

A: I heard voices. Sometimes in the middle of the night. They were hard to hear, but I think it may have been a young girl's voice, or maybe a young woman's voice. Definitely not a man's voice.

Q: Voices?

A: Yeah, and Mrs. Williams. I heard her too.

Q: Do you think she did something to Charlie?

A: I don't think she did.

Q: But you think someone did?

A: I don't know.

Q: What about your dad? He and Charlie got into a fight last night, didn't they?

A: Yeah, but my dad deserved it. Besides, they seemed fine afterward. And my dad would never kill someone, not even Charlie.

Q: On that note: When you first saw the body in the pool were you surprised to see who it was?

A: Actually, I wasn't. I can't say why but I sort of expected it. Hey, can I go now? I need to use the bathroom.

Q: Sure. Thank you for your answers Ben. And if you want to talk to us more, we're here.

* * *

MOLLY EVANS

RELATIONSHIP TO DECEASED: FRIEND OF FAMILY

Q: I'm asking everyone general questions. Are you doing okay?

A: No. I'm not. I just can't believe it. What a terrible accident. Poor Kate. And to think she was worried about me.

Q: Worried why?

A: I've not been getting along with my husband. He can be a handful.

Q: Handful how?

A: Sam has anger issues. He always has. It gets worse the more stress he is under.

Q: Does he ever get physical?

A: No, not with me.

Q: With others?

A: Well, I've only seen him get physical once, maybe twice. And one of those times was last night. Was it an accident? Charlie?

Q: We're not at liberty to disclose anything right now, Mrs. Evans. Have you been here before?

A: No, I didn't even know it existed until a month ago. We should have stayed home.

Q: Did you know about Lacie?

A: No. I was hurt, and maybe a little pissed, when I found out. I mean, I'm supposed to be one of Kate's best friends, and she never shared that with me?

Q: So what happened here last night?

A: Oh my God. I really don't know. The place looked great, we drank and had dinner. Everyone was tense though. We were all on edge, waiting for the other shoe to drop so to speak... So much happened here in such a short amount of time. But no one ever expected someone to die.

Q: What did you expect?

A: We all felt it, the electric tension, and the house felt dark... but someone dead? That is a shock to all of us.

Q: Tell me about Charlie and Kate.

A: Well, they seemed normal at first. But then all the stuff about the missing sister came out. That was weird. They argued a lot about that. Charlie seemed worried about something. Kate got weirder about it as the days passed.

Q: Weird how?

A: I don't know, she seems so scattered. She wasn't the Kate I knew.

Q: Did you see her leave the party at any point?

A: Only when I got up to get a drink, after dinner, I noticed Kate was off to the side of the pool, and it looked like she was speaking to someone. I couldn't see who though.

Q: Try and remember any detail you can.

A: That's all I remember. I mean except how agitated Kate seemed.

Q: Agitated?

A: Unsettled…that's a better word.

Q: When did you leave the party?

A: After dessert, Sam was getting so tired and cranky. He wanted to go to bed, so I accompanied him. He needs his sleep. He was annoyed, Charlie sort of told on him. But that's how they always were with each other. God, this is awful.

Q: You mentioned earlier that Charlie seemed worried. Do you know what he was worried about?

A: Well, he and Kate seemed to be arguing about the house and her sister. I think Kate thought he was keeping something from her. I thought maybe he was hiding something from her about his past. He wouldn't be the first husband to do so.

Q: Had you heard anything about Charlie's past?

A: No, not until Sam brought it up at dinner. It was just old drama—something about Charlie in high school. But it really set Charlie off.

Q: How did everyone else react?

A: I think we were all confused. I don't know… I can't really remember. So much has happened since then.

Q: Well, if you do remember anything later, just give us a call.

A: I will. You do think it's an accident right? I mean this house. I don't know, it gives me the creeps.

Q: It's too early to tell, but if you remember or hear anything from the others, please do let us know.

* * *

ANDREW WILLIAMS

RELATIONSHIP TO DECEASED: SON

Q: I'm very sorry for your loss.

A: My loss. That's what you call him. Now he's a loss. My dad just died. Fuck. This can't be happening.

Q: I'm sorry. I can't say I understand. It must be painful.

A: It's bullshit. He was a good swimmer, a great swimmer. No way he drowned. Something happened to him.

Q: We will do our best to figure out what happened. What can you tell us about last night?

A: The whole thing is just bullshit. We never celebrated her birthday before. I would ask why but now I know. It just came and went most years, without even a mention. I got used to it, and then this summer, she just acted like it was the most normal thing in the world to celebrate. I went with it, didn't ask questions, was excited even to spend time with Ben. But this house is strange, we all felt it. Mom was different. Sure, she seemed happy, but it wasn't real. She was pretending. I could tell. Dad was in a good mood, smoking. Everyone was drinking a bit too much maybe. I just thought everything was cool, but I swear I felt like something could happen.

Q: *Felt?*

A: *Yeah, can't explain it, it felt like a simmering pot about to boil over.*

Q: *Did you and your dad speak after dinner?*

A: *I just asked him about Chloe. She was at the beach. We were worried about her.*

Q: *Why? Where did she go?*

A: *She was just upset; she found something out about her family, and she needed to think.*

Q: *Tell me about Chloe. Do you like her?*

A: *I don't know her that well. We just met. But she seems great. Although I think she was looking for something here at the house. I am not sure what.*

Q: *Looking for something?*

A: *She was curious about this place, she said. I guess there were ghost stories she had heard. Something about the Villa being cursed. We just thought it was weird at first, and that she was just trying to scare us.*

Q: *And now?*

A: *We should have believed her.*

Q: Okay. Let's get back to your father. So did you actually fight with him last night?

A: What? No! We didn't.

Q: I'm just trying to figure out what happened. It's a part of the process, piecing together the evening. Were the two of you out by the pool at some point?

A: That's where the party was mostly! Everyone was there.

Q: I understand. Did you talk to your dad about anything else?

A: I don't remember.

Q: Something that made you upset?

A: No. He was upset. I was just telling the truth.

Q: About what?

A: Nothing. It doesn't matter now. Can I go? This is bullshit.

Q: Can you just let me know the topic?

A: It was nothing, I told you.

Q: And your mom?

A: This is all her fault. She shouldn't have made us come to this place. We should have just gone to Nantucket as planned.

Q: Where were you when the body was found?

A: What? I was sleeping. This is the worst day of my life.

Q: Thank you, Andrew.

* * *

SUSAN DRESDEN

RELATIONSHIP TO DECEASED:

CARETAKER OF VILLA MAGDA

Q: *Do you know where Chloe is?*

A: *I am sure she is around. Sometimes she disappears for a few hours to take some time for herself.*

Q: *Anything else you can tell me about last night?*

A: *I just can't believe it.*

Q: *Where were you?*

A: *I was mostly in the kitchen, cooking and cleaning up. I just went outside a few times, I don't like when there's too much drinking or arguing.*

Q: *Arguing?*

A: *I heard voices raised quite a bit.*

Q: *Do you know who was arguing?*

A: *They all were.*

Q: *Did anyone come into the kitchen?*

A: *Not really. Andrew came by to get something from the fridge. And Katie walked through a few times to check on us, and she went back outside.*

Q: *Where was she going?*

A: She said she was going to talk to Alice.

Q: Did she come back?

A: No, she must have been on the phone, so I didn't talk to her.

Q: Who was she speaking with on the phone? Alice?

A: I don't know. I know so little about her now. Our little Katie. It makes me a little sad to think of all we missed out on.

Q: If there's anything else you can remember, just call me.

* * *

DOUG DRESDEN
RELATIONSHIP TO DECEASED:
CARETAKER OF VILLA MAGDA

Q: How long have you been a caretaker here?

A: Forty years.

Q: What can you tell us about last night?

A: Susan and I were happy to have Katie back at the house after so many years. We missed her. We just wanted her to have a nice time. She hadn't been here and, well, she was so excited to be back. She looked beautiful.

Q: Did you see anything unusual?

A: Well, we're not used to parties anymore! They all seemed to be having a good time. It got a bit loud, so we retired to our house.

Q: Did you speak with Charlie during the evening?

A: Of course! We knew Charlie since he was just a boy. He was always troubled, but Katie loved that boy, man.

Q: Troubled?

A: We had heard rumors about his anger problems as a teenager, but he always treated Katie with love. She loved him with her whole heart.

Q: Do you remember what you spoke about?

A: Oh, I'm sure it was about Aria. Charlie seemed really angry last night, though. I wouldn't be surprised if he got into it with someone.

Q: Angry? About what?

A: Who knows. That boy did always seem to find trouble.

Q: Like what?

A: Well, this hasn't been proven, but Susan and I did always suspect there was something going on between him and Lacie.

Q: Something romantic?

A: Some thought that. She made him angrier than I've ever seen, that's for sure.

Q: Where were you when the body was found?

A: Asleep. We woke up from the shouting.

Q: If you remember anything else, please do give us a call, Doug.

* * *

KATE WILLIAMS

RELATIONSHIP TO DECEASED: SPOUSE

Q: *I'm truly sorry for your loss and apologize in advance for the questions. I just have to be thorough.*

A: *Thorough...*

Q: *You said you went to bed before your husband?*

A: *Yes. I was in bed, I must have drifted off by the time he came up.*

Q: *You're sure he came to bed? Kate?*

A: *I thought so, but I'm not sure. Now I really don't know.*

Q: *Was he acting different or at all peculiar at the party?*

A: *He drank maybe more than usual.*

Q: *Someone said the two of you had been arguing?*

A: *We had a small argument, yes.*

Q: *What about?*

A: *I would rather not say.*

Q: *Look, I'm sorry and I know how hard this is for you, but I need to have all the information in order to understand what happened to your husband.*

A: *It was about my sister.*

Q: *Your sister. Lacie?*

A: *Yes.*

Q: *Why would you argue about her?*

A: *Because he lied to me about her. And I wanted to know why.*

Q: *Lied about her?*

A: *About that day. About her. About all of it. I'm sorry, I can't do this right now.*

Q: *What is your relationship like with your son?*

A: *My son? What does that have to do with anything?*

Q: *Please Kate, I know this is hard.*

A: *We have a wonderful relationship. Always have. He's just been busy with his friends.*

Q: *Chloe?*

A: *And Ben. Chloe—did you find her? She was obsessed with my sister, the cold case.*

Q: *Do you know where she is?*

A: *What? No. Why would I know where she is?*

Q: *Where were you when Charlie was found?*

A: *In my room. Asleep.*

Q: *And you don't know where Andrew was?*

A: Andrew? I am sure he was in bed; it was late. Will that be all for now? I really need to take care of my son.

Q: Yes, that will be it for now. And again my condolences. I'm very sorry.

A: I know.

24

MONDAY

"Gretel knew the witch's intentions, and said,
'I don't know how to do it; how shall I get in?'"
—*HANSEL AND GRETEL*, GRIMM BROTHERS

The house had finally settled. It was satisfied, happy to see another tragedy. Happy to have created chaos once again. Kate had been happy for so long away from here. Why had she returned? It was inevitable, she thought. She was called back after her mother's death, now beckoned to uncover the truth, and instead, secrets were spewed out like a snake's venom, infecting everyone in the house. Kate and her sister, Sam's gambling, and Molly's drinking, Alice's secrets, and Charlie's lies. The house was content. Charlie was just another casualty of Villa Magda.

Lacie had once described Villa Magda as tortured. She had been so young to think that, but she said she felt it. Kate looked at the house. The irregular shape, the labyrinth of rooms, the secret passages inside the house that Kate and Lacie would play in, and the lonely tower where the attic was. Kate hated Villa Magda just as much as her great-grandmother must have. It felt like a prison. It lured them in and then spit them out shells of their former selves. Charlie had said they shouldn't come. She wished she had listened to him. And where was Alice? She didn't mention her to the police, she didn't want to do that just yet. They didn't ask. Kate was so angry with her. She suspected that she may have some answers to what happened to Charlie. Kate had always wanted to burn Villa Magda to the ground after that summer. If she had, Charlie would not be dead.

Charlie had never been clumsy, and he was a fabulous swimmer. He hit his head on the side of the pool, that much was clear, but what was he doing by the pool in the middle of the night? She remembered hearing voices that night but thought she was dreaming. Had Charlie been meeting someone by the pool? If so, who? Kate couldn't believe any of this was actually happening. All she wanted to do was talk to Charlie, and now she never would again.

* * *

The doorbell rang. Kate had barely slept. The couch in the living room had made for a lumpy bed, but it was better than facing going to her own bed without Charlie. She had tried to close her eyes but the pain was so strong in her chest. How would she ever survive this? How would Andrew? The pain made her head dizzy and the room felt hot, her thoughts confusing and exhausting. Lacie. Charlie. The two closest people in her life, apart from Andrew. Gone. Forever. It couldn't possibly be true.

The doorbell rang insistently again and Kate got up to answer it. She shuffled to the door in a daze.

It was Darien. "Hey, Katie. It's me."

Seeing him brought a spark of guilt, but Kate was still relieved to see him. He calmed her. She needed that more than ever now.

"I know this seems like a nightmare. I promise I'll do all I can to make this easier." He pulled her into a hug and she breathed into his chest. Kate doubted anything would ever be easy again.

Suddenly, the shrill ringtone of her cell phone, coming from her robe pocket, caused her to jump.

"Kate Williams? My name is Dr. Miles. I'm the medical examiner. I found some things and want to go over them with you."

Kate was silent, having heard the words but not really understanding the meaning. "Things? Like what?"

"It's a normal procedure. Can you come by our office today?"

Kate took a deep breath and nodded. "Yes. I can be there in an hour." Kate hung up, lost in her thoughts.

"Everything okay, Katie?" Darien asked.

"I'm not sure," Kate replied. "The medical examiner asked if I can come by. Something about Charlie."

"I can meet you. It usually helps to have a friend beside you. Do you know where it is? It's in downtown Augusta," Darien suggested. "And Kate?"

"Yes."

"It's going to all be all right."

Nothing had made any sense since they arrived. Kate needed to get her bearings so she could figure out how this was all connected. She felt a chill pass through her bones as she passed by

Alice's room and thought she saw a figure standing in it.

"Alice," Kate said as she quickly turned around only to realize that no one was there. Kate pushed Alice's door open and found the room was empty. None of her clothes were in the closet, and the bed was neatly made, as if it hadn't been slept in. Alice was gone.

* * *

Andrew had wanted to come with her even though Kate had insisted against it. But convincing a seventeen-year-old of anything was nearly impossible, so they drove in complete silence, hardly looking at each other. Like Kate, Andrew was numb. Kate wanted to wrap her arms around him and tell him it would all be okay, but she'd feel like a fraud if she did. She could tell Andrew was angry and sullen. She wanted him to come to her when he was ready.

Kate glanced at him. She couldn't take the silence anymore. "How are you?"

Andrew just shook his head. "Dad's dead."

Kate felt her heart clutch in her chest. She couldn't fix this.

"Have you heard from Chloe?" she asked, genuinely concerned.

"No. But she warned me that Villa Magda was fucked up." He spat out at her. "You brought us to this evil place. It's on you."

Kate pulled over to the side of the road.

"There is nothing I can say, Andrew, except that I didn't want any of this to ever happen. I wanted you to be spared any hurt, but I realize now that no matter how hard I try, I can't promise you that you won't be hurt in life. I can promise you that I will continue to love you for as long as you allow me to." Kate said, tears streaming freely down her face.

"I miss him," Andrew said as he allowed his mother to hug him.

"I know. I do too."

There was not much more she could say to him. All she could do was cradle him in her arms and share the unbearable pain.

* * *

They pulled into the parking lot of the medical examiner's office. The red-bricked building stood in the middle of the square, right next to the police station. She signed in at the desk, and the lady there said Charlie's name as if it were among products on a shopping list. Kate felt her body stiffen. Just hearing Charlie's name brought a sharp pain to her chest, as if a knife were plunged into it. And to them, he was already just a thing.

Kate and Andrew were led into an office and they sat down on one side of a desk and waited.

"Mrs. Williams?" A husky voice shot through the air. A hand stretched forward, and Kate took it and looked up. Standing in front of her was a short, stout woman, much smaller than the voice that came out of it, with short dark hair that spiked out on the sides. For a moment Kate wondered if it spiked out like that naturally or if she put some gel or spray to make it stand up. Her thick eyeglasses were perched high on her nose. She pushed them up further, making her eyes look bigger.

"Hi, I'm Dr. Miles," she continued as she stretched out her hand to Andrew and then sat down behind the desk. "I just needed to show you a couple of things directly." The medical examiner spoke in a clear voice. She handed Kate photos of Charlie.

There was a knock on the door, and Darien walked in.

"Dr. Miles, is it okay if I join you?" he asked.

The doctor nodded.

Darien smiled sympathetically at Kate. "Are you doing all right?" he asked.

"Can I see Charlie?" Kate asked Dr. Miles.

Dr. Miles glanced at Darien.

"Please, I need to see my husband," Kate pleaded with Darien. She pushed the photos away from her on the table. He nodded towards the medical examiner.

"Follow me, this way please." Dr. Miles led them towards the back. The doctor handed them each a blue robe and plastic gloves. They quickly slipped them on.

They entered through a metal door and heard it click shut behind them. Inside, the room was cool, and there was total silence except for a slight buzz of a machine. And on the table was a sheet with a body underneath. She pointed to a spot next to the table where they could stand. Then she nimbly moved over to the other side and pulled on fresh latex gloves and a plastic shield in front of her face. Kate wasn't prepared to see Charlie like this. She thought she would be when the medical examiner first asked her to come down, but now she wanted to turn and run away.

Kate took a deep breath and sighed heavily.

"I know this can be very difficult, but I did find some irregularities on the body."

"What does that mean?" blurted out Andrew. "Irregularities?"

Kate could feel her body tense up as the medical examiner paused. Darien took her hand in his and squeezed. She felt the sudden warmth surge through her and a wave of calm settled in.

Kate was grateful that he was there. "You got this Katie, breathe, okay?" He looked at her with those warm eyes. Kate did as he said. She would get through it. She had to for Andrew.

"Andrew, are you sure you want to be here, I would rather..." Kate began.

"I want to be here, Mom," he said firmly as he took her other hand in his.

Kate nodded. "Please just make this quick."

The medical examiner very methodically explained.

"We believe your husband was hit in the back of the head, which is how he ended up in the pool. There is some indication that there may have been some struggle before he fell. Looking at the wrists of the deceased, there is bruising, indicating that someone may have been holding him down or struggling with him. His right knuckles are bruised, as well as his jaw." She hovered her finger over Charlie's face. "There is also a slight darker coloration here on the left shoulder blade, from a blunt trauma or force to the back."

Kate looked at Darien. Her mind reeled.

"I'm not sure I understand what you are implying," Kate said carefully.

"Most of the bruising may have come from the fight he had with Sam earlier that day," Darien suggested.

"We think there may have been a struggle of some sort minutes before his death," the examiner said.

"What? Like somebody pushed him? Who would do that?" Andrew's voice was loud. His face was turning red as he turned toward his mother, pulling his hand from hers. "Mom! Who did this? I thought he fell. Did you see anything?"

"Andrew, please go outside," Kate said, grabbing his hand.

"I didn't want you to see any of this." Andrew brushed her hand away and stormed out of the room. After the door had closed, the medical examiner continued.

"There was a high quantity of alcohol in his system. In addition to the marks that I mentioned on the wrist and the back, there are some fresh scratches on the right neck, but they appear to be from an earlier time than the others." The medical examiner was moving around the table and indicating areas on Charlie's body with her gloved hands. "See here."

"Earlier? Like a few days?" Kate was getting more agitated.

"Not very long before but at least a few hours would be my guess. Possibly the day before. I'll run some more tests, but that would be my first estimate," she continued in her poised voice.

Kate felt like she was in a surreal movie, looking onto her own life from above.

"The fight he had with Sam, maybe this is from that, too?" Kate said.

"We have collected samples from almost everyone at the house. If it's Sam's, we will know. These scratches seem to have come from someone—or something—shorter than Charlie." The examiner lowered her gaze.

"How do you know that?" Kate asked.

"The angle, and the depth. But the scratches could be from something as inconsequential as a low-hanging branch. It's just, we still need…"

"A sample of my nails, my DNA?" Kate realized.

"Yes, I'm afraid so. And also of your son. This is all very standard procedure, but we have to ask that you let us take some skin samples from your nails, not because we suspect you of anything at all, but to rule you out. In my opinion, there is enough indication of foul play to initiate further investigation. I will be giving my report to the officers later today, but I wanted to give you a chance to process and ask any questions beforehand."

"Rule me out?" Kate said. "I didn't scratch him."

"Even if you did scratch him, it doesn't prove anything, but it gives the police a better place to start. A timeline of events."

"Well, the answer is no, I didn't scratch Charlie, I would have remembered something like that, don't you think?" Kate was angry. She felt betrayed suddenly.

Out of the corner of her eye, Kate saw Darien shoot a look at Dr. Miles.

"What, what was that look?" Kate asked.

"It's just…" Darien said.

"Just what?" Kate asked. "Darien, tell me what this is. Stop with the games."

"Just that you have had problems with memory in the past, and well, maybe you have again. Charlie mentioned to Aunt Susan that you've been under a therapist's care, one that specializes in memory retrieval."

"He told her that?" Kate said, her voice rising.

"He was concerned, and so are we," Darien continued.

"Well, it hasn't worked has it? All that bullshit therapy and I still have one big, gigantic hole in my mind!"

"It's okay," Darien said, trying to calm her.

"No, it isn't, what if it's all true? What if I did do something terrible to Lacie and now Charlie?" Kate cried.

"Look, this is all normal."

"Can you stop saying normal?" Kate screamed at Darien.

Kate felt as if she had been punched in the stomach. *Problems with memory.* This was because of Lacie. Her memory lapses created large gaps in her life eighteen years ago, and now, was she forgetting chunks of this week?

Darien suspected she had something to do with Charlie's death, which was clear to Kate. Charlie had struggled. But with whom and why—those were the questions. Sure, Sam had been angry, but to kill someone would take a lot more than an argument between friends. There were more and more questions and no answers in sight. Someone may have killed Charlie, and she was sure that same someone had something to do with Lacie's disappearance. This was too much of a coincidence to not be suspect.

After dropping Andrew off at the house, Kate realized she might have to turn to the one person who seemed to know everything about that summer.

25

"'Stupid goose,' said the old woman,
'the opening is big enough, I could get in myself.'"
—HANSEL AND GRETEL, GRIMM BROTHERS

The house was dark, but Barbara's car was in the driveway. Kate took a deep breath and rang the bell. The door opened, TV blaring from inside. Barbara looked nervously past Kate's shoulder.

"What are you doing here?" She asked.

"I was hoping I could talk to you," Kate said, her heart beating frantically.

"You were? Well, I'm busy now," Barbara snapped, slamming the door in Kate's face.

Kate rang the bell again and again. Finally, Barbara threw open the door.

"What?"

"Please, I just need a minute."

"Well, you weren't so accommodating when I asked you to talk for the paper," Barbara said sarcastically.

"Look, I don't know if you know this, or if you will care, but Charlie is dead. We found him in the pool this morning. It might have been an accident but…"

"Charlie, oh my God," Barbara said, her tone changing. "I didn't know."

"Your brother is investigating the case, but I just feel like this all leads to Lacie somehow."

Something in Barbara's expression made Kate think that she thought so, too.

"You know something, Barbara. I know you do. You've been obsessed with my family for years—I've seen your website. How long before something about Charlie's death shows up on your blog?" Kate could feel herself going overboard, but she couldn't stop. "Where are you getting your information?"

"It was all my father thought about for years! His entire office was covered with information about Lacie's case. I just wanted to help find out what happened to Lacie."

"You can still help me find the truth. Please just tell me what you know."

Barbara paused, her brow furrowed as she peered at Kate. "You really don't remember, do you?"

"Remember what?"

"I thought somehow you fooled everyone," Barbara continued, her eyes studying Kate.

"I don't know what you mean," Kate said, pleading with her. "Fooled…?"

"Your sister, your little sister…" Barbara started.

"What?" Kate asked.

"Look, I don't know if this is just some act you've put on to hide all of your guilt all these years, or you really have blocked it all out," Barbara said. Kate could tell she was scared.

"I don't understand. What happened to Lacie?" Kate asked. She wanted to shake this woman. "If you know, you have to tell me."

"She was pregnant," Barbara blurted out. "And you knew too. You knew all along. You hid it from everyone, including yourself apparently. We had to deal with your little secrets and clean it all up! Now, please leave." She slammed the door, leaving Kate standing there speechless.

* * *

Pregnant—the words echoed loudly in Kate's mind. Lacie, innocent Lacie, had been pregnant that summer.

And Barbara mentioned her father's obsession with Lacie. Could there be more information in his office that wasn't in the official case file? Kate recalled her conversation earlier in the week with Darien, when he mentioned he had moved into his childhood home. Kate remembered going there for a party Darien had had over the summer.

Now, Darien's house looked weathered and in need of updating. Kate parked the car a few houses down. Kate tried pulling on the door, hoping it was unlocked, but it wasn't. Kate rummaged in the bush next to the house where the key had been when she was a kid. Nothing there. She looked around and noticed another bush with magnolias. She didn't remember it, but she felt behind it, and there it was, the key. Kate looked around, making sure there was no one out on the street, and then put the key in the lock. The door creaked open. The house stood as if it had been frozen in time and was just as Kate remembered it. Antique furniture strewn about in the living room with no particular theme. A leather armchair, a grandfather clock, and a television. She walked toward the basement door, where Barbara and Darien's father had had his study. A bird chirp startled her, and Kate realized it was just the clock on the wall. She hurried down the stairs, keeping in mind she may have very little time until Darien came home.

The door to the office was unlocked and in it, Kate found a large wooden oak desk with papers scattered across it. The office was as messy as the rest of the house, with photos and newspaper clippings framed and hanging on the wall. She didn't know the first place to look—it was a bit like finding a needle in a haystack—but she opened the cabinet first. Tax papers and documents, large folders with bills and other normal, everyday clutter lined the drawers.

Frustrated, Kate looked in the last two drawers, and still there was nothing that seemed to relate to her sister or the case. Feeling foolish, she realized she was grasping at straws. Why did she even think she could solve the case when the police hadn't been able to? She wasn't Nancy Drew or Veronica Mars. It had been a long shot, and she had been terribly wrong. Charlie would have told her not to come, that it would be a waste of time and dangerous. But now Charlie was gone and there was no one to guide her, not even Alice. Kate could not get the image of Charlie's lifeless body floating in the pool out of her mind. His beautiful face with the blunt hit to his head. Kate would do anything in the world to tell Charlie just how sorry she was and that she forgave him no matter what happened all those years ago. She just wanted to hold him one last time and be a family again. Coming here had been more than a mistake; it had been life changing.

But they thought she had something to do with Charlie, didn't they? She saw the look on Andrew's face when Officer Mallory said that it may not have been an accident and when the medical examiner confirmed it. Her own son, doubting her. It broke her heart in more ways than she could bear. She had just shut off her light and gone to bed. If only she hadn't, maybe Charlie would still be alive.

How could she think she could just break into Darien's house and find the answers she so desperately craved? Her heart sank, she might never find out the truth about Charlie or Lacie. As she passed the desk, she caught a glance of her image in the mirror. Her face was tired, haggard even. She had aged more in the last week than she had in the past ten years. Her eyes were hollow and dark, rimmed with red and blotches of purple. A bookshelf caught her eye in the mirror behind her. She noticed how neatly the books were arranged. She was impressed and appreciated the order for a moment, since everything else seemed so out of place. She turned to leave and then stopped. That's when she saw it. The book had been staring right at her all along. It was Lacie's favorite book, right there in the bookcase. *Hansel & Gretel.* It was just like the one from Lacie's library, a special edition that Lacie had gotten on her birthday. Kate felt an intense chill go through her as flashes of her sister reading it on her bed came to mind. Lacie had never been the same after reading that book. *It doesn't mean anything*, Kate thought. So many loved that classic and had it in their bookshelves. Didn't they? Kate looked at the book and pulled it out carefully. Her hands were shaking. It was a hardcover, yellowed with a gold border. She opened it gently. The pages were dog-eared in some places. It had been read and reread.

As Kate flipped the book closed, an inscription on the front page caught her eye. There was a heart drawn next to it. The inscription read: *A+A (secret friends) 4ever. Thank you A for being my special friend. I would be so lonely without you. Love, Alice.*

Kate's hands shook. It was Lacie's handwriting. She knew it. But she'd signed it as Alice. Alice—why would she have done that? Kate could hardly see straight, her vision blurring through her tears. Was everything she ever knew one big lie? They had been friends all along. Did Alice do something to her sister? Was she responsible for Charlie's death as well? Waves of fury engulfed Kate. She shook her head. Alice. Alice. Alice held the key all along, and now she was gone too. Kate looked in the book again, and then a photograph fell out. It was Lacie holding a baby, her baby. She was in a room. Kate had seen that room before but it wasn't in Villa Magda. There was a small table with a tea set in the background. What was this book doing here and the picture of Lacie with her baby?

Kate heard the door screech open upstairs, and her body froze. She quickly put the book and the photo in her bag as she listened to footsteps above her. Kate quietly moved out of the office and into the basement, finding a small door. She opened it and slipped into a dark room. There was a washer, dryer, and a small crawl space. More footsteps echoed above her, and Kate opened the door to the crawl space and crept in. It was hardly big enough for her body. The footsteps grew louder as they moved down the stairs and Kate slipped further in, wondering what Darien was doing at home in the middle of the day. Charlie's voice rang in her head: *"I told you so. I told you so. I told you so."*

26

"Gretel gave her a push,
and she shut the oven door
and left the wicked witch to burn miserably."
—*HANSEL AND GRETEL*, GRIMM BROTHERS

After what seemed like forever, Kate didn't hear any movement in the house. She finally opened the door and stepped into quietness. Down the hall, the study's door was ajar. The lights were off, but as Kate peered in, she noticed the contents of the once-neat bookcase were now strewn across the floor. Papers littered the ground instead of the desk, and the desk's drawers had been rifled through. Clearly, whoever was in the house was looking for something specific. Kate wondered if they'd found what they were looking for, as she thought about the photo and the book in her bag.

The lights were all off as she crept up the stairs. She reached the kitchen and opened the back door and, without looking behind her, ran as fast as she could to her car. She threw herself into the front seat and collapsed, she couldn't trust anyone anymore. Lacie had been pregnant. According to Barbara, Kate herself had known some of this and her own brain was something she couldn't trust. Everybody had been keeping something from Kate—even Darien. And now she had confirmation that Alice had lied to her all this time. She needed to find her and get the truth from her once and for all.

Her head hurt as she tried to focus. She feared she was losing her memory again. Darien had mentioned her memory being so fragmented, but she had thought she had a handle on it. Alice was there when Lacie was gone, before Kate had left for home. Alice was there whenever Kate needed her or had some issue. But isn't that what best friends do? Why was she suddenly suspicious of that? All these years, Alice had never done anything to hurt her...had she?

After she calmed her breathing, Kate drove directly to the police station. She'd made the decision while in the crawl space that she needed to see Officer Mallory. She would ask her about the book, about Alice. Surely, if Lacie had been friends with her, the police would have known, Kate thought. And Kate couldn't help but feel that the book and the photo might have something to do with Charlie's death.

Kate burst through the front door of the police station just as Officer Mallory was leaving.

"Mrs. Williams," Officer Mallory sounded surprised.

"I need to talk to you." Kate breathed out. "I found something."

Officer Mallory looked around and kept her voice low, "Why don't we talk in my office?"

"There was a photo of my sister," Kate fumbled with her bag, pulling out the book and the photo. "I don't know why he had it, but I thought it could help—"

"He, who?"

"Kate!" A deep voice made Kate jump. Darien strode toward them, a smile on his face. "I thought you'd gone back to Villa Magda after the medical examiner's."

Kate's heart jumped in her throat, but she tried to relax her face. "I wanted to see Officer Mallory. Something about Charlie."

Darien shared a look with Officer Mallory. "I'm sorry," Kate interjected as they both looked at her. She imagined how she must have looked to them. Definitely a crazed suspect. But she was desperate. Darien's eyes jumped to Kate's hands and he turned to Officer Mallory. "Don't you have your meeting with Dr. Miles? I can handle this."

"Of course. Thanks, Chief Anderson." Officer Mallory nodded at them. Kate's eyes silently pleaded with the officer, but Officer Mallory left, leaving her alone with Darien.

"You okay?" Darien asked as the officer left the room. "What's wrong?" Concern laced his voice.

Kate didn't know how it would look once she told him that she had broken into his house, but he had already seen her with the photo and the book. He would understand—at least she hoped he would. She opened the book to the page where Lacie had written, and let him read it. He glanced at it, then looked at Kate, frowning a little in confusion.

"Where did you find this?"

"In... your father's office. I know it sounds crazy, and I'm sorry, I should have told you I was going there, but I had to see

your father's case file, his personal notes. Barbara said your father
had been obsessed with the case." Kate rambled on, knowing
just how crazy this was all sounding.

"Wait a minute, back up. You broke into my house?" Darien
shook his head. "Kate, that's illegal. How could you?"

"Come on, Darien. You all think I killed my husband, pos-
sibly my sister. I have no choice but to do what I can to prove
I didn't. Look, isn't it strange that this book was in the office?"
Kate was pleading.

"My father kept a lot of random things in the office; maybe it
was something he picked up at the church book fair for my sister."

"With her dedication? It's Lacie's handwriting," Kate said,
her voice trembling.

"I suppose, but there must be some explanation. Maybe my
father had it with his things from the case?"

"But why did he keep it?" Kate probed.

"I'm not sure, and we can't very well ask him now, can we?"
Darien said, annoyed.

"Another thing, it's signed by Alice. You know Alice, she's
my best friend."

"I mean, I remember her name coming up. Don't even
remember how actually, but no one seemed to know who she
was," Darien said.

"Didn't you see her at the party?" Kate asked. "She was there,
but now she is gone. Just up and left, and she never told me
she knew Lacie."

"At your party? No, I didn't see her or meet her. But then
again, I hardly spoke to any of your friends. You were all so preoccupied," Darien said flatly, looking at Kate closely. He then took a
deep breath. "Kate, have you called a therapist?" he asked carefully.

"My therapist? No, I haven't. What does that have to do with anything?" Kate asked, getting upset.

"Maybe you need to make sense of some of your thoughts." Darien said. "It is the anniversary of your sister's disappearance, and you just lost your husband. You are bound to be suffering and in need of some guidance."

"Look, Alice has something to do with all of this. This is Lacie's handwriting, and she signed it 'Alice.' It has to mean something," Kate insisted.

"That is odd, granted. Something to possibly look into. And you say she left after the party?" Darien asked as he tried to usher her out the door.

"I mean she may be back at the villa; I don't know, I've been gone since this morning." Kate was tired. It had been a long day. She needed sleep to gather her thoughts and make sense of all of this.

"Kate, I know you're going through a lot, but this all does sound a little far-fetched. I mean, I'm not sure this proves anything other than you may have a bad friend who knew your sister, but murdering her or your husband…" Darien spoke carefully. "It's unlikely."

"So, it's more likely that I did it? I harmed him?" Kate asked in an accusatory tone.

"You were concerned that Charlie had been hiding things, things about Lacie. You told me so yourself," Darien said.

"That doesn't mean I killed him!" Kate screamed. But the truth was, she didn't know anymore.

"I have been looking for anything I could find since I arrived, any clue about what happened to Lacie, and all I've found with any bit of certainty is that Lacie signed her name Alice. This has to be something. It just has to be. Please." Her voice was cracking from fatigue.

"Okay. Okay. I will speak to Barbara and see what she knows or why she is pursuing this. My sister can be a little eccentric and somewhat of a conspiracy theorist," Darien said.

"She told me Lacie was pregnant. Did you ever hear that?" Kate asked.

"She said what?" Darien asked incredulously.

"She did," Kate insisted. "That's why I went to look at the files! That's when I found this photo."

"I've never seen this before." Darien looked confused. "I'll take care of it," he said as he finally guided Kate out the door. "Now, you go get some rest, stop thinking about it. I will get to the bottom of it. Just trust me, okay? And if your friend returns, call me right away." His dark eyes bored into her. "I have always just wanted to be there for you."

Kate forced a smile as he eased away from her.

"Let me hold on to this," Darien said, lifting up the book. "This was a good clue to find. I'm surprised I hadn't found it before. We may be closer than ever to answers, I won't let anyone know it was you who found it. Don't worry about that."

Kate felt a surge of relief. Someone was in her corner, and together they would figure out this mystery once and for all. Now all Kate had to do was find Alice and get some answers from her. She had an idea just where she might find her.

* * *

Kate arrived at the house. The sun was starting to set and all was quiet. She had lost all track of time. As she went upstairs and passed Molly's room, she caught a glimpse of her friend packing.

Kate stopped and saw that her eyes were swollen and red.

"You've been gone all day," Molly said as she carefully folded a top into her bag.

"I had to go to the medical examiner's office." Kate spoke as if she were talking about buying eggs. It seemed strange, this new reality they had all been pulled into.

"Where is everyone?"

"Sam left with Ben. I stayed to pack. Ben wanted to go. This was all too much for him. He had a panic attack."

"I'm sorry. Molly—" Kate said. "I didn't mean for any of this to happen."

"The police have our information, and we promised not to leave the country." Molly shook her head. "As if any of us would ever hurt Charlie."

Kate nodded. "Is Andrew here?"

"He's in his room. It's locked. I tried to see if he was okay. But he didn't answer. Asleep maybe, poor kid."

"I don't know what to say," Kate said. "I would never—"

"Stop, Kate. Just stop. Please don't say anything. You know, when you first invited us here, I was looking forward to spending time with you and helping you through this. I was hoping you would open up to me about your mom and your childhood, but as more of what happened to your sister came out, I kept wondering about you, who is this Kate that I don't know, don't recognize? We have known each other for years, but I am just now realizing that I don't really know you." She was looking at Kate with sadness. "I couldn't understand why you had us come here. I mean, this place isn't happy. It may have been once, but it isn't. I felt it when we first arrived. I told Sam I thought maybe it's haunted, but you know Sam, he just thought I was being me." She took a deep breath. "But I wasn't. I was right. Don't get me wrong, it's a beautiful house, but it's a sad house, and you knew that and brought us here anyway."

"Molly, I—" Kate tried again, but Molly wouldn't let her speak.

"A few nights ago, I had too much to drink again. I thought just this last one, one more drink won't hurt anyone. I'll stop tomorrow. I can. At least I convinced myself I could. It's what addicts do—we lie to ourselves, sort of like you lying to yourself that you weren't coming here to find your sister." Molly gazed off into the distance, her face flushed.

"That night I went downstairs to the kitchen to get a bottle of water. Maybe an aspirin. I heard a voice. So I waited on the landing and…and it was you, Kate. I can recognize your voice anywhere. I was relieved it wasn't some ghost I had conjured up in the middle of the night, my imagination or my drunken stupor running away with me."

Kate wasn't sure what she was trying to say, but the look in Molly's eyes scared her to the core.

"I wanted to see who you were talking to, so I tiptoed down the steps enough to see the kitchen." She took a deep, shaky breath before finishing. "I saw you, and…no one was there. It was just you." There was fear in Molly's eyes as she spoke. "Of course, I thought I was imagining it at first. I mean, you're not crazy. You're Kate. You're the grounded one. Yet, there you were, having a determined and full conversation with nobody."

Fear grabbed Kate by the throat, but she tried to shake it off. This was absurd. She couldn't trust a word of what Molly was saying; she had to still be drunk.

"Molly, that's crazy. You're not well."

Molly scoffed. "I know, right? I thought something was wrong with me, but then...well, I started watching you more closely, listening closely. And you did it again. In the garden. I followed you. You were alone, and you were talking to yourself again. You kept saying the name Alice. As if that was who you were speaking to."

Kate's heart stopped. What was Molly saying? "Alice," Kate said, searching her friend's face. "I don't understand."

"I told Charlie, and not for any other reason than I was genuinely worried about you. But he knew. He said you had done this before, that you had gone to see someone to talk about it, and that you had lapses in memory. He asked me not to say anything to you and said he had it under control, that this other person was a coping technique for you. It didn't happen often, he said, but he imagined it had to do with the house."

Kate's head was spinning. Charlie knew...what? He knew Alice, certainly. But instead of saying that, he'd been talking about her and her mental health with Molly?

Before she could wrap her head around it, Molly continued.

"But he didn't have it under control at all, did he? And now I think that it's my fault he's dead, that maybe you or Alice—or the both of you, I don't fucking know—had something to do with this. All I know is that I need to leave and get the hell out of here before I go crazy myself. I am going to a hotel for a few days. When you and Andrew are ready to leave Maine, I will drive back with you. But I think you should come to the hotel with me. You and Andrew shouldn't be here alone in this house."

"I would never hurt Charlie," Kate said quietly. "And Alice is my best friend; you know her, she was here." But she no longer believed it herself.

Molly looked as if she had seen a ghost.

"No, Kate, she wasn't. Not for the rest of us at least. There is no Alice. We've never met her. She doesn't exist."

Kate suddenly saw images of her sister. She was talking to someone, but no one was there.

"Can you guess my name?" Lacie teased.

"Lacie," Kate said.

"No, my other name, my true self. Think hard, Kate."

Kate repeated the name over in her head. Lacie. Lacie.

"Mix the letters," Lacie said, exasperated. "It's right there."

L A C I E.

"A L I C E. See, when jumbled, I am Alice."

Kate was shaking her head as the memory faded, reality settling like a brick in her stomach. No…no, it couldn't be. She could see Alice as clear as day. She was her best friend. This couldn't be.

Kate had been grasping for answers, and it had been there all along—her sister *was* Alice. An imaginary friend, a replacement for her sister to ease her guilt.

"She'll grow out of it," Susan would say, when Lacie made them call her Alice. Who knows if she would have, but it was clear that Kate never let it go, never let Lacie go—she kept her here as her best friend, Alice.

Her heart was beating loudly, the blood rushing in her ears.

"You need help, Kate, real help that none of us can give you. Charlie tried but coming here was a terrible idea. He should have stopped you, but you said you were ready," Molly continued.

Tears were running down Kate's face. "He told you that?"

Molly nodded. "He loved you, you know. I want to stay

and help you, I do. But I'm truly terrified of you, Kate. This is not something anyone, let alone me, has the strength to cope with. Charlie's dead. Game over for me. I'm sorry." Molly shut her suitcase and looked at Kate. "We should leave. You should stop searching for whatever it is you were looking for here. Get whatever help you need." Molly walked out of the room, pulling her suitcase down the hall.

Kate watched her leave. Her friend, her real friend who was flesh and blood and not some figment of her imagination, whom she needed now more than ever, was gone too. She and Andrew were the only ones left.

* * *

"*The mind is a tricky place, filled with rooms, rooms we keep things stored in,*" *the voice said.*

Kate's mind wandered as she saw Alice standing in front of her, her beautiful face smiling as she tilted her head, studying Kate.

"*Some of these compartments contain our memories: memories of our friends, our families, our loved ones. They can also contain traumatic events. How big these compartments play a role in their influence on your life. For some, the compartments may differ in both quality, quantity, and relevance. You created many more compartments, Kate. Alice was in one of them, and when your sister disappeared, she took over.*"

She remembered so much, it was like a few compartments had been unlocked or kicked over, reality flooding in. Alice was there whenever she wanted her to be. She needed her. She was her sister, her confidante, her best friend—albeit imaginary.

Kate stood up. The house was quieter than ever. Molly was right—she had to leave. But if she couldn't be sure of what was real and what wasn't, how could she be certain she hadn't done anything to Charlie? She had been so angry with him the other night. But had she been mad enough to kill her husband?

Kate walked into the dark hall and saw a figure, pale and slight—a figure she knew was Alice. But suddenly, there were two of them standing side by side: Lacie and Alice.

"It's all pretend, isn't it?" Kate said out loud. She looked at her beautiful sister and her friend, standing there in the dark. They were one and the same.

"My sister, and my best friend," Kate whispered to herself.

"Shh... listen..." Alice said as she put her finger to her lips.

"Silent," Kate whispered to herself. She remembered.

Susan looked at the girls, their small faces filled with anticipation. "Who can tell me the anagram for silent?"

Lacie loved playing this game as she sat and ate her berries.

Lacie looked at her and proudly shouted, "It's silent, the anagram for Listen is Silent!"

"That's right," Susan said. "You are so very good at this."

"I'm Alice," Lacie had said.

"You're who?"

"Alice. Mix the letters up for Lacie. Isn't that so great? I'm an anagram too."

The memories were flooding her brain all at once. Susan. The writing in the bathroom. Silent... Did Kate write that on her own mirror? The room Lacie was in with her baby, she knew that room. It was a room where they had spent a lot of time as children, a place where they both felt safe to be themselves.

"Susan," Kate said, a sudden realization coming over her. Susan knew all of their secrets.

Kate rushed down the stairs and out the front door. She

looked back at the house. The sun had already faded behind the trees, and Villa Magda looked like a giant animal when dark. It watched from the attic with glimmering eyes. The lights were on in the cottage, and Kate ran toward it, thinking of all the things Susan had said to her. They used to play games together, pretend games. *Listen.*

Kate knocked furiously on the door. "Susan," she called out.

After a few moments, the door opened. It was Susan, her face weathered and stoic. She saw the fear in Kate's eyes and smiled sadly. "I knew you would come."

Kate took a deep breath. Susan, the woman she had trusted for years. What was she hiding? She could feel the terror envelop her suddenly.

"The anagram game we used to play—Alice. You've known about her, haven't you?" Kate cried.

Susan stayed silent and just looked at Kate, her face still.

"You were Lacie's secret keeper. I remember now," she said, out of breath from running.

"Come in, Katie, I suspected you would come sooner or later." Susan was half smiling. "It's been a long time, and we have a lot to catch up on. I think you need a nice hot cup of tea."

Kate looked back at the villa in the distance as she entered the cottage.

27

"Be comforted, dear little sister, and sleep in
peace, God will not forsake us."
—*HANSEL AND GRETEL*, GRIMM BROTHERS

As soon as Kate stepped inside, she was transported back to her childhood; there was a sitting area and living room where Kate and Lacie spent many days drinking tea and playing games when their mother needed them out of the house. Susan motioned for Kate to sit down.

"You knew all along," Susan said. "We weren't sure how much you would ever remember, but you knew about Lacie. For a while, you went along with it. We didn't think that so much fuss would have occurred as it did. I mean of course we knew that people would ask and there would be questions, but we had hoped that we could manage it."

Kate felt her stomach drop. "I knew." It wasn't a question. The realization was devastating.

She had known that her sister, her little sister, had been pregnant. Now that it was confirmed, Kate could visualize it. Lacie was sitting on her bed, crying and writing in her journal. Kate was worried that something was going on with Charlie, but she was more worried about Lacie. She tried to console her, but Lacie was distraught, scared.

That night, Kate slipped into Lacie's room and read her journal. Entries about Charlie and then... those words.

"I haven't gotten my period and told Susan. She thinks I might be pregnant."

Kate hadn't known what to think when she read that. She thought that Lacie was playing games again. So, Kate had gone to see Susan.

Susan told Kate that they needed to help Lacie together. Keep her secret from her mother. And so they did. They decided to hide her. It was the only way.

"We had to make sure. We took care of it quietly. Your mother would have sent Lacie away and gotten rid of the baby. She said she was worried about it ruining Lacie's future, but I think she was really worried about other people finding out. She was always such a selfish woman. We couldn't allow that to happen. So, we hid her. Lacie sent a letter to your mother, saying she was running away. It was all we could think of. We would have her back afterward, we thought. But your mother, called the police. We were careful, it was difficult, and we didn't really know what we were doing. We just wanted to help Lacie." She sipped some tea and then continued.

"We had never had children of our own, and we were going

to just keep the child ourselves. We never meant to hurt anyone." Susan's voice was trembling. "I promise you that."

"But the police said she just disappeared?"

"It was a hard secret to pull off, but we were quiet, and Lacie was so good about it. She loved it here, being out from under your mother's thumb, and of course having all the attention on her."

Kate sat down, her legs shaking beneath her. "I just don't remember any of this."

"No one knew. We were her secret keepers," Susan said proudly. "We took that role very seriously."

"Did you… did you kill Charlie?" Kate had so many questions she needed answered, but at this moment, that one mattered the most.

"No, no, of course not. I know this is so much for you to take on, you must believe that Doug and I never meant to hurt anyone."

"I don't believe much of anything, this is all so confusing. What happened to her the months before she gave birth?" Kate had too many questions now flooding her brain. "Where was she all that time? Here?"

Susan took a deep breath. "You really don't remember? I wondered, over the years, if you ever would. We just assumed that you were traumatized from the guilt. You knew there was so much more you could have done for her, but you just left."

"She was here all along," Kate said.

Susan nodded. "Come, I'll show you." Kate followed her to the back of the cottage where there was the door hidden by pantry shelves. Like Villa Magda, the cottage was full of secrets. Kate stopped coming to the cottage after Lacie had vanished. It was too painful for her.

Susan slowly opened the secret door.

"She stayed here, and we took care of Lacie together for a while, and then you had to leave. She was devastated, losing you, but we told her you would be back."

"You took a young girl and played pretend with her life!" Kate felt her blood run cold. "You were manipulating both of us, just so you could have the baby you always wanted. Just because you couldn't … We trusted you. We were both just kids."

Lacie had been here all along, locked away like some doomed princess in a castle. And Kate knew. Kate could have helped her. But instead she was too weak and pretended not to know. Her anger toward herself began to rise in her throat. She wanted to scream and run out of there, take Andrew, and never look back—but she needed to hear more. She needed to know what exactly had happened to Lacie. So she followed Susan just as Lacie had done all those years ago, behind the door.

"But what happened to her then? Where is she now?" Kate stammered, already knowing the answer in her heart.

On the wall hung a photo. There they all were—Susan and Doug with Lacie. And then there was another photo of Chloe and Susan. Chloe looked just like Lacie.

"Chloe…" Kate said right before she heard a shrill crack, a searing pain shooting through her head, and it all went dark.

* * *

Images of Lacie running in the woods in her white dress swirled around in Kate's head, along with Alice's voice chanting in a grating rhythm.

She was as pretty as a swan
Which made her sister want her gone
So she locked her in her room
And slowly brought her to her doom.

Kate was running after her, but she only got further and further away until all Kate could see was a tiny white dot in the blackness. Kate pried her eyes open, adjusting to the darkness. She could hear voices: Susan, Doug, and someone else.

"You didn't have to hit her so hard," Susan said in a low voice.

"She's starting to remember and put everything together. We just can't take the chance anymore, this has to be over with her now. Why did you let her come back to the house in the first place?" the voice said.

"We tried. We told her we would take care of everything, but she insisted on seeing the house one last time. You know Katie, once she puts her mind to something, there is no talking her out of it."

Kate felt intense pressure in her temple and a warm gooey substance on the side of her head, probably blood. She slowly looked around the dark room, her eyes adjusting until she could make out her surroundings. Her hands were immobile, and it took her a moment to realize she had been tied to a small cot. Was it the same cot where Lacie had slept? The room looked like a replica of Lacie's room up in the villa: books, an art easel with a painting of the house. Nothing had changed. They had kept the room like this for years. Kate tried to pull on the rope around her wrists but it was firmly tied. She hoped that Darien would come looking for her—or someone, anyone. She couldn't disappear like Lacie had, alone here in this room.

"She's awake," Doug said.

"She's going to need stitches."

"Aunt Susan. We don't have time for this," the voice said firmly.

"We can't keep her here too long," Doug said.

Kate saw a bassinet in the corner. The baby. Lacie's baby. Chloe? Could it actually be true?

Kate looked at them, hardly able to get words out, searing pain shooting through her head. The voice. Aunt Susan. A man. Kate realized in horror whom that voice belonged to.

"Darien…" she said as she focused on the third dark figure. The voice. *Mix the letters, make out the name.*

D A R I E N / A D R I E N.

The name on the Reddit thread, Adrien_A_69—the *A* in the book. He had been with Lacie. He was the boy she was referring to; he was why Susan was her special secret keeper. *He* was the father of Lacie's baby, not Charlie. Kate struggled to look up, squinting through the pain, and saw him standing there.

"Why did you give me the file?" Kate had a feeling she knew, but wanted to hear him explain.

"You already had it in your head that Charlie was lying. I needed to nudge you in that direction," Darien said. "I wish you would have just stayed away. You shouldn't have come back… you had that memory issue, and that was fine with us. But this afternoon, when you came to the police station, you said her name. You said Alice. And you had the book. And I knew we couldn't just let you go." His eyes bored through her.

She took a deep breath, mustering up every ounce of strength she had—and screamed. She was as loud as she could manage, but she knew no one would hear her. Everyone was gone, everyone but Andrew. Her blood ran cold. What if they hurt her son? Darien hit her hard to get her to stop screaming.

"Quiet down!" His voice was loud and hard. Kate winced.

"She loved Darien. They were both just lonely kids," Susan said.

"I wasn't ready to have a baby and neither was she, but she got it in her head that we would get married. I mean, she was sixteen, and I was only seventeen. I had dreams of leaving this town. I was scared. We thought that we could change her mind. I tried telling her it would be okay, but she started getting angry, cruel even. She said she would tell everyone we kidnapped her. After the baby was born, it got worse. She was supposed to go back home and pretend nothing had happened, but she was making all these demands."

"So you killed her," Kate said, suddenly seeing where he was going.

Darien stared at her, his voice flat. "I didn't want that to happen, none of us did. But I would have gone to jail. Susan and Doug would have lost everything. And it was almost too easy to keep it a secret. Your father fled like a coward and took you with him, and Gail was always too drunk to notice anything. But over the last few months, she started getting suspicious. The only way to keep our secret was to stop her from digging. But then you showed up."

She'd thought she wanted answers, but the truth was tearing her apart, nausea rising in her as she thought about them murdering her little sister. "You were supposed to look out for her," she cried as she looked at Susan and Doug. She swallowed down her fear and looked up at Darien, another truth dawning. "You killed my mother. And you killed Charlie."

"Charlie was purely an accident. The night of your birthday, he called me to come back. He knew about the baby and wanted to find out how much I knew. Chloe had confronted him, she figured it out. We were always afraid she might. But she thought Charlie was her father. We had no choice when it came to your mother. She was starting to wonder why Chloe looked so much like Lacie. She wanted to see her, talk to her. At first, we let her, but then she started asking too many questions. We were worried that she was going to say something to you."

"Her tea. You poisoned her," Kate realized, turning to Susan.

"She already wanted to die; Doug and I just helped her."

"She loved you. How could you?"

"She never loved us," Susan spat. "We were just 'the help,' and she never failed to remind us of that. Gail didn't love Villa Magda; she just loved the status it gave her in town. Your mother never cared about the town until she had us put on her stupid little garden parties with her rich friends who thought they were better than us. We weren't family until she had no family."

"I never knew you felt this way," Kate whispered.

"We didn't think you would ever come back. You had been gone so long." Susan ignored Kate's comment. "I told you we would take care of the memorial, her things. You should have just stayed away."

"You gave me those files, the photo, all lies, to get me to remember a different past. To manipulate my memory," Kate said. She was filled with rage, she wanted to kill him. As always Charlie had been trying to protect her. "Is this what Carl was trying to tell me, that day in the house?"

"We didn't intend for him to find out, but he walked in one day and found Lacie in the house. We couldn't risk him telling anyone, so we paid off his brother to keep Carl quiet as best he could," Darien said, his eyes wild. He reminded Kate of a feral animal.

"Where is Chloe?" she demanded. Kate remembered what Ben had told her: "*She's obsessed with you and your sister.*"

"She's safe with Barbara," Darien said, leaning close to Kate's face. "I loved you, Katie. We were supposed to be together, but then Charlie came along and you fell in love."

"So you went after my sister to make me jealous?"

"I tried, but Lacie became obsessed. She gave us no option, we did what we had to do."

"And now you're going to kill me, too," Kate said.

"I don't want to. I really don't. But you know all our secrets. We can't trust that you won't say anything." His voice was cold.

Kate felt the horror of what they were saying fill her. "What about Chloe—she knows some of the secrets."

"We'll worry about her later, she doesn't know enough now to hurt us," Darien said as he untied Kate's hands. "And she will now think that her aunt killed her mother and father."

Kate was terrified. "You're all crazy. This can't go on forever, all these secrets. This entire town, one big secret."

"You're right. They'll die, finally, with you. You are the only one that we have to worry about, and after tonight we won't have to ever again," Darien said as he sighed, his eyes glittering and sharp. Kate could practically see the adrenaline pumping through his veins.

"When we were kids, you wanted to burn Villa Magda down to the ground. Well, why don't we make that happen?" Darien said. "It's just you and Andrew, the rest of them are gone, and you can join Lacie and Charlie."

Kate stood up, her head still burning with pain. She longed for Charlie; he would have saved her. Her poor dear Charlie.

"It would've been different, if we had continued after that day in the garden, when we kissed. I know you felt what I did. You lingered, but then that was it. You ignored me after that as if it never happened," Darien said.

Kate looked at Darien. "I would have never been with you. You're just a weak loser," Kate spat at him.

Darien slapped her, drawing blood on her lip. He shoved her toward the door, digging his fingernails into her arm.

The house loomed above, waiting, as they left the cottage. This was its final moment. Kate wondered what Lacie had been thinking in her final moments. She wanted desperately to know what happened, how she had died, but was afraid to know the horror of it. She asked anyway.

"How did you kill her?"

"Lacie loved when I made her blueberry pie, it was her favorite," Susan said as she looked at Kate. "I couldn't bear to let Darien kill her; I just wanted her to go to sleep like a princess, just like in her fairy tales. The garden grows some deadly nightshade. They look like blueberries, and they're just as sweet. We only needed a few, placed in a slice of her favorite pie. She went peacefully. By that time, you had stopped writing to her, stopped asking us about Lacie. You left her and then forgot about her."

"How could you?" Kate looked at Susan, her caretaker, her second mother. She wanted to throw up. Susan looked away. "We loved you, trusted you."

Kate's eyes overflowed with tears, she couldn't see straight.

"Where is she? Where is Lacie?" She demanded. "Where the hell is my sister?"

"We took her out on the boat," Doug said.

The light suddenly went on upstairs.

"Help!" Kate started to scream. Darien yanked her back, clamping his hand over her mouth.

"Be quiet." Darien growled as he shoved Kate through the kitchen door, his hand smothering her mouth.

Kate pushed against his hand, the smell of gasoline filling her nostrils as Susan and Doug poured it throughout the house. Footsteps stomped upstairs, and Kate prayed Andrew would find a way to escape.

"Andrew, run!"

"Come on, Kate, don't make this harder than it has to be."

She had to get to Andrew. Darien jerked her toward the pantry, his fingernails digging into her skin.

Smoke started to fill the house, and Susan and Doug called out for Darien. Kate worked on loosening the rope knotted around her wrists. Every inch of her body throbbed with pain, and it took all of her strength not to cry out.

"Mom," Andrew called from upstairs. "What's going on?"

"Get outside!" She coughed. Her fingers closed in around the last knot on the rope.

"Get inside!" Darien shouted as he opened the pantry door and a large creature flew out. Kate instinctively ducked and it hit him directly in the face. Another bat, Kate thought, as she finally ripped her hands free. She shoved Darien and ran out into the hall. Darien stumbled backward as he swatted at the bat that flailed violently around him. Kate flew up the stairs, the air growing thicker with black smoke with every step. Kate registered Darien's voice behind her right as he grabbed her leg. Kate fell forward, but kept hold of the handrail, which gave her enough leverage to kick back as hard as she could. Her foot made contact with Darien's chest, causing him to fall down the steps with a thud.

Kate rushed toward the end of the hall where Andrew and Ben's bedroom was, but it was empty. The dark smoke was filling her lungs, and she could barely see Andrew's silhouette as he emerged from Alice's room in the middle of the hallway. He was doubled over, wheezing.

"Mom," he cried, as Kate saw Darien's shadow creep up behind him.

"Andrew, watch out!" Kate called but it was too late, Darien hit Andrew over the head with the gasoline can, knocking him to the ground.

"No, you son of a bitch," Kate screamed, lunging at him. He easily caught her arms and yanked them behind her back.

"This would have been easier if you had listened to me earlier," he growled and dragged her towards Lacie's room.

"Andrew…" Kate cried. But Andrew was out. Kate whimpered as Darien shoved her inside and threw her to the ground. He closed the door behind her and locked her in with the missing key.

Kate collapsed on the floor. She was getting tired, and her head was pounding. Kate feared it was over. Lacie, Charlie, and now she and Andrew would all die here at Villa Magda. There was nothing she could do. She was trapped.

She saw a figure standing there in the corner. It was Alice, but this time Kate knew she was not real.

"You have to get to a window," Alice said.

"I can't!" Kate cried, her head spinning.

"Wake up!" Alice screamed at her. "Get up now."

Kate just wanted her to disappear.

"Andrew is lying out there, you have to get up now."

Kate tried with all her might to move, but she couldn't.

"The secret door. Remember it?" Alice said.

Kate thought of the secret passageway in Lacie's room where they would hide when playing. Kate opened the closet and crawled to the back. Through the darkness, her fingers found the wall panel, and she pried it open. She squeezed herself into the space and dragged her body forward. Spiderwebs stuck to Kate's face as she crawled toward the door that led to her room. Kate found the doorknob and threw the door open. She rushed out and found Andrew lying in the hallway, writhing in pain.

"Andrew," Kate coughed. She took his face in her hands. "Please, honey." She begged him to open his eyes. "I need you to get up."

Andrew moaned but remained on the ground. Kate could see that the fire was now ablaze downstairs and quickly spreading.

"You don't have much time," Alice warned.

Kate grabbed him under his armpits and pulled him like a ragdoll into an empty bedroom. Her lungs felt like they were going to explode. She opened the window and picked him up with all the strength she could muster.

"Andrew, listen to me. You have to climb out of the window and jump," Kate cried.

"What? What about you?"

"I'll be right behind you, I promise."

"But, jump?"

"The fall won't be bad, trust me," Kate pleaded.

She could hear the faint roar of a fire engine in the distance. Then it all went black as Kate heard the faint chanting of the final verse of the town's taunting rhyme swirling around her.

Lacie fell in love too soon
A boy in town made her swoon
But something with him was amiss
Because he killed her with a kiss

28

ANDREW

"'Hansel, we are saved! The old witch is dead!' Then Hansel
sprang like a bird from its cage when the door is opened."
—HANSEL AND GRETEL, GRIMM BROTHERS

The house watched as it always did, relishing in the chaos it had
once again caused. Emergency vehicles crowded the driveway.
Their lights flashed as the firefighters tried to get control of the
fire. The hope they'd had when they arrived was gone, taken
by tragedy and sadness.

Andrew watched his mother as she was given oxygen in
the back of an ambulance. He had been horrified when Chloe
told him everything she knew after the article came out. She
had found information she said would lead to finding her birth
parents. He never expected to find out that Chloe was part of
his family. At first, he'd thought Chloe was just acting crazy

and that Ben may have been right about her. But when Carl told Chloe that Lacie was her mother, Chloe went to Barbara, knowing she had been researching the case for years. Barbara told her that she needed to speak to Charlie, which was when she found him at the beach. That same night, Andrew realized, his father was dead.

He'd immediately thought it could be Chloe. She had left. Maybe she killed his father. Their father? Andrew didn't want to think of it anymore. He was too angry at all of them and just couldn't wait to leave this place. He was asleep when he heard Molly and his mother fighting. He'd tried to listen. Alice? *Who was Alice?* he thought. It quieted when he heard a voice, a girl: "Listen..."

"Chloe?" At first he thought it could be her, that she had come back. There was noise coming from the attic—footsteps. Was Chloe up there the whole time? He'd raced up to the attic and found the small tea table and trunk, but no Chloe. *So where did the voice come from?* he'd wondered. And then he heard the shrill scream in the deep night.

His mom was going to be okay, the paramedics told him. They also said that had they not gotten out when they did, they would have died in the fire.

Officer Mallory and other officers had separated Susan, Doug, and Darien. They were all cuffed and being questioned. They would be paying quite a price for all they did. Barbara was finally ready to tell the truth. She'd kept the secret for too long. Barbara had come across Lacie sobbing one day that summer, and Lacie had confided in her that she was pregnant. She was afraid that Kate would tell their mom, and Lacie begged Barbara not to tell anyone. But over the years, Barbara's guilt over hiding the secret had turned into an obsession with the case. She spent years trying to find Lacie, and through her denial, she had failed to see what was right in front of her. But with her family now behind bars, she could finally be free of it.

SIX WEEKS LATER: KATE

*"'But now we must be off,' said Hansel, 'that
we may get out of the witch's forest.'*
—*HANSEL AND GRETEL,* GRIMM BROTHERS

Molly had suggested Kate see a new therapist, one that had
been recommended to her by their friend Sarah Rock. She was
going to a Tulpamancer support group. She could hardly even
pronounce the word, let alone figure out what it was, but Kate
had learned that there were many adults like her, Tulpamancers,
who had imaginary friends who were called Tulpas. Tulpas were
so lifelike that the Tulpamancer could hear, see, and sometimes
even touch them, as if they were real. Tulpamancers had no idea
that their friends weren't real. Kate worried that she was crazy,
but her therapist reassured her that it was a coping mechanism;
she needed Alice to cope with the series of traumatic events

that occurred in a short amount of time. As a way of reassuring Kate, she had mentioned that even Agatha Christie had several imaginary friends.

Kate entered the room. The doctor was sitting in the center of the room, her auburn hair pulled back tightly and her smile warm and inviting. There were twelve people in the room, each of them telling their story about the friends they relied on, their friends in childhood who had stayed with them.

It was her turn. She looked at the doctor sheepishly, scared to discuss Alice out loud.

"It's okay. You can share. No one here will judge you."

Kate looked to the back of the room and saw Alice there, sipping a latte, dressed in a beautiful white dress, her hair perfect. She smiled.

"Her name is Alice," Kate said.

Dr. Helena Robin

First Session with Katie Williams:

Patient suffers from declarative memory disorder. She has created a Tulpa to cope.

Memory disturbances are predominant in the presentation of post-traumatic stress disorder (PTSD) and are part of the diagnostic criteria. The re-experiencing symptom criteria of PTSD include intrusive memories of the traumatic event, and the avoidance symptom criteria include the inability to recall important aspects of the trauma. In addition, patients with PTSD often complain of experiencing everyday memory problems with emotionally neutral material, although these problems are not included in the diagnostic criteria. Documenting these types of memory deficits related to PTSD, and understanding the reasons underlying these deficits, has become a primary focus for researchers for the past 20 years, in part because memory problems can lessen a patient's engagement in, and response to, treatment.

Intentional retrieval suppression can conceal guilty knowledge in ERP memory detection interactions between environment, cognition, and culture.

Work with Kate and her imaginary friend (Tulpa) Alice is progressing. Kate created false memories of meeting Alice shortly after her sister went missing. She believes she met Alice while searching for her sister, however it is my understanding that Kate manifested Alice later, closer to the birth of her son, as a way to explain the missing memories of her sister. (Note: Alice is an anagram of her dead sister Lacie, who disappeared when they were teenagers.) She recently found out that Lacie was killed. She struggles with needing Alice and wanting her gone. Alice helps her cope with her guilt and she fears losing her sister all over again.

Note for upcoming sessions: need to explore trauma related to guilt and grief of loss of husband.

Need patient to trust me and rely on these sessions. Will encourage her to rely more on her Tulpa (Alice) so that I can study the relationship further. There is someone I have in mind to help and stimulate her Tulpa so we can further analyze the relationship on my terms.

Patient has not wanted to address the topic of her husband just yet and all that happened. I am certain that we will get to all of that in due time. I can be patient. The work here is that important to the study.

TWO MONTHS LATER

*"Then all anxiety was at an end, and they
lived together in perfect happiness."*
—*HANSEL AND GRETEL*, GRIMM BROTHERS

The rain beat down on the pavement as Kate got into the car outside her home in Connecticut. It was a cold, gray, November morning that would have been better spent with a cup of tea in front of the fireplace. It sure wasn't the ideal day to drive all the way up to Aria to meet with the soon-to-be new owners. Or maybe it was. She somehow felt relieved that the sky was crying tears, a mirror to her heavy heart. Andrew had insisted she go through with the sale. The fire had damaged the kitchen and most of the second floor except for Lacie's room. The buyers would build their own home. Kate hoped it would be a happier home.

"No need to live in the past, Mom," Andrew had said

gently but firmly, "You need to, *we* need to move on. I'll be there, I promise."

And he was going to be there. Andrew was out of school on Thanksgiving break, and he was picking Chloe up from her college. They were driving up together to meet Kate at the house. It would be one of the few times Kate had seen Andrew since he had begun the fall term, and the first time she had seen Chloe in months. As Kate drove, she was reminded of the mantra her therapist had suggested she repeat when she was facing a difficult situation: "Negative thoughts only have the power I allow them." Even though today was going to be tough, Kate tried to focus on the positive and make it a good day. They would get to say good-bye to Charlie together.

After several hours of busy highways, Kate turned onto the Maine road that led toward the home. Her heart was beating faster as she glimpsed the sea stretching out on the side of the road. That night seemed like so long ago, yet only a few months had passed since she had almost died. And even though that had happened, the ocean still gave her a sense of both peace and excitement, a feeling of being part of something bigger than herself, that all was as it should be, the waves rolling in no matter what.

The car drove down the long driveway, and she parked in front of the house. She was the first to arrive. Andrew had texted that they were about an hour away. As she got out of the car, she could feel the cold damp air around her and she shivered. Her body was cold and sweaty, remembering the last time she had been here. Her head felt dizzy, and suddenly Kate felt scared. Shuffling onto the porch, she sat down on the stone steps and hugged herself tightly, protecting her wounded heart. Lacie was still here. She could feel it. She did believe in ghosts, after all.

She believed that Lacie needed her to remember. "I'm sorry. I'm sorry I forgot you Lacie. I promise I never will again," Kate said.

She looked up when Andrew and Chloe arrived. Molly had wanted to come as well, for moral support. She had since separated from Sam and stopped drinking completely. Kate welcomed her company and friendship; she was a true friend. One that didn't just go when the going got tough—and it had. She was better than any imaginary friend could ever be, Kate thought to herself.

"Mom!" Andrew's deep voice said.

Part of her still imagined Andrew as her little boy with the sweet little curls, but she was proud of the man he was becoming. He gave her a warm hug and she held him close.

"Mrs. Williams," said Chloe. Kate stretched out her arms toward her. They embraced gently.

"Aunt Kate," Kate said as she looked at Chloe lovingly.

"Yes, Aunt Kate." Chloe smiled.

"Come on, if we are going to do this, let's do it now before the new owners show up." Andrew took Kate's hand. Out of his bag, he picked up a dark urn. Charlie's ashes.

"Oh, Andrew, I don't think I can…" Kate began as her eyes welled up with tears. But Andrew wasn't taking no for an answer.

"Mom, it's for Dad. We need to do this. And you are stronger than you think. You can do this."

Not a day went by that she didn't miss him. His touch, his sparkling eyes, his voice. Sometimes she talked to him, but she knew that he wasn't there, it was just in case he was. She wanted him to know how much she loved him and always would.

Andrew led Kate down the path, and she could only follow. When Andrew insisted on something, she just couldn't resist.

They walked down to the ocean and stood on the sandy beach. The wind howled and the waves crashed against the rocky far end of the beach, over and over again, creating a rhythmic beat to their heavy hearts. The rain had just stopped, and the clouds were lightening up. Suddenly the sky opened up just a sliver and one ray of sun shone down in front of them on the ocean. They stopped and breathed together for a moment.

"That's beautiful," whispered Chloe, as if she didn't want to invade the moment.

"He's here," Kate exhaled. She felt a sense of peace coming over her—somehow things would be fine.

Andrew nodded and took out the urn. He looked at his mother who signaled to him to go ahead. And then he lifted the lid and held the urn high. He slowly tilted it and let the ashes fly in the wind out to sea. Kate felt her cheeks warm with tears. Charlie would always live with them in their hearts and memories, and he was alive through their beautiful boy.

"Chloe has brought a poem for us, if that is okay," Andrew said softly as he took his mom's hand. Kate nodded and wiped her eyes.

Kate stood quiet and still as she listened to Chloe, looking out over the ocean as the sun fully broke through the clouds and a seagull swooshed by, settling on the water. She nodded to her and as their eyes met, a warmth settled in her chest.

"I wish I had known her, my mother," Chloe said, as she finished and folded the paper.

"You look a lot like her," Kate said, smiling.

As she looked out over the sparkling ocean, she thanked Charlie for giving her the most special gift, Andrew. And she felt all would be okay.

"Mom," Andrew's voice interrupted her thoughts. "They're going to be here in just a few minutes. We should get back to the house."

"Yes, of course." Kate was ready to move on from the house. She took Andrew's hand in one hand and Chloe's hand in the other, and together they turned to leave the beach.

Kate noticed a large man standing in the garden. He smiled at her and Kate smiled back. She walked towards him.

"Hi, Carl," Kate said.

Carl nodded and handed her a piece of yellowed paper, ripped along one edge. "This is what I had for you. I was gonna give it to you that day in your room." Kate unfolded the paper carefully, afraid it would crumble. It was torn from Lacie's diary. But it was a letter to Kate.

September 10th

Dear Katie,

I miss you. I'm sorry for trying to come between you and Charlie. He loves you so much, and I was jealous of that. I don't want anyone to come between our special bond. Susan tells me you went back home and that you won't be back until Christmas. I don't know if I can wait that long. Thank you for keeping my secret. I love you and can't wait to see you when the baby is born. You are going to be the best aunt ever.

Love,

Your Alice

Kate looked back at Carl, tears swimming in her eyes. "Thank you for bringing this to me," she whispered.

"I'm sorry for scaring you that day."

"You were just trying to warn me. I should have listened to you."

Carl shrugged. "I promised Lacie I would get this letter to you. Even though it's been years, I still wanted to keep that promise. I'm just sorry it had to end this way."

Kate enveloped him in a hug, tears threatening to stream down her face.

Just then, a car honked from the driveway. Kate looked to find Carl's brother sitting behind the wheel of their old pickup. He gave a small wave, a small, sheepish smile on his face.

"I'm moving into a nursing home in town. If you and that boy of yours ever come back, make sure to come visit me."

Kate's voice was thick with emotion. "I will."

As he walked away, Kate looked up at the house. The "Sold" sign in the large driveway. The broker said they were lucky to get the offer they did, but Kate didn't mind; she was glad to be rid of it. Kate sighed. She saw images of herself and her sister as they chased each other in the garden, free and innocent, and knew that a part of her soul would forever be there, trapped in the corridors and secret rooms, in the garden and labyrinth, playing forever with her sister, Lacie, and best friend, Alice.

"Time to go," Kate said. She saw Molly standing there, greeting the buyers, doing what friends do, helping each other through the good and bad times. Kate walked past the labyrinth toward the car. She hadn't needed Alice for months, but there she was, standing, smiling, and encouraging her as she always did. But Kate knew now that she would not be needing Alice anymore. She was ready to let her go.

Andrew looked at her.

"You okay?" Andrew asked.

"I am," Kate said, and really meant it for the first time in a very long time.

With the ocean at their backs, they walked away from the summer house, ready for the new season in their lives. Maine would live in her heart, even though she would always be "from away." And Villa Magda, with all its secrets, ghosts, and tragedy, would be someone else's worry now. Her home was with Andrew. Kate was ready to belong wherever she was. A seagull circled above them, and she finally felt as free as the bird.

Villa Magda, now empty and damaged, stirred again. It had almost burned to the ground; the kitchen, living area, and most of the second floor were hollow shells of the rooms they used to be. The books in the library couldn't all be saved except for a few scattered among the ashes. Kate had felt some secret relief when she saw the flames in Villa Magda. She felt that with the house gone, so would much of the pain it had caused. But the foundation was still there, and the heart and soul of the house were still intact. The house had watched as the people that lived there once again were overcome with tragedy, distress, and doubt. The irony of it was that the house had been built for love. But it had not been a healthy love, it had been an obsessive, unrequited, and then jealous love.

Yes, indeed Max had built the house for Magda to prove his undying love and adoration to her. But a house can also become a prison, and for Magda, it became exactly that. She had wanted to leave so many times. Her friendship with Marshall the farmer had been her only reprieve. She had looked forward to his visits. They talked about the weather, the crops, and Aria. She told him about Germany and her home and how she missed it. His visits became more frequent, and Magda noticed that he would stay longer than needed. She welcomed it and even encouraged him to stay, inviting him for tea. Max soon caught wind of Marshall's visits and was not happy with them. He confronted Magda angrily one night in their room. She was so upset and could hear the children crying. Max told her that he would lock her away in one of the secret rooms he had built, a room that was so deeply within the walls of the house that no one would ever find it or her. Magda shivered at the thought and planned her escape. She would leave as soon as she could, take her children with her, and run off back to Germany. So, she waited several weeks, until she knew she was ready. She would take none of her belongings, just her children and their small things. That night, she woke quietly within the halls of Villa Magda where her husband's obsessive love had been suffocating her. She was scared of what her husband might do if he found out, but the fear of staying was greater. She snuck out of her room on the second floor, the same room that Lacie would occupy years later. She crossed over to her children's room. The moonlight shone into the room as she quietly brought her lantern to their beds. But the beds were empty. They were gone and behind her stood Max. Magda's heart sank as Max led her downstairs to the secret room under the library, a room he had built for this very purpose. A room she would be locked away in, like a doomed princess, forever. Magda knew as Max shut the door behind her that she would never leave Villa Magda and that she would forever haunt its halls and rooms, waiting for the day when she would be free.

* * *

By the following summer, work had started on the house. The new owners decided to rebuild. After removing the damaged sections, construction workers began demolishing all that Max had built, including the secret rooms. As they entered the hidden room below the library, they saw a small bed, table, and a notebook filled with journal entries. And by the door were the bones of a young woman as if looking for a way out. It was Magda. And she was finally free.

Into the woods she went to play
Dressed in white that summer's day
But little Lacie said farewell
For off the cliff she fell, fell, fell.

Little Lacie went to run
All she wanted was some fun
She disappeared into the woods
Now little Lacie's gone for good.

She was as pretty as a swan
Which made her sister want her gone
So she locked her in her room
And slowly brought her to her doom.

Lacie fell in love too soon
A boy in town made her swoon
But something with him was amiss
Because he killed her with a kiss.

TULLAN HOLMQVIST is a writer, investigator and actor. Tullan wrote the award-winning thriller *The Woman in the Park* with producer Teresa Sorkin, and also writes screenplays, TV series, children's stories, and essays. She has performed in film, TV, and the theater, her first love. Her work as a private investigator has included global fraud investigations, financial due diligence, and art cases. Tullan holds a master's degree in political science from the University of Florence, Italy; literature and language degrees from the universities of Florence and Aix-en-Provence, France; and screenwriting and acting studies at New York University, Boston University, HB Studio, and with Michael Howard. Originally from Sweden, Tullan also grew up in Nigeria, Italy, France, and Austria and now lives in New York with her husband, composer Giovanni Spinelli, and her children, Max and Leo.

TERESA SORKIN is one of the founders of Roman Way Productions. She has a passion for creating, writing, telling, sharing, and producing great stories. Her first novel, *The Woman in the Park*, is a psychological thriller that she co-authored with Tullan Holmqvist. Teresa is also included in *Moms Don't Have Time To: A Quarantine Anthology* along with fifty other authors. Teresa grew up in New York City and graduated with a Marketing Degree from New York University. She was an entertainment journalist and producer. She currently lives in Manhattan with her husband, two children and their dog Coco.

BOOK CLUB QUESTIONS

1. Did you notice a connection between this book and the authors' previous book, *The Woman in the Park*?

2. Were there any passages or scenes that stuck with you? If so, which ones and why?

3. There are many supernatural elements in the book. Have you ever experienced anything unusual after a loved one has died that couldn't be explained?

4. What do you imagine could happen in a sequel?

5. If you have read the first book, what do you think Dr. Helena Robin has planned for Kate?

1. Lacie believed in fairy tales. Modern Disney fairy tales usually end with a happily ever after, while stories by the Grimm Brothers get fairly dark and disturbing. How would you classify the ending in *Lacie's Secrets*?

2. If you had been invited to spend the week at Villa Magda with Kate and her friends, would you have stayed the whole time? If not, what would have been the final straw for you? But if you did stay, how would you have helped Kate?

3. Were you surprised at whose body was in the pool? If so, who did you think it would be? If not, why did you think it would be that person?

4. Why are the police investigation questions so important to the narrative?

5. What twists did you figure out before they were revealed? Which ones surprised you?

SETTING AND THEME

1. What are some of the prevailing themes in the book?

2. Gothic fiction is a genre that heavily utilizes tropes. What tropes of the genre stuck out to you when reading *Lacie's Secrets*?

3. How does Maine affect the book's story? Was the town a character as well, and if so how?

4. How does the isolation of Villa Magda drive tensions between the characters?

5. Ultimately this is a story about toxic love. How does love play into the house and its secrets?

CHARACTERS

1. Why do you think Kate felt it was necessary to go back to Villa Magda after so many years?

2. Did you feel Charlie was supportive of Kate? If so, how?

3. How does childhood trauma affect Kate? Her memory?

4. Why was Magda such a crucial figure in the novel? How did Max's love affect her and the house?

5. How would you describe Kate's feelings toward Lacie? Did they change throughout the book?

6. Darien has a hidden dark side. Did you expect him to be different from how he seemed in the beginning?

7. How do the main characters change as the week in Maine progresses? What do you think causes the changes?

8. Can you think of an example of one character manipulating another? Did you, as a reader, feel manipulated by the unreliable narrative?

9. What motivates different character's actions? Do you think those actions are justified or ethical? Do you think you would have reacted differently?

10. Once Alice's true identity was revealed, how did that change your view of how she and Kate interacted?

11. How is Chloe's character important to the plot?

12. Who in the book would you like to meet? What would you ask or say to them?

13. If you could insert yourself as a character in the book, what role would you play?

14. Kate has an imaginary friend. Have you or anyone you know ever had an imaginary friend?

15. If this were made into a movie, who do you think would play each character?

ACKNOWLEDGMENTS

FROM TULLAN

I am so grateful for the wonderful companions along my path during the creation of this story about family, sisterhood, home and the love that lives on.

Thank you to my fabulous writing partner Teresa for our exciting book journey together.

Deep gratitude to Jane Wesman for her gracious guidance and to the marvelous and supportive team at Beaufort Books, Megan Trank, Olivia Fish ,and Eric Kampmann.

My love to my family, my joy and inspiration, my home—my sons Max and Leo, my husband Giovanni, my sisters, Malin and Linda, and their children, Sebastian, Daniel, Miles, Elsa and Alice. To my angels, especially my beloved mamma Carin and pappa Bo, you are always with me. Love conquers all—*Amor Vincit Omnia*.

FROM TERESA

Thank you to my smart and amazing writing partner and friend Tullan.

I am grateful to Beaufort Books and our editing team Megan Trank and Olivia Fish who have truly believed in this novel and helped make it what it is. And thanks to Eric Kampmann for all his wisdom and to Jane Wesman our agent whose wisdom has guided us.

This is a novel about family and memories and I am so immensely grateful to my children Jaden and Isabella for believing in their mom and inspiring me each day and to my husband who stands by me endlessly. My love to my family, my joy and inspiration. I truly can say that no novel is written without the help of a village and I am so happy to be part of this one!